BLACK MAMBA

BLACK MAMBA

WILLIAM FRIEND

Atlantic Books
London

First published in hardback in Great Britain in 2022 by
Atlantic Books, an imprint of Atlantic Books Ltd.

This paperback edition published in Great Britain in 2023
by Atlantic Books.

1 2 3 4 5 6 7 8 9

A CIP catalogue record for this book is available from the British Library.

Paperback ISBN: 978 1 83895 660 8
EBook ISBN: 978 1 83895 657 8

Printed and bound by CPI (UK) Ltd, Croydon CR0 4YY

Atlantic Books
An Imprint of Atlantic Books Ltd
Ormond House
26–27 Boswell Street
London
WC1N 3JZ

www.atlantic-books.co.uk

For my parents.

One

Alfie

This morning, I heard the name Black Mamba for the first time, and it made me remember some dreams. Not mine; dreams that my daughters had. Visions that splintered their sleep.

It began nine months after the accident. Every night, during the devil's hour, I'd wake to find the twins standing motionless at the foot of my bed, their faces veiled by the dark.

Daddy, there's a man in our room.

Those words became familiar, like a choral refrain, and could stir my body whilst my mind, or the better part of it, remained asleep. I'd shift beneath the cold, stiff sheets, flatten my nose against the pillow and sigh. *No there isn't*, I'd say. But my arm, half dead with sleep, would lift the duvet all the same and let the girls clamber in, to nestle in the cleft where their mum had once slept.

Naturally, the first night was different. On the first night, the twins' mere presence at my bedside, sudden and unexpected, sent a shot of adrenaline through me.

'Daddy, there's a man in our room.'

The sentence jerked me upright, like the tug of a noose and the floor falling through beneath my feet.

'A man?' I said.

'A man.'

And the girls stood so still, and their voices were so flat and toneless and dead that I could scarcely breathe; yet somehow I gathered the strength to tiptoe out of my room and towards theirs.

'Stay here,' I whispered, but they wouldn't let me leave them, so we shuffled together down the staircase, their tiny hands squeezing mine as we listened. And it was only the silence – the pure, solid hush of night – that began, finally, to calm me. Blood flowed back to my face and neck, and I started to feel like an adult again. Like a father.

'Are you sure you weren't dreaming?'

'It wasn't a dream. It was real. He was there.'

Into their room we went, and the snap of the electric light instantly illuminated everything, revealing nothing, no one. I flung open the wardrobe doors; lifted the duvet, with its chalk-blue swirls, to search beneath their bed. Unvacuumed carpet and misplaced toys – but no one there.

'What did he look like?'

'He ... he ...' Their voices quivered, as feeling returned, and they fumbled for their words. 'It was dark. We couldn't see.'

Down another flight, to the ground floor, where we flooded each room with reassuring light. We checked everything: windows, doors, locks. Nothing was open, nothing was smashed. Bewildered, the girls turned to each other, half in search of support, half in suspicion. We retraced our steps.

'Where did you see him?' I asked. 'Show me.' And, just like that, all synchrony in their words and movements fell apart.

'He was out here,' Sylvie said, her finger charting vaguely across the landing. 'We saw him through the doorway.'

But Cassia jerked her head and cried, 'No, no, he came into our room!'

'But the door was closed.'

'Exactly.'

And suddenly they both seemed very tired. I stroked and kissed their heads; strands of their static blonde hair gleamed in the low light.

'It must have been a dream,' I said.

'It wasn't a dream.'

'Let's get you back to bed.'

'Why can't we sleep with you?'

The girls' night visits persisted for several weeks, and I dozed through each one more deeply than the last, until the visits themselves took on a dreamlike quality; until sometimes it was only the girls' presence the next morning – their tiny bodies curled up next to mine – that reminded me of their appearance in the night, and of what they'd said.

Then the visits stopped, just as they'd begun: suddenly and without explanation. I woke each morning to an empty bed, and the memory of the whole thing started to fade. I never asked the girls if the nightmares had ceased. They must have, or else why had the visits? Nor did I question why they'd begun in the first place, nine long months after the accident. I pushed those thoughts to the back of my mind – assuming it had all meant nothing; assuming it had run its course.

It was only this morning, when Marian came round with jam tarts and tears, and the girls told me about Black Mamba, that I remembered, in a rush, those moonlit serenades from a month ago – the girls' dead eyes and voices, and the things they'd said, echoing in my head like a leitmotif; strings that keen and tremble long after being touched.

Julia

I've come to the house – not because I want to, but because he's asked me to.

Hart House, No. 4, Allington Square, London: the house where I grew up. I loved it once, as we all did, and part of me still does. My happiest memories are connected to this house, as well as the most frightening, which makes for what people in my profession call a 'compound emotional response'. In every room, the walls are pale and blank, but they bear, in my mind's eye, the imprint of a thousand smiles; a palimpsest of all the birthdays I've celebrated within them – nearly 100, for no fewer than seven people.

Two of those people are dead now. I see them in the walls here too.

Alfie opens the front door with a soft smile.

Pretty, in a manly sort of way. That's what I thought of him when we first met, almost a decade ago. Now he's pretty but damaged, his face lined, his sandy hair mazy and thick. He looks more grizzled than he used to, though not as a result of maturity, but of trauma. I'm not judging. I look dreadful too, or at least assume that I do. I haven't looked in a mirror properly since the accident.

'Thanks for coming,' he says, taking my coat. Still a gentleman, I think, even after all that's happened.

No – more so, I realise, sadly. He was never like this when Pippa was alive. I'd come to visit, and Alfie wouldn't so much as look up from the telly. He'd just call out, cheerily, from where he lay on the sofa, one twin tucked beneath each brawny arm, and jut out his cheek for me to kiss. Now I watch him fold my scarf before draping it carefully over the bannister, and his tenderness is hard to bear. We move into the kitchen, and I distract myself by looking at the girls' latest drawings, pinned to the fridge by magnets.

'They're in bed,' I hear him say. I nod without turning. Sylvie has drawn a whirl of falling petals, with hard black outlines and softly smudged interiors. Cassia has drawn blue crystals, cold and clear. The girls' names, in the far corners, are calligraphed with letters that put my own crabbed scrawl to shame. I brush my hand reverently across the paper.

It's dark outside, and cold in the kitchen. I hear the clink of mugs, the flick of the kettle. Alfie's brewing tea. Normally when we're together, we drink – really drink – but not tonight. Today is the first of the month, just like the day of the accident. Wine would feel inappropriate, as it often does when you need it most.

I assume he needs it. Maybe that's just projection. I should try to find out.

'How are you?' I ask, keeping my back turned.

'Fine,' he answers, speaking into the sink. His voice is flat, unreadable, but I don't argue. For all I know it might be true, on most days at least. I'm fine most days too. The anguish has finally eased. I know, instinctively, that he's at his worst when he's around me, just as I'm at my worst when he invites me to Hart House.

He pours some tea into my favourite mug, black and speckled with stars, and we sit at the table. The stars appear only when the mug is hot; by the time around half have been snuffed out, it's safe to drink.

'How are you?' he parries, eventually, fiddling with the handle of his own mug, which looks tiny next to the span

6

of his palm and fingers. Alfie's a big man; a smart one, too, and softly spoken.

'I'm fine, too, I guess. Keeping busy.'

He nods, tightly. There's something on his mind, something he wants to tell me. This wasn't a routine invitation; I thought that on the phone this afternoon. Something about his voice – breathless, catching – struck me as off.

'At the clinic?'

'Mm,' I say. 'Finally seeing a full roster again. More or less.'

After the accident, I couldn't work for months. I took long-term sick leave, which only made things worse. I needed to work and I needed therapy, but – given my day job – both options felt closed to me. Like a cold, there was no cure; I just had to wait it out. Things are better now, at least a bit. I can work through my pain. I can talk about it. Other people can give me theirs again.

I sip some tea to mask the awkward silence, and burn my tongue. The stars are still shining furiously. I only have myself to blame.

'Have they called you again?' I ask. 'KCL, I mean. About going back.' Alfie's worked at universities for as long as I've known him.

'No, no,' he says quickly. 'There's no pressure. Not this year.' Whatever's bothering him, then, it isn't that.

I push my mug to one side, and do what I do with all recalcitrant clients: fight the urge to fill the awkward gaps; use the silence against them.

Eventually, he cracks. 'Marian was here this morning,' he says tentatively, and at last I begin to understand his mood. *Mum*. I touch his wrist and nod, sympathetically. No one could ask for a trickier in-law, even in better circumstances; I love her, but that much even I admit.

There's more, of course. I see it in his hesitation. Something has happened. Something bad or, at the very least, concerning. But I won't rush him. He'll tell me when he's ready.

We sit in silence, stirring our tea. It's ten months today since my sister's death.

Alfie

Julia eyes me across the table. It's a funny word, eyeing, but that's what it feels like. It's something more invasive than looking. Her stone-blue eyes are questing, questioning. She has the look of a poised cat who can swivel her ears towards sound without tilting her head. What does she want from me?

She wants me to carry on talking.

Ah, yes. Marian. This morning.

I gulp some tea – black – and burn my tongue. We only had enough milk for one, something that never happened when Pippa was alive. Or maybe it did, and I just don't remember, which is even worse.

Where to begin?

With the bell, rousing me from a sticky sleep. I'd been

dozing in front of the telly with the girls, marinating in sadness. *My* sadness, for the girls were no more or less sad than usual. Why should they have been? They didn't know that today was the first of the month. Or if they did, it meant nothing to them. The sun had still risen in the morning, and I was still the only parent they had left. To them, today was just another day. That's what I told myself when they asked if they could watch cartoons.

'Of course we can,' I said. But then I turned the volume of the telly right down, as if a sick relative were in the room, so they knew that something was wrong. Saying nothing, they snuggled with me and watched the near-silent screen while I dozed and drew comfort from the heat of their small, perfect bodies. I was being selfish, but I couldn't help it. It was the first of the month, we had nothing to do, and the most important person in the world was dead. It felt wrong that they were running cartoons on TV.

When the bell rang, I didn't want to answer it. I didn't want to move, think or talk, and I didn't care who it was. But it rang again, piercing and insistent, so I swabbed the dribble off my chin, tidied the living room, and then finally answered the door – hopeful that whoever it was would have given up and gone away.

When I realised it was Marian, I only wished I'd waited longer.

Should I tell Julia that? I'm about to, but then reconsider. Julia and Marian have always been close. Not affectionate or tender, perhaps. But close.

I stick to narrating the bald facts. I keep my resentments to myself.

There she stood, breathless on the doorstep, her cheeks pinched and raw in the cold air, her greying hair wild and on end. Wreathed in black furs, she clutched a bulky basket, full of misshapen jam tarts.

'Grandma's here,' I called out weakly to the twins, before deciding that would do for hello. Retreating into the darkness of the hallway, I waited for Marian to follow.

'Oh Alfie,' she said, voice wavering as she stepped over the threshold, groping for my hand. It would almost have been moving, had she and Pippa not detested each other quite so nakedly when Pippa was alive.

I led her dutifully into the living room. Before the accident, we'd get the same wistful remark whenever she walked on the mahogany floorboards – *This room looked so much better with a carpet* – but today we were spared that. Instead, she simply staggered through the doorway and collapsed onto the sofa, exhaling loudly, her limbs jutting out like a wet crow's feathers. It's petty, but I was gratified that neither of the twins had responded to my call. Even upon their grandmother's sharp descent onto the sofa, their eyes remained glued to the television.

'You don't mind,' she said to me breathlessly – a statement, not a question – 'me stopping by the house.'

The house. That's what Marian has always called it. Not *your* house, *the* house. When Pippa was alive, it didn't matter. It was Pip's family home, after all – the house where she and Julia had grown up. But now that she's gone, it's starting to sting.

Chickens coming home to roost. When Marian offered to sell us Hart House, we knew what the trade-off would be, and we could have said no. But with two small children, and jobs that fulfilled us rather than paid well, it was the only way we could afford to live in London. Marian gave us an excellent price and, in exchange, she came round whenever she pleased; made us feel like guests in our own home; criticised every tweak we made to the décor. We never agreed to those terms. Pre-sale, they were all unspoken. But still, we never complained. We'd known what Marian was like when we signed the contract. We never felt we'd been tricked.

If anything, it was the opposite: the guilt was all ours, and it pricked especially when Marian reminded us, always with tears in her eyes, of the reason she'd been forced to sell us her beloved home. Marian had been widowed by the age of forty, and suffered a stroke by the age of fifty, leaving her plagued by headaches, joint pain and chronic fatigue. Both her daughters had flown the nest. When Sue, her sister-in-law, who'd been lonely for years, offered her companionship, Marian felt she'd no choice but to go.

Julia's mug is cooling at last. She holds it, obscuring a few stubborn stars, and begins to drink in earnest. Not for the first time, I feel an urge to confide in her – to explain how Marian's refusal to acknowledge that Hart House is no longer hers is starting to sting. When Pippa was alive, I belonged here because she did. But now, every 'the' from Marian's lips makes me feel unwelcome. Like I'm an outsider. Like it's time for me to pack up and leave.

What would Julia say to that?

She'd reach across the kitchen table and squeeze my hand. She'd tell me I was being silly – paranoid, even.

Yes. But what would she be thinking?

That Hart House was her inheritance. That Pippa and I had got it for a snip. That it wasn't rightfully mine. That it never would be.

That's paranoia too, I realise. Julia would never think like that. For one thing, the girls have always loved Hart House – perhaps more than any of us – and I belong wherever they do. All the same, I steady myself, and confide nothing.

Marian – still being ignored by the twins.

'Well? How are my little angels?'

In my exhaustion I, boringly, did the right thing and thumbed the remote. TV off, the twins gave Marian their full attention. They hugged her, kissed her, and prised the basket of jam tarts expertly from her wrinkly fingers.

'A bit of help for you, Alfie dear. You must be really struggling.'

I lifted the basket out of the girls' reach. 'Thanks. We're doing fine.'

'Philippa was such a wonderful cook,' Marian said.

Yes, I thought, airlifting the tarts to safety, *largely because she wasn't taught by you*, and a picture popped into my head of Pippa stifling a smirk that made me want to cry. Pippa always said that her mother had witch-like powers: not only did Marian burn everything she cooked, she had an unnerving ability to make others burn their food too. Sometimes she would turn up unannounced on our doorstep around dinner time, disrupting Pippa's cooking at the pivotal moment. Other days, she would telephone at breakfast and detain her daughter just long enough that ribbons of black smoke began to unfurl from the toaster, making the twins shriek. Oddly, though, the tarts looked fine. Tempting, even.

'Susan's been such a help,' Marian said, revealing the tarts' true source, and right on cue her eyes began to fill, her irises blurring in a ghostly, watery hue. 'Everyone has. Everyone's been so kind ...'

'I'm sure.'

I could almost hear their voices. *Poor Marian ... Her daughter dead so young ... And after losing Eric too ... So awful ... Oh yes, unspeakable ... Poor Marian ... Mm, yes, poor Marian ...*

Poor Marian. Black furs and tears were mere residue of the figure she had cut ten months ago, at Pippa's funeral. Like a mummer playing a character in a morality play – Lamentation, Misery, Without Hope – Marian had shivered and swayed, head to toe in pitch-black cloth. When I tried to give the eulogy, it was drowned beneath the weight of her wails. The church was too small. No one else's grief could fit.

'They're not a meal, mind,' she continued. 'They're a snack. The tarts.'

'Yes.'

'My girls are eating full meals, aren't they?'

The house. *My* girls. I drew a deep breath, and reminded myself that it was all in my head. 'Of course they are,' I said.

'Of course they are ...' Marian murmured the words back to me as if barely conscious of their meaning. She was still breathing unevenly, but she'd fought off the tears and her eyes were once again focused and clear. Silently, her gaze roved across the stacks of books that I had hastily constructed, and lingered on the dust that had been displaced.

'And the cleaning ... ?'

'All in hand,' I lied. 'I'm hoovering this afternoon.'

At last she exhaled properly and lay back on the sofa, closing her eyes and nodding in approval.

'I'll stick the kettle on,' I said.

And at that, her eyes flicked open again, and instantly refilled with tears. She clasped the twins close to her. 'If only she could see you now ... Philippa, I mean. She'd be so proud of you three. I just know it.'

She hated being called Philippa, and she hated you, I thought.

'Thanks, Marian,' I said.

Julia's tea is finished. Or cold. She's stopped drinking, at any rate, and her expression is tight and tense, which confuses me. I've rambled on about her mother's visit for a good ten minutes, delicately avoiding full-on criticism, only ever hinting at annoyance. A model of diplomacy, or so I thought. Her face suggests otherwise.

'What's wrong?'

'Nothing,' she says. 'It's just ...' She hesitates. 'I don't understand, that's all. Why have you asked me here?'

'Oh,' I say. 'Do I need a reason?' I must look crestfallen – crushed, even – because she swiftly backpedals.

'Of course not,' she says, before lowering her voice, I assume not to wake the girls. 'I'm sorry. I didn't mean—'

'It's fine.'

She scans my face, foraging for something. 'It's just that I know there's a problem. I could hear it when you called. Don't sugar-coat it, please. Just tell me.' Now she looks grim, as though steeling herself. 'What did she do?'

'Who? Marian? Oh, God. Nothing at all. It was ...' I grasp for the right words. 'The tarts.'

Julia's eyebrows jump. 'The tarts?'

As soon as Marian left, all eyes fell upon them. The twins have only just turned seven and stand a little over four feet tall. The top kitchen shelf, where I'd placed the basket, remains, for now, just out of reach.

'Daddy?'

'Yes?'

The twins exchanged a glance, which is all it ever takes to synchronise their speech, and seemingly their thoughts. 'Can we have one now?'

'No,' I said, naturally. It was almost lunchtime. But then I thought about how good they'd been with Marian, and how much I loved them, and how their mum was dead, and I gave in. 'Well, all right. Just the one.'

'Each?'

I turned and reached up towards the magic shelf. 'One each.'

'One each, and one for Black Mamba.'

And there it was. I'd never heard that name before in my life, and, because my back was turned, I had no clue which girl had said it.

I turned to face them. 'One for who?'

'Black Mamba.' This time the twins spoke together again, in near perfect unison, as they have since they were little. Pippa and I were used to it. Only strangers found it unnerving.

'What,' I said slowly, 'like the snake?'

They nodded and smiled.

'He's our friend,' said Sylvie.

'You can't see him,' said Cassia, 'because he doesn't want you to.'

The basket was now in my hands; the girls' palms extended in my direction. Their demand for an extra tart for their invisible friend hung in the air. I handed them one each. 'Snakes don't eat pastry,' I said firmly, and kissed them on the tops of their heads.

Sylvie seemed satisfied, but Cassia kept her palm outstretched. 'What do they eat then?'

I sighed. The thought of admitting my ignorance, and shattering the precious illusion of a father's omniscience, felt impossibly heavy. So I said, 'All right then,' thinking again that their mum was dead, and little else mattered. 'One for Black Mamba.'

Julia

'Black Mamba?' The words feel peculiar on my lips. Exotic, yet familiar; strangely fallen out of place.

'Yes. I looked inside their bags. They've been learning about snakes at school. I guess he's ... an imaginary friend.' Alfie speaks slowly. His worry is palpable in every breath, but a hardness is setting in. He's sitting up straighter in his chair, and his thick arms are tightly folded. It's my fault – I shouldn't have been impatient; asking him outright why he'd summoned me here.

Fine, he's thinking, *you didn't want to come. You don't want to help. No need to make it quite so obvious.*

'Are you asking me what I think as an auntie?' I say. 'Or do you want my professional opinion?'

He shrugs. 'Either. Both.'

I try not to sigh. It wouldn't be productive. And besides, maybe he's right to be annoyed. True, he summoned me – but it was my choice to come. 'Lots of kids have imaginary friends. It's a normal part of play.' I lean forward, squeeze his wrist. 'I'm sure it's hard to see them playing again. Isn't it?'

Silence. And then, stiffly, he nods. He's not exactly laying his vulnerabilities bare, but he is, at last, showing some ankle.

'I understand,' I say, emboldened. 'I see it all the time. Among parents I work with – bereaved parents. You try so hard to cheer your kids up, to help them bounce back, and when they actually do, it hurts like hell. I get it. I really do.'

'I'm sure,' he says, withdrawing his wrist.

There's nothing I can say to that. I know he's still angry with me for ducking out on him when Pippa died. After the accident, Alfie had wanted me to counsel the girls, and Mum badgered me on his behalf whenever I saw her. *You're a family therapist, for heaven's sake. You've helped hundreds of kids. Why not your own flesh and blood?*

I just couldn't. It wasn't about ethics, or my own well-being. Even when I was steady enough to start seeing clients again, I refused to treat my nieces. I needed to hold them, and Alfie – and Hart House – at arm's length. Mum's never understood, and I've never explained it. How could I? Where would I begin?

Alfie rubs his face and sighs, his body loosening. 'I'm sorry,' he says at last. 'It's just not like them. They've never ...'

'What? Had an imaginary friend?'

He pauses, then says decisively, 'Yes.'

I shouldn't have jumped in. He was going to say something else. The golden rule with clients is to let them speak; force them to find their own words.

'Not once, ever,' he continues. 'It's not like them.'

I feel myself frown. There must be something else that's upset him. 'They used to play make-believe, though, didn't they? When they were younger.'

'You know they did.' His tone isn't angry, as such. Just cold. 'Before Pippa died.'

Ah, I think. *Is that it?*

Pippa.

My sister always loved playing make-believe. When she had kids, it made her a natural with them. I close my eyes, and a series of memories – still images – whirr before me, like frames on one of Dad's old photo reels.

Click. There's Pippa and the twins, crouched in the courtyard behind the house, playing shopkeepers. The girls are tiny, maybe two or three. Their blonde hair, in coils, sits like icing on the tops of their heads, and their tiny pink fingers are a blur – frozen in a flurry of movement, busily dishing out rubber vegetables in exchange for plastic coins.

Click. The girls are older now, four or five maybe, and their hair has darkened, becoming wild and unbrushed – and there's Pippa, smiling at them, lying in Peter's Park, her own hair blending with the long grass. Bright streaks of paint adorn all three of their faces; I remember that because Pippa painted my face too. We were playing Queens of the Amazon, warrior princesses, leaders of tribes.

Click. Now the girls are older still, six or thereabouts, and they're indoors, in the kitchen where Alfie and I are sitting at this very moment. A stuffed toy is lying on the kitchen table, a white polar bear, and the girls are wearing thick winter coats, fur-lined, with the hoods up. Pippa has a bowl of water in her hands, and a damp cloth. They're scientists – I remember suddenly – scientists on an expedition to the Arctic, tending to an injured bear.

I'm close to tears as the camera in my mind's eye whirrs again. I know what the final image will be: the last game of make-believe that Pippa ever played, just moments before the accident. I want to see it. I don't want to see it. I want to see it.

Click.

'Auntie Julia?'

My eyes snap open and I hear feet on the stairs. *Sorry*, I mouth to Alfie, and he shrugs. I was right: my voice did wake the girls.

We rise abruptly, our chairs scraping against the kitchen floor. Sylvie and Cassia rush in, still wearing their pyjamas: matching onesies, already too small for them. Blue cotton, dotted with gambolling lambs; a present from my mother at Christmas.

'Auntie Julia!'

We cuddle, and I feel the lingering warmth from their beds. The girls seem bigger than when I hugged them last, and the predictable guilt envelops me. Still, it's a wonderful hug.

Sylvie pulls away first. 'What are you doing here?'

Her face looks different too. Some of her freckles have faded, and a little puppy fat has been shed, sharpening her cheeks. Aside from their blonde hair, the girls have never much resembled Alfie, but the more they mature, the more they look like their mum; the more they look like me.

'I've come to see your dad.'

Sylvie tosses her hair, harrumphs. 'Him? But what about us?'

'We've missed you.' Cassia's voice is gentle. She doesn't let go of me, but she loosens her grip, and tilts back her head until her clear blue eyes meet mine. When the twins were tiny, and Sylvie would cry incessantly – always wriggling; her little body forever becoming too hot and itchy – Cassia was Pippa's salvation. She was so placid, so quiet and still. Even after the terrible twos were over and Sylvie mellowed, those reputations stuck. Cassia was the calm one, Pippa's rock; Sylvie was the handful Alfie indulged. I've always tried to treat them equally.

'I'm sorry. I was going to check on you. I promise.' A little reluctantly, Cassia allows me to prise myself free from her embrace. I take both girls firmly by the hand. 'Come on. Let's get you back to bed.'

The girls nod, chewing at the ends of their wispy blonde hair. I look at them closely, but nothing about their expressions or behaviour seems unusual, nothing that helps me understand their dad's concern. I walk them back up the stairs and Alfie trails us, like a shadow – big and awkward, not fitting in with the three of us; not seeming to want to. I hear his soft breathing behind me and my arm hairs rise like spindles.

Hart House is big enough for the twins to each have a room of their own, but they've always shared, and they say they always will. Their bedroom is on the first floor; it's the one I shared with my twin, when we were little.

Pippa. It's pointless to compare my grief with Alfie's, but it *is* different. The bond between twins isn't a myth, and losing mine is a layer of pain he cannot see. I open the bedroom door and my gaze is drawn, instantly, to the wide window and the view outside – unchanged since the day I left it. Peter's Park is dense with trees, which, from this height, crowd out the flowers from view: sycamores and weighty magnolias and, just in sight, at the park's far edge, the red horse chestnuts, beneath which Pippa fell ill. I tread hastily towards the window, which I note, with momentary surprise, has been left ajar. Moonlight is pouring in; the tree-tops are swaying in the night breeze. I glance at the twins.

'Did you open this?'

They shake their heads, watching me silently as I pull it to, and draw the curtains. Then I usher the girls back into bed and pull the covers to their chins. The blue swirls of the duvet undulate as they snuggle and nest. Alfie sits on one side of the bed, I on the other. Tucking them in doesn't feel strange; I've done it before, a thousand times. When they were tiny, I was babysitter-in-chief. The girls would come to stay with me and Mum, when I still lived here with her; they'd fall asleep in this very room. But tucking them in with Alfie, in my sister's place ... I kiss my nieces on the tops of their heads. Their hair smells different too.

Once it had the scent of crushed flowers; now it smells of cheap shampoo. Alfie's not hard up, just lacking in knowledge, so this is another casualty of the accident, albeit a minor one. I'm sure the girls haven't even noticed.

They share a double bed, the same one I shared with Pippa when we were small. Just as they've never wanted separate rooms, they've never wanted singles. I switch on the side lamp, illuminating the girls' faces in soft amber light, filtered through the cloth of the lampshade. It makes their hair look dark and bright at once – like cords of black and gold, threaded together – and the walls of the bedroom, which are plastered with the girls' drawings and sketches, are tinged in a gentle orange glow, as though the four of us are huddled in a fire-lit cave, primitive etchings surrounding us like we're a stone-age family.

I should wait till tomorrow to question them. When the conditions are better; when we're all less tired. But the window being open has unnerved me, and Alfie, judging by his shallow breath, is still on edge – so I smooth the covers down over their bodies and smile, implacably. Game face on: firm auntie and shrink, melded into one.

'So,' I say. 'Your dad tells me you've made a friend.' The twins' eyes are inscrutable. I broaden my smile and continue. 'Black Mamba. Tell me about him.'

They glance at each other. To confer, the twins never need to speak. A look is always enough. Even when they were very young, decisions about what toys to play with, which children to sit with, whether to stay in a room or leave it, whether to comply with a demand or resist, could all be made through a momentary locking of eyes.

'What do you want to know?' they answer in unison.

'Well, he's a snake, yes? A hissing, slithering snake.'

They smile and nod, enjoying my playfulness.

I furrow my brow, exaggeratedly, and endeavour to keep my tone mild. 'Can he talk?'

'He can talk to us,' Sylvie says swiftly. 'He can talk without moving his lips.'

'He sounds clever. And how did he get into the house?'

Sylvie blinks, seemingly uncertain. She turns to her sister.

'Why, through the door, of course,' Cassia says quietly. Her mouth is twitching slightly, as though she's tickled by her own private joke.

'Not through the window?'

'Of course not,' she says, still smirking.

'Of course not,' I repeat. 'Silly me. He sounds amazing. Although ...' I shake my head, screwing up my face, as though suddenly wracked with concern.

'What? What?'

'Well, he *is* a snake, isn't he? And snakes can be scary. Aren't you scared of him?'

Without hesitation, they shake their heads. 'We like him. And he likes us. He wants to stay.'

'Oh, so he's here now?'

'Yes.'

'But it's bedtime. Don't you think it's time for him to leave?'

They turn to Alfie. 'Can't he stay, Daddy?' Perhaps it's my imagination, but I think I hear a change in Sylvie's voice – suddenly it's more high-pitched, more babyish. The problem is never that a parent *has* a favourite; it's that their children know it.

Alfie doesn't answer, so I switch off the side light and kiss the girls one last time. 'Good night, angels.'

He leans in and kisses them too. 'Nighty night.'

We head towards the door.

'Please, Daddy,' Sylvie wheedles in the dark. 'Can he stay? Just for a bit. Like a sleepover, with a friend.'

That's it, I think instantly. That's what I've been missing. The source of Alfie's unease.

'Of course,' he whispers back. 'A friend of yours is a friend of mine. He can stay as long as you like.' He reaches forward to close the door. 'Sweet dreams.'

As soon as it's shut, I say it aloud: 'It's not the fact that he's imaginary, is it? It's the fact that he's a friend.'

Alfie laughs hollowly and nods. 'Stupid, isn't it?'

The girls have never had friends, not really. They're rarely invited to birthday parties or sleepovers. They've always been insular, uninterested in anyone except each other. Whilst Pippa and I yearned, from an early age, for a life outside the walls of Hart House – a life beyond each other – Sylvie and Cassia have never seemed to have that need. Pippa loved them more than anything, and they loved her too, of course, but they always loved each other more.

'It's who they are, Jewel,' she used to say, dreamily, if I ever queried it. 'They're more alike than you and I ever were. They're like two halves of one whole. They're two people and one person at once.'

And now they have a friend.

'Did I do the right thing?'

We're retreating down the stairs now, quietly – I more quietly than him. After all these years, I still remember every board that creaks.

'About what?'

'Black Mamba. Was I right to say that he could stay? Should I be playing along?' I reach the bottom, and turn to find Alfie at a halt, three steps up, one arm resting on the bannister.

'Sure. I see no harm in it.'

With his free arm, he runs his fingers through his sandy hair. 'What do snakes eat, anyway?'

'They're carnivorous. Small mammals, that kind of thing.' I fetch my bag from the kitchen, then return to the hallway for the rest of my things. 'Thanks for the tea,' I say, shrugging on my coat.

He's still by the bannister, but staring at the walls now, deep in thought, only dimly aware that I'm still present. I put on my scarf. I know we won't see each other again for a while, a few weeks at least. We're always at our worst around each other. Maybe we won't see each other again until next month. Until the first.

'Are you leaving?' Suddenly, he's out of his reverie, and

there's an urgency in his voice that perturbs me. 'There's one more thing.'

I've already turned to go.

'It's probably nothing.'

Somehow – I don't quite know how – I sense what he's going to say.

'This isn't the first strange thing they've said. About a month ago, they went through a phase of having nightmares.'

'Nightmares?' The adrenaline heightens my voice, but I keep it steady, just about.

'Yes.' There's a long, sick silence. 'They said there was a man in their room.'

And there it is.

'I'm sure you're right – it's nothing,' I say. 'I have to go.'

'Julia?' Alfie's voice rises, in confusion and concern – but I'm already gone, out of the front door and into the cold night air. The door slams shut behind me, echoing through the square. I rush towards my car, mind reeling. *I'm never coming back*, I think, though I know I'm coming back. I have to now.

I open the car door and fall inside. It's colder outside, but the cold inside feels worse: clammy and still. 'Oh God,' I moan, leaning forward onto the steering wheel. 'Oh God, oh God.'

It's happening again.

Two

Alfie

We were happy here once, and the twins were happiest of all. Even from the youngest age, they adored Hart House. 'It's special,' they'd insist, and we never demurred.

Every floor of Hart House is slender and pinched, its rooms all squashed together, but the building itself is tall, impossibly tall, with a winding staircase driven through its centre like a screw in a press. The house is crowned by a tiny attic and a terrace, and the master bedroom, on the top floor, has a skylight, through which Pippa and I would watch clouds drift by, or count the stars, or, during summer, lie in wait for a plane to bisect the brilliant blue. When the girls were out with Marian or Julia, we'd pull ourselves up through it and sit on the terrace. On hot days, we'd drink cold beer, and sometimes I'd stand, knees shaking, and lean against the baking tiles of the attic roof, to take in the view: Peter's Park, lounging before us like a paradise, and around it, endless rings of houses, stretching all the way to the city skyline.

'It's beautiful,' I'd say. 'Come, look.' But Pippa never would; she couldn't bear to touch the attic roof. So what if she hadn't seen with her own eyes what happened in there? She knew.

The façade of Hart House is white and peeling, and the walls inside are mostly pale. Colour in Hart House never seems to stick; yellow fades quickly into cream and red fades quickly into rose. Not that it matters – no two rooms look alike, even those painted the same chalky grey, for the light inside Hart House is magical: it dapples the paintwork, plays tricks. The living room, on the ground floor, has a large bay window that opens out on the park, and the walls always gleam, like a jug of milk in sunlight. By contrast, the bedroom I shared with Pippa has thin, narrow windows that face in the opposite direction, towards a nest of sloping rooftops, and the walls are always icy and bloodless.

Eric died in the attic, Pippa in the cellar. Both rooms are closed now, sealed off. Part of me would like to sell this house, but I couldn't do that to the girls. They've already lost enough.

I wake with a jolt, not knowing if it's Monday yet or Sunday still. Black Mamba's eyes – piercing yellow, blackly slit – meet mine, coolly, in the dark.

Everything hits me at once: an empty bottle, which I was holding when I fell asleep, is rolling towards the edge of the kitchen table. I lunge and catch it, just in time. I must have knocked it on its side in my sleep; perhaps that's what woke me. I stretch, and check my watch blearily. Six minutes to midnight. I cast Black Mamba a filthy look, then head to bed.

Ascending the spiral staircase, I listen for a sign that I've woken the girls. Silence – but on reaching the first floor, I peek inside their room anyway. For a moment or two, I stand in the doorway and watch my daughters sleep, their golden hair spread on the pillows, their limbs entwined beneath the duvet, which rises and sinks with their chests; blue chevrons and parabolas dip in and out of view as the coverlet ripples in the moonlight. Even in sleep, their breaths are unified.

I woke them at eight this morning. Or rather, I woke Sylvie. Cassia was already stirring, but when I entered the room she remained hunkered beneath the duvet, cloaking herself in her sister's warmth. Sylvie has always taken after me in that respect – groggy in the morning.

'Was Auntie Julia here last night?' yawned Sylvie, once I'd roused her. 'Or was that a dream?'

'It wasn't a dream,' I said. 'It was real.'

'She put us to bed?'

'She did.'

'And then she left?'

'Of course.'

I looked around the room and winced. *Thank God*, I thought, *for darkness*. The night had hidden from Julia the worst of the mess. Recently, the girls' carpet has come to resemble a graveyard of outfits, worn and discarded: yesterday's, and the day before that's, and the day before that's. Pippa's absence is everywhere; we're drowning in it.

After the accident, I expected chaos, so I was glad of chores – at first anyway. I thought that pressure to *just keep going*, for the sake of the girls, would keep me steady. But none of the clichés have any truth to them, or at least they didn't for me. After she died, my life just carried on as it had before, identical in every respect, but with Pippa hollowed out of it. Every day was appallingly ordinary. Outside Hart House, the sun shone and millions of Londoners went blithely about their lives; inside, every time I did a job, another needed doing, or re-doing – and none of it meant anything without her.

Still, the light of day can shame, at least a little. As the girls stirred, I got down on my hands and knees and began to tidy. 'Come on,' I said.

Cassia rose first, and plonked herself beside me on the floor. Sylvie groaned and stretched. Cassia picked up a stray crayon from among the debris, and began to doodle on some paper. Sylvie yawned.

Kneeling on the floor, as if to pray, I swept crumbs into my hand. 'Looks like Black Mamba enjoyed his tart,' I said drily, dropping the pile into the bin. I scooped up the surrounding socks and knickers and shook them gently over the basket's wicker rim. 'But I don't think we should give him any more.'

Cassia drew studiously, as though she hadn't heard, but Sylvie cocked her head.

'No?'

'No. Pastry's for humans, after all. Not snakes. And look!' I jabbed a finger at the only uncluttered spot in the bedroom: a barren patch of carpet in the corner. 'He's already starting to get fat.'

'Who is?' Still drenched in sleep, curled up and blinking like a baby mammal that has just been born, Sylvie seemed to straggle one beat behind the conversation, ever playing catch-up.

'Black Mamba,' I said. 'Can't you see? Soon he'll have to shed his skin, or he'll go pop.'

Sylvie's mouth fell open, as she finally realised what I was doing. She sat up sharply in bed and turned, in amazement, to her sister. Cassia looked up from her doodle and fixed me with one of her coldest stares.

'Why are you pretending you can see him?' she said. 'You can't. He doesn't want you to.'

Half-statement-of-fact, half-warning, Cassia's words shut down the conversation. They were the sound of a well being covered, a curtain being drawn.

A friend of yours is a friend of mine, I'd said last night. But I'd been wrong about that too.

'I'm just being silly,' I replied.

Now the rules are clear, I thought. *He's real, but he's ours, not yours.* I tried not to mind, and more or less managed it. The twins have always excluded me. They excluded Pippa too, when she was alive. It's what they do; it's who they are. It isn't that strange.

After the tidy-up, we went downstairs for breakfast. We'd run out of cereal, so I made pancakes instead – thin, crispy, dashed with lemon. Black Mamba, having heard my comments on his weight perhaps, didn't ask for one.

He waited until we were all seated at the breakfast table before he made his next demand.

'A portrait? On the kitchen wall?'

'It's only fair,' Sylvie litigated on his behalf, as I drizzled syrup over her stack. 'We've got a picture of Johnny' – their pet rabbit, who died last spring – 'and a picture of your dog from when you were little. Black Mamba's our friend. He should be there too.'

I struggled to refute her logic. 'Fine,' I said, reminding myself of Julia's words. *I'm sure you're right – it's nothing. I see no harm in it.* 'But how can we take his picture if he's invisible? Remember, I can't see him, because he doesn't want me to.'

Cassia's eyes narrowed as she scoured my face for signs of mockery, and I tried to look innocent. Success. Her mouth puckered in a pouty smile; perplexed but pleased.

Sylvie arrived at the solution. 'We'll draw him then! With artists' pens.'

'Yes,' Cassia said, her voice soon rising exuberantly. 'Yes, yes, yes!'

'Black Mamba likes that,' Sylvie said, smiling know-ingly as she cut into her pancakes. 'He says that we should both draw him … and *you* can judge which picture is the best.'

'I'd be honoured,' I said. 'It'll be nice to see what he looks like.'

While the girls finished their breakfast, I crept into the hallway and, a little reluctantly, unlocked the cellar door. The stone steps that lead down to the cellar form a grubby companion piece to our spiral staircase, and the cellar itself is deep and sunken. A long, curved groove bites into the ceiling, where infrared lighting used to hang, back when Eric used it as a darkroom. Now a bare bulb, draped with cobwebs, provides the sole illumination. The only other vestige of the room's former life is the matrix of wires, from which Eric used to peg his photographs, hanging unused and useless, casting shadows that criss-cross the floor.

When Sylvie spoke so lustily of 'artists' pens', I knew immediately that she wouldn't be fobbed off with crayons; only Pippa's finest would do. All her art materials lay in boxes lining the cellar walls, their lids thick with dust. I sifted through their contents quickly. I knew what I was looking for: the lacquered set that I bought Pippa for her last birthday. As soon as I found it, I fled the cellar, locking the door behind me and trying not to think of how it wasn't just her last birthday, but her *last* birthday, and trying not to think of how she died.

By the time I returned to the kitchen, the girls' plates had been licked clean, so we went upstairs and assembled the studio. A light, airy room on the second floor of our house – a room that Pippa only ever used for hanging laundry – seemed the perfect candidate, once the clothes horse had been removed. Deep pocks, like moon craters, dotted the carpet where it had stood. Sylvie and Cassia clutched their mother's pens reverently, marvelling at their lightness and sheen, the delicacy of their nibs, and we spread out some paper on the carpet. Solemnly, I placed a cushion in the middle of the room, onto which Black Mamba could slither.

'On your marks … get set …' I began, but Sylvie's pen had already touched down.

'Go!' she screeched, leaving her sister in the dust.

They drew, feverishly, for almost half an hour. I was forbidden from viewing their labours, so I sat on the opposite side of the room, watching the supple movements of their fingers and seeing lines emerge, but – upside down – understanding nothing; the perfect summation of what it's like to watch the twins do anything.

They inherited their skills from their mother. Pippa wasn't just a keen painter; she was a professional one. People *paid* for her work, and it was easy to understand why. When I first saw Pippa's art, it left me stunned – dumbstruck that such a gift could sit within a person. (This was in the early days, when things were simpler. When we laughed all the time, fucked all the time; when I was only just starting to fall for her.)

She never taught our girls to draw; she just drew with them, for hours on end. Whole weekends were swallowed up in craft, and the house became awash with paper. Not once did I see her model a technique, or lecture them. Instead, she inspired, praised, patiently kept them on task, and I marvelled as their talents emerged.

I've never been able to hold a pencil straight. I could have drawn with the three of them for just as long, or twice as long, and never come close to their level. So I left them to it. I watched and wondered – excluded by my nature and by choice – as Pippa lay next to our girls, the three of them following their imaginations, wherever they led.

When it was time for me to judge, the girls rotated their drawings with their unnerving knack for synchronicity, and I was permitted to part the curtain, and look into the most holy place.

'Oh wow,' I said. 'They're incredible.'

Incredibly similar.

'How did you—' I broke off, unsure how to phrase the question. The girls had both drawn the same elegant black snake, curled up in a weighty heap in the centre of the cushion, his skin patterned like diamonds. His eyes were aflame; his tongue, protruding slightly in both pictures, was as black as his body. But what caught my eye was the tail. Both girls had drawn the very end of his tail as pointing upwards, as if gesturing, nonchalantly, off the edge of the page.

'What?' Sylvie asked.

I didn't answer, but, subconsciously, I must have traced the tip of his tail with my finger.

'He was pointing at you,' Cassia explained. 'Because you're the judge.'

'Right,' I said. Black Mamba's golden eyes stared back at me, glowing off the paper. I turned, instinctively, to the empty cushion. The girls hadn't said anything to each other while they'd busied themselves with their drawings – not a word about how the snake was positioned. Had they looked at each other's work; had one twin copied the other? Or was it just a product of their twinship; the identical contours of their minds, effortlessly mirroring each other's thoughts, ideas, desires?

Before I could think on that further, another question.

'Whose is best?'

I turned back to face the girls, who were looking at me expectantly. How do you choose between your children? Or their drawings – which feels like the same thing. My answer's always been to let them choose themselves.

'Cassia, yours is nice,' I began. 'Lovely cross-hatching. But Sylvie ... these colours! *My word ...*'

The emphasis was enough.

'I win,' Sylvie said: a performative speech act.

Cassia – calmness personified, Pippa's rock – came to my rescue. 'Perhaps mine can hang in our bedroom,' she suggested.

'Good idea,' I replied, and Sylvie, after only the briefest of pauses, graciously nodded her head.

The framing ceremony for the winning portrait took place in the late afternoon. A dark frame, which brought out the intense yellow of Black Mamba's eyes, was selected, then affixed with hammer and nail between a picture of me, as a boy, with the beloved spaniel of my youth, and a picture of the girls clutching Johnny – Sylvie by his underbelly, Cassia by his powdery tail – in the final days of his life.

They didn't cry when he died. They just stared, blankly, at the empty carrier beside my feet, and asked me questions. *Where's he gone? Can he come back? Will we ever see him again?* I fumbled for answers – feeling my way through a gravel of hard truths and white lies. It would have been easier, perversely, had they been more upset. I could manage a strong arm around the shoulder; intellectual enquiry was harder to cope with.

And I couldn't ask for help from Pip, who lay catatonic on the sofa; too distraught to speak, her eyes red beneath their swollen lids.

The girls were pleased that Black Mamba had his spot in the hall of family pets. I was grateful for their happiness, and resented it at the same time. After putting them to bed that evening, I climbed back down the spiral staircase and returned to the kitchen. Opening the fridge, I pulled out a bottle of wine and poured a large glass. Alone at the table, I stared at the pictures on the wall until night fell, and only Black Mamba's fiery eyes remained visible – pinpricks of colour in the night.

*

Those same eyes watch me now – sharp and brilliant, lemony ink pressed firmly onto paper, though this time by Cassia's hand. Her drawing hangs just above the girls' shared bed. The coils of Black Mamba's body are hidden in shadow, but his cool unblinking stare shines out, identical in every respect to the one in the kitchen, at least in this light.

I want to rip it down, I realise suddenly. I want to rip both drawings down. But how could I do that to the girls? How could I take anything from them, ever again?

I have to go – if I linger in their room any longer, they'll wake. I close the door gently, and ascend to the top of the stairs. Wind whistles softly in the attic above my head, as I pad into the master bedroom. I can't call it 'our bedroom' anymore, but neither can I call it mine, so master it is.

I sink into the mattress, my teeth unbrushed and sour with the taste of wine, and fall asleep.

The next moment, we're at a beach, confronted by the vastness of the sky and the sea, stretching out to a seamless horizon. And it must be Britain because the sky is ashen and we're wearing coats. The twins skip about, invigorated by the cold, damp breeze, whilst Pippa and I walk arm in arm along the promenade, clinging to each other for warmth.

Collier Beach. Its name comes to me with ease, like a playing card turned over. We've been here many times; I recognise some of the shops, and the shape of the shingle. There's a beach vendor on the promenade, selling novelty items. We buy the girls balloons – big ones, cherry red – but when Sylvie touches the string of hers it bursts. I don't hear it pop. I feel the cold and the wet, but I hear no sound, like we're in a silent picture. I look down at the sorry remains of the balloon at Sylvie's feet – scraps of red rubber, like exploded flesh – and even Cassia stops skipping temporarily, sensing danger. I have no clue what to do, but I also know, distinctly, that it doesn't matter. Pippa scrapes back her raven hair, shoves me her things to hold, and bolts down the beach. When she reaches the edge of the water, she combs the shoreline until she finds a large pink shell. Bending, she dips it gracefully into the sea.

Then she returns, as if she'd never left, and presents it carefully to Sylvie. The shell overflows with creatures – sea horses and fish and brightly coloured worms that look like strawberry laces, glowing and wriggling. Sylvie's face lights up. She turns immediately to brandish it at Cassia, to make her jealous.

But Cassia isn't even looking. She's still playing with her red balloon. The strong wind tugs at the string, and before we know it, the current has lifted her clean off the ground; with every fresh gust, it carries her further away. And she's smiling – smiling and smiling, and I've never seen her look less interested in Sylvie in her life.

Sylvie reaches up for her twin's leg and starts to pull her back to earth. Impatient, she throws the shell to the ground, where it smashes. I hear the sound at last, like an egg breaking. No: louder, worse – like bones cracking. And I hear the hum of the wind, and the roar of the waves. And Pippa's voice.

'I'll get you another,' she says to Sylvie, as Cassia's feet touch the promenade once more. 'I'll get two.'

'No,' I say. *'No.'*

Pippa hears my fear, but laughs and shakes her head, like she can't quite comprehend it. Then she races back down to the sea, and picks up two more shells.

'No,' I cry again. But I'm stranded on the promenade with the girls; stuck behind the iron railings that separate land from sand. All I can do is watch.

Pippa wades out to sea, turning to wave at us, still clutching the shells.

'Drop them,' I shout, but she can't hear me, and before I can take another breath I see her look down into the water. For a moment, she looks inquisitive, her face full of wonder, but it soon turns to panic. Then she's snatched beneath the surface.

I scream as she disappears into the ocean's depths. I scream until a gust of wind blows the ash from the sky into my mouth.

I wake up, sweating – Pippa's frightened face etched on the backs of my eyelids. It takes a moment of slow breathing to remind myself where I am. I place a hand on my chest, and focus on slowing my heart. Thump-thump-thump. Thump.

Thump.

How much time has passed since I checked on the girls? An hour? Two? As I exhale, I study my surroundings: the narrow shape of the window frame, the chequered pattern of the bedsheets, the shadowy outline of the dresser. Their familiarity restores me, comforts me. I can see them fairly well, even in the dark.

Abruptly, realisation strikes: I'm not in the dark, at least not completely. The bedroom light is off, but a bright sliver is running along the bottom of the door to our en suite – a crack through which light seeps like sand.

It's Pippa. That's my first thought. It's an automatic reflex, and a cruel one. That's something you can't prepare yourself for: the pain that's self-inflicted. The unbearable cruelty of dreaming and waking – of forgetting, and half forgetting. And remembering.

'Sylvie?' I call out. 'Cassia?'

Silence.

'Are you okay?'

The light in the en suite flicks off, the door opens, and a dark shape moves across the room as my daughter, whichever one it is, leaves the room. Ordinarily, I'd get straight up, find out who it was, check she's all right, but I'm so tired I sink back into the folds of the bed. All I want to do is return to sleep – to a dream or a nightmare; any place where Pippa isn't dead forever.

I don't want to be a single parent when I wake in the morning.

Sometimes, I don't care if I wake in the morning.

When I wake for the third time, the bedroom is bleached with daylight, so bright it hurts my eyes. I stir slowly, emerging this time from a different kind of sleep: deep and dreamless – as though my mind is rising, sluggishly, from the cellar of the house. It must be late, because the light from the sun outside is almost white. I feel guilty for leaving the girls to fend for themselves, but when I hurry downstairs, I'm relieved to see their bedroom door is shut and they're not yet up and watching the telly. I go to the kitchen to prepare them some breakfast.

'Room service,' I say, knocking lightly on their bedroom door, tray in hand. I push the door open and find the girls still half asleep beneath the covers. Cassia's drawing of Black Mamba hangs at a skewed angle over the bed. In daylight, it looks shallow and innocuous, almost comically so. Embarrassed, I quickly look away.

I set the tray gently on the bedside table, then clamber into bed between the girls, making them squeal in protest. Beneath the covers they grab hold of me and tickle. The despair I felt last night is still there, but it has retreated, and I find myself laughing, joining in with the game, begging them to stop. When we're all worn out, I pull the girls close to me so that I can feel their heartbeats, and hear their gentle breathing, like two seashells pressed against my ears; the sound of the sea.

Suddenly, I remember my dream last night, and how I woke from it. 'Who used the loo in the night?' I ask the girls vaguely, indifferently.

Cassia's head rises. Strands of her wispy hair fall into my mouth.

'Which loo?'

Mine, I think – and wince. 'Mummy and Daddy's.'

At that, Sylvie sits up too, bemused. The girls stare down at me where I lie, squashed against the headboard. 'We didn't go to the loo last night,' they say in unison.

'One of you did.'

Sylvie, ever groggy, sinks back, indifferently, beneath the sheets. But Cassia remains upright, her face inscrutable. 'Perhaps it was Black Mamba.'

I dredge her hair out of my mouth and tuck it behind her ear before pulling her gently to the pillows. 'Don't be daft. Snakes can't switch lights on, remember. They don't have hands.'

Cassia's face is barely an inch from mine, so I see immediately the flicker in her eyes. 'Black Mamba's not a snake.' There's indignation in her voice, but more than anything, surprise. 'He's a man.'

I hear the words, but it takes me a moment to absorb them. 'A man?'

'A man,' she repeats solemnly, before adding, wideeyed: 'A *magic* man.'

'He can *turn* into a snake,' Sylvie explains, half yawning, her voice muffled as she speaks into the sheets. 'He can turn into whatever he wants.'

'A man?' I repeat, as if in a stupor – until, finally, it dawns on me. 'The man in your room,' I whisper.

'That's right,' Cassia says, delightedly. 'The man in our room.'

Three

Julia

I'm home – 'home' being my north London flat. Just three rooms, but tastefully done out, or so I like to think. I'm not my sister. Decorating three rooms is the limit of my artistic capability. Any more space, I tell myself, and things would start to look threadbare. A couple of *nouvelle vague* film posters hang above the sofa. On the mantelpiece sits a row of succulents in tiny terracotta pots. Door locked, chain fastened, I kick off my shoes, dump my bag on the sofa and pour myself a glass of wine from the half-empty bottle in the fridge. Home.

Except I'm not, not really. Home is Hart House, even after all these years; even after everything that happened there. I draw back the gauzy netting that droops over my flat's solitary window, and gaze over the city rooftops. As ever, no stars are out to light the headlands; the horizon is a thick, dark band of winter mist and pollution. But the knowledge that Hart House – like Parliament or

Tower Bridge – is out there somewhere, sitting quietly in the darkness, waiting for me, wriggles in the pit of my stomach.

Instinctively, I distract myself the best way I know how: with more work. My leave of absence has only just ended, but already I'm slipping back into bad habits. I pick up my bag again, open my laptop, and write notes on today's crop of clients – Andrew and Jen, who don't like their kids; Doug and Louise, who don't trust their kids; Simon and Ralf, who can't decide whether to have them ...

There's a restaurant at the bottom of the building so my flat is always overheated, even in winter, and the air shot through with faint cooking smells. After an hour, the hunger pangs are so great they force me to stop. I slip off my clothes and eat a microwaved lasagne in my underwear. Then I run a bath, taking a second glass of wine with me into the en suite. I strip and lower myself gingerly into the tub, allowing each limb enough time to adjust to the water's heat. Then, my body fully submerged, I feel my muscles relax and I focus on the sensation of the water against my skin. To the extent that I allow myself thoughts, I keep them simple and brief:

I have a body.

I *am* a body.

This is what it feels like to be me.

Except, before I know it, I'm in Hart House again, recalling the summer when Mum spent each day coaxing me and Pippa to lie on the living-room floor, side by side.

'Close your eyes,' she'd say eagerly, and we obeyed.

The carpet felt warm and soft, and sunlight, streaming in through the open bay window, lit up the backs of our eyelids in a pinkish glow. Mum would pace around us, carefully adjusting the positions of our legs, arms, hair and fingers, until – to her exacting eye – Pippa and I were perfectly in sync with each other, our posture identical.

'Now, clear your minds,' she'd say excitedly. 'Focus on your bodies, and how they feel. Try to relax.'

The theory was that by adopting the same pose, identical in every respect, our minds would meld into one, and thoughts would be free to cross from Pippa's mind to mine, and back again, via a psychic bridge. This was just one of Mum's many theories about how the mind works that I've yet to see borne out by science, despite all my years working as a psychotherapist.

'Think of an animal,' she'd urge one of us, before instructing the other to 'allow the image to come through'. Pippa and I were happy to oblige. I remember screwing up my eyes, trying to welcome her animal in.

A beaver? No. *A pony?* No. *An otter?*

'Don't block the energy,' Mum would warn, anxiously, if the number of failed guesses started to mount. 'It won't work if you do.'

Most of the time, though, one of us obviously did block the energy, as results were decidedly mixed. The summer wore on, and we tired of playing. Yet Mum's enthusiasm for the new game remained undimmed, and she sighed whenever we messed about or fidgeted. Sometimes she even started to cry, and her tears soon made us behave. Pippa and I were good girls; we couldn't bear to see our mum upset – not after Dad died.

Correction: not after what Dad *did*.

Whenever Mum cried, we'd pull ourselves together and approach the game with renewed focus, until her excitement returned, redoubled. Breathless, she'd instruct one of us to picture a person in our mind's eye – anyone we knew – and to focus minutely on their hair colour, their eye colour, their skin, and let the image float across.

Once, and only once, I thought of Dad. I pictured his black bushy beard, and the unfaltering smile that always masked whatever was going on beneath: the spools of worry in his head; the coils of regret. I pictured him so exactly that I, too, began to cry, and had to screw up my eyes even more tightly to fight back the tears.

But then Pippa began to speak – an image was coming through – and she spoke of a man with a dark beard, and I backed off immediately, shocked and panicked, and thought of someone else.

The tips of my fingers have wrinkled up like raisins, and I'm beginning to feel cold. Focusing on my body has ceased to be a source of relaxation; my mind is racing with thoughts of the house – the things that Pippa saw there, or said she did; the things the girls have seen now too.

A man in their room. I didn't press Alfie for details. I couldn't bear to.

Shivering, I rise out of the bathtub, heaving water with me. A little slops over the edge, and I see something scuttle, out of the corner of my eye. There's a daddy-long-legs spider on the bathroom floor. When I was very small, I believed they had that name because Daddy always killed them. They have another name, those spiders, but it eludes me; like a dream, slipping from memory.

The daddy-long-legs darts again, towards me this time. The urge to stay in the safety of the tub is there, of course, but I repress it. Years of living alone and, before that, living with Mum's histrionics have inured me. I drain my wine glass, turn it upside down, and imprison the spider underneath. These things are surprisingly easy when you don't have a choice.

Trapping insects was my job for years, even before Pippa left home. I somehow inherited all the jobs that Dad had once done. Pippa wasn't expected to help; I was the older twin – by all of three minutes – and apparently that meant something to everyone but me. The perils of growing near the exit are not explained to children in the womb, but perhaps they should be.

I inspect the creature as best I can through the curved glass, which has steamed up a little in the bathroom's heat. *Cellar spiders.* That's the other name they go by. I reach hurriedly for a towel. Now it's not just the water that's making me shiver.

I pad into the bedroom, drying myself hurriedly before flopping onto the bed. A photograph of Pippa, Alfie and the girls, all smiling sweetly, stares at me from the top of the dresser. I close my eyes tightly, trying not to think of how – and where – my sister died.

It's no use. Outside, darkness has fallen; there's no pinkish, summery glow to illuminate the backs of my eyelids. In the gloom, all I see is Pippa's face, beaming; the face of my twin, like mine in several ways, but different in many more. It's the face of a woman who never had to trap her own spiders, I think, a little coldly. And then I remind myself, forcefully, *I love that face* – and it's on that thought, tonight, that I shall fall asleep.

Before I slip under the duvet, I check my phone. Alfie hasn't called while I've been in the bath.

When I'm writing up notes, my clients' feelings are so often obvious to me – clear cut. My own are much harder to parse. As I get into bed, I try to identify them. There's relief that he hasn't called, certainly – but somehow, alongside it, disappointment too.

And something deeper still: a sliver of dread.

When she sold Hart House to Pippa, shortly after her stroke, Mum moved into the basement flat beneath the church that we attended as kids. I still have to remind myself that it's a real church; it never felt like one when we were growing up. We visited churches when we holidayed in Scotland, so I knew, even then, what a real church was. Real churches, I thought, resembled sleeping stone beasts, with enormous rib-vaulted lungs. They were tall buildings, broad and buttressed – their walls made of impossibly large stones, each bigger than a bull's head. Real churches had naves and apses, and were ice cold – festooned with carved bosses, rood screens and gothic spires.

Our church was a terraced house. A small brass plaque next to the front door was the only clue to what lay inside. THE LORD'S SERVANT AT ENDOR, the plaque read, and then, in smaller letters underneath: A CHURCH OF CHRIST.

This morning, as I walk up the short flight of steps that connects pavement and porch, I linger for a second in the building's shadow. The words on the plaque are still there, but the brass has oxidised and spotted. The knocker has corroded too. I tap it sharply and step back to see the curtains twitch. The inhabitants of the Lord's Servant are faceless behind the ivory netting, but nonetheless I smile. They can see me, but I can't see them. Or, at least, I see them only dimly – *through a glass darkly*, as the Lord's servants might say. Just like we see God; just like we see the dead.

Right on cue, the curtain trembles, and then, a moment later, the door opens.

'Julia!' Auntie Sue smiles, then frowns – delighted, though clearly mystified, by my presence. She lifts a hand, blushing slightly, and gently pats down her delicate carapace of white hair. 'Well, what a nice— Heavens! It's Wednesday, isn't it?'

'Yes,' I say. 'Wednesday.'

'Marian!' Auntie Sue ushers me inside as she calls back, cheerily, over her shoulder.

'Yes?'

'Julia's here. It's Wednesday.'

'What?'

'It's *Wednesday*.'

'Julia?'

Mum's rooms are downstairs – she calls it 'the dungeon', a little ungraciously, given that Sue lets her live there rent-free – but her voice is coming from the ground-floor kitchen: Auntie Sue's kitchen. The distinct smell of meat, charring, wafts towards me. The clear demarcations of domestic space, so rigid when Mum first moved in with her sister-in-law, are slowly dissolving. Or *being* dissolved; perhaps that's a better way to put it. Mum has a special knack for breaking down boundaries.

I scowl as she emerges from Auntie Sue's kitchen and bustles down the hallway like she owns the place, her crown of dirty-grey hair bobbing imperiously. *This must be a good day*, I think. *No joint pain, no migraine, no fatigue – the effects of her stroke, so present on days when she's angry with me, miraculously at bay*. Only when she gets closer, and I see that her eyes are red and puffy, do I rebuke myself. I'm being unkind, too cynical. I'm forgetting her fragility.

'Darling ...' Mum enfolds me in a tight hug. Though it's been ten months, it still feels strange; she was never this tender when Pippa was alive. That's a way in which both she and Alfie have changed. Sometimes, it's as though they've each split, in my mind, into two versions of themselves – one from before the accident, one from after.

When I'm released, Auntie Sue twirls around me, unwinding my scarf. Sue's lived here as long as I can remember. No. 2, Crescent Place. Every inch is familiar to me, from the shapes and faces in the wood panelling to the strawlike scent of the carpet. While the rooms in Hart House are big and airy, with high ceilings and white walls, No. 2 has always felt cosy and hunched. The walls are painted in primary colours – faded now, of course – and the furnishings are eternally soft; though they, too, have begun to seem shabby and worn. Unlike Hart House, which changed in décor when Pippa and Alfie moved in, No. 2 has stayed the same over the years – doggedly so. The world outside has moved on, but the Lord's Servant has refused to move with it.

'Come in, come in.' Sue ushers us both into the sitting room, her inner sanctum.

'Oh, please,' I protest, 'there's no need. We can go downstairs.'

But Auntie Sue covers her ears, smiling, and shakes her head.

'Are you sure?' I ask, even though the three of us are already inside. 'We don't want to intrude.'

My use of 'we' must sound barbed to Mum, as her eyes narrow. I didn't mean it to, but still – I can't quite shake the feeling that whenever Sue leaves the house, Mum abandons her dungeon immediately and comes in here to sprawl on the chaise longue.

My aunt shepherds me into an antique chair, lavishly upholstered. 'Something to drink? Or eat?' She leans forward in a stage whisper. 'Any fruit cake?'

Auntie Sue's fruit cake was a staple of my childhood – enormous chunks of glazed cherry walled in by moist sponge, dense and drenched in alcohol. She made one for me and Pippa, I recall, on our fifth birthday. I stared at it in wonder. It was the largest cake I'd ever seen, too heavy to lift. I remember sitting by my sister, the whole congregation gathered around us, as if in homage. I remember the pleasure I felt – all eyes upon us – as I took my first bite.

'Go on, then.'

We were around five, I suppose, when we began to realise that our church was different in more ways than one. It wasn't just the building that we prayed in, the curious anonymity of it. The absence of a pastor, or any kind of single figurehead, became ever more striking as the years flowed by. Everyone – our parents told us firmly – has a direct connection with God; and so, at church meetings, everyone's feelings were weighed in equal measure.

'Herbal tea? We've got peppermint, sage, chamomile, and . . .' Sue closes her eyes, her mouth moving chaotically as she tries to trick her tongue into saying the words that her mind can't reach. She bends down and slaps my knee. 'Lemon balm!'

She laughs, and I can't help but laugh too. When Pip and I stopped going to church, seeing our aunt each Sunday was the only thing we truly missed. Although the

Lord's Servant had no leader, at the heart of everything was Auntie Sue. During my girlhood, she always seemed larger than life, with her reams of coiffed blonde hair and her perfect teeth. She was a gifted organiser; she ran the church almost by herself. She was my dad's big sister; a successful estate agent – it was she who acquired Hart House for us – and an endless fount of wisdom. The comparison between her and my mother was never favourable.

Of course, the years have reduced her, as they have the brass plaque outside. These days, Sue stoops, you can see her scalp, and church business is mostly managed by her daughters.

'Just a builder's, please.'

'Lovely. I'll bring in a tray. Then leave you two in peace.'

I move to say, for a second time, 'No need,' that she's welcome to stay, but then I see her glance at Mum and I understand. We don't need peace; Sue does. I sympathise, having lived alone with Mum myself for many years. My aunt's in a worse position than I was, though, as she doesn't have the option of moving out. This is, after all, her house.

While Sue and I have been talking, Mum's been rocking on the edge of the chaise longue and tapping her knee.

'Everything okay?' I ask her, as Sue leaves the room.

She nods, almost imperceptibly.

'Are you sure?'

Mum scowls but doesn't answer. She won't start on me, I know, until Sue has returned with the tea – then left for good.

I sigh, lightly, but say nothing. I recognise this mood, of course; Mum cycles, broadly speaking, between two. Ever since Dad died, she has lived in a state of complete inertia, punctuated by manic episodes of intense frustration with the inertia that she perceives all around her. Since her stroke, and Pippa's accident, those peaks and troughs have only become more pronounced.

The sound of Sue busying herself in the kitchen travels faintly down the hallway, underscored by my mother's endless tapping. As we wait, I scan the room's familiar contents. The bookcase, with its leather-bound volumes. Plants in porcelain, little knick-knacks, potpourris: the same bowl for decades, now almost scentless. No photographs, but, above the mantelpiece, three framed pictures. On the left, a poor watercolour of the Transfiguration: the spirits of Moses and Elijah, long dead but radiant, appearing next to Christ, to the amazement of His disciples. On the right, an oil print of King Saul, seeking out the wise woman at Endor – her arms aloft as she raises the spirit of Samuel from the pit.

And between them, elevated in a brass frame, a black-and-white drawing of Michael, my cousin, age seven – a pencil sketch from the year he died.

Michael was Sue's only son. I never met him; he died before I was born. I saw a photo of him once, and recognised him instantly, so I think the likeness of the drawing must be good. Then again, I saw that photo for only a couple of seconds, when I was a child. I know where it will be: in the attic, in a locked red box, marked with a pure white cross, where Sue stores all her photographs. Despite the prominence of the black-and-white sketch, in all these years I've never once heard her speak of her son.

'It goes best with butter and cream.'

Sue's back. She sets the fruit cake, and its artery-clogging accompaniments, down on the coffee table with a smile. When we were younger, my aunt made it so often that Mum would even call her 'Fruit Cake', on occasion, but I haven't heard her use that sobriquet in years. Since Sue's forgetfulness began, I guess it seems inappropriate.

Mum ignores the cake. She's fidgeting now, as though scalded by the chaise longue; she's desperate to speak. Her grief is the reverse image of my aunt's. While Michael's death has been shrouded in silence all these years, my sister's is a scab at which Mum just can't help but pick.

'I'll leave you two in peace,' Sue says again, backing out of the room without turning away from my mother, as if she were a queen.

As soon as she's gone, Mum's tongue at last breaks loose.

'I thought you weren't coming.'

I breathe, and sip my tea calmly. 'I always come.'

'Well, thank the Maker. We need you, Julia – now more than ever.'

We. Now it's Mum's turn to whip out a provocative plural.

She leans forward, teetering even more precariously on the edge of her seat. 'Have you been to the house this week?'

I swallow hard. She knows about the nightmares – if, indeed, that's what they were. *She knows about the man in their room.*

'Julia!'

'Yes,' I answer, trying to steady myself. 'Yes, I have. I saw the girls one evening.'

'And?'

'And ...' I'm reluctant to finish but, after a moment, I say truthfully: 'I thought they seemed okay.'

Mum shakes her head balefully. I'm not surprised. This has been her refrain for the past ten months: how the girls aren't coping – and how I'm, in part, to blame.

In the weeks following Pippa's death, I built a wall between myself and Hart House and its inhabitants. But I couldn't cut Mum out of my life and, every time I saw her, her words poked tiny holes in that wall's great structure. She'd whisper of the twins' pain, their endless tears. She'd describe how Sylvie's meltdowns, formerly a preserve of her infancy, had returned. She'd explain how Cassia's calmness had morphed into detachment. How she wouldn't speak of Pippa at all, not to anyone. Not even to Sylvie.

I refused to counsel the girls, but I couldn't refuse to hear of their distress – or of Alfie's anger at my detachment, which Mum conveyed with particular, unfeeling persistence. Or at least, so it seemed at the time. It's hard to keep these things in perspective.

'Honestly,' I insist. 'They seemed all right.'

Mum shakes her head again, more fiercely this time. 'It's not them I'm worried about. It's Alfie.'

I start; this is new.

'He isn't coping. Philippa kept that house steady. Now it's a mess. I've offered to help. Believe me, I've tried. I've brought round food. I've said I'll clean. But all I get is deflection. *It's all in hand. We're doing fine.*'

'He doesn't want your help, Mum.' I try to keep my tone neutral.

'Oh, I know.' Any attempts at neutrality on my mother's part always end in failure. 'He wants *yours*, Julia.'

My eyes narrow, instinctively, as I study my mother from across the room. I think of her efforts to get Pippa back to Hart House, after I left it – in the end, she practically gave it away – and I recoil at her trying the same thing with me. Visions flood my head of lying on the floor in Hart House beside my twin, watching Mum's hands move in a blur about our bodies, shifting our limbs this way and that.

She meets my stare head on, her own eyes narrowing, like a chess player considering her next move. Alfie's rage and disappointment failed to make me budge. Would his desperation?

'I think, Mum ... he's okay without me.'

A brief silence, and then – I should have seen them coming – a trickle of tears.

'Please, darling. Trust me. Something's wrong in that house. A gulf is growing between Alfie and those girls ...'

She breathes heavily, stroking the fabric of the chaise longue. 'I can feel it like a groove beneath my fingers ...'

'A gulf between them?'

Mum nods gravely. 'He was coping better,' she whispers, 'when they weren't.'

I shudder. For the first time, her words ring true; they correspond with what I saw and felt myself, when I visited Hart House. I rebuke myself again, more harshly this time. I'm being unkind again, too cynical. Forgetting how much she cares.

I sip some more tea and mumble vague promises. To escape her gaze, I check my phone, and immediately go red.

'What is it?'

I thrust the phone back into my handbag. Alfie has rung me three times in the last ten minutes.

'It's nothing.'

'Julia—'

'Just ... a situation at the clinic.' I gulp down the rest of my tea. 'I need to go. Enjoy the cake.'

Mum groans, but leans over the coffee table and cuts herself a weighty slice. Her frustration has finally peaked; already, I can see inertia beginning to return. 'When will I see you next?'

'Wednesday week.'

'Too long,' she answers, with her mouth full.

'It'll come round soon enough.'

Mum grunts, dejectedly. 'Promise me you'll think about what I've said.'

I'm already at the door, turning the handle.

'I promise.'

When I enter the hallway, I start. Sue's waiting for me, with my scarf and coat. 'Take care of yourself, Auntie,' I say, giving her a hug. The soft wool of her cardigan compresses beneath my fingers until I reach, with shock, her tiny, twig-like arm.

'You too,' she says gently. Even though she's frail, the light in her eyes is undiminished. 'Don't worry about Marian,' she adds. 'The Lord will comfort her. He *does* comfort her.'

'Yes?'

'Oh, yes.'

'And does He comfort you?'

I'm not quite sure what makes me say it, and for a split second I worry I've made a terrible mistake. I've never raised Michael's ghost before, never made even the slightest allusion. But it's okay – Sue just smiles and takes my hand.

'Yes,' she says again, even more emphatically. Her eyes shimmer, and I wonder if she can remember her son's face as something separate from the pencil sketch – the cherublike smile, the smudged curls. Suddenly, her grip tightens, and she leans in. 'It wasn't his fault,' she whispers. 'You should know that. Even if he won't listen. I've tried telling him, of course, but you know how he can be.' Sue's voice is firm but quiet, as though she's unveiling an age-old secret.

It takes me a moment to realise that she's not talking about Michael. She means my father. I don't know what to say. I've heard her speak of the dead as though they're still living a few times before – 'All part of the dementia,' Mum says – but never like this.

'I'm sorry,' I whisper.

Sue just smiles again, and shakes her head. 'That's the point: you shouldn't be. Nor should he. It was no one's fault.'

There's silence – taut and vulnerable, like skin pulled tightly over bone – and then she speaks again.

'I'm sorry too.'

It's dark by the time I'm back at the flat. Before I switch on the lights, I spot the eye of the answering machine, blinking red. Landlines are a relic, I know, but Mum insisted I keep it, in case of emergencies, and after her stroke I couldn't deny her that. I think again of Alfie's missed calls, steadily mounting. I didn't call him back. I should have, straight away when I left Mum's, and part of me wanted to, to hear his voice. But I still can't face what's happening in that house.

I feel my way through the shadows to the kitchenette and open the fridge. My bare arms are bathed in cold light. I reach for the bottle of wine, almost empty now, before turning back to press the button. A high-pitched, automated tone, then – *Alfie.*

'It's me. Listen, can you come round at the weekend? I'm worried about the girls. Remember the nightmares I told you about? The man in their room? Well, that was him: Black Mamba. The snake. Their imaginary friend. Please come. I know you said not to worry, but ...'

I replay the message, several times, to absorb its contents and their meaning. *The man in their room ... was him. Their imaginary friend.* I rub my forehead, attempting to self-soothe. This is good news, I tell myself. Whatever the girls saw in their room at night, it's not the same thing Pip saw, all those years ago; it can't be.

Yet I still feel flushed with unease.

I replay the message again – not to listen to the words this time; instead, just to hear Alfie speak.

When I first met him, almost a decade ago, I was instantly struck by his voice: deep, rounded and smooth. He was young – younger than Pippa and me – and his voice was like a brand-new cello, barely used. The years have altered it, of course; hoarsened it, roughened the edges. Cigarettes, alcohol and grief. But beneath the abrasion, I can still hear the voice that attracted me the first time I heard it.

We met for lunch in Soho: Pippa, Alfie, Mum and me. The restaurant looked more art gallery than eatery, and the tablecloth was impeccably pressed. Pippa hung off Alfie's every word, and he off hers. Their eyes moved in tandem; they smiled at their own private jokes. They were two souls, moving as one. I'd never seen a performance like it.

Pippa talked about the two of them moving in together, renting a flat, and Mum, who'd barely recovered from Pippa leaving home, smiled tightly, like she'd bitten into a lemon.

'You know what they say,' Mum had mused, elliptically. 'If you want to make God laugh, tell him your plans.'

Alfie swirled the wine in his glass and answered, 'If you want to make Alfie laugh, tell him about God,' and Pippa snorted into her napkin.

When I'm done listening to the recording, I delete it and lie on the sofa, determined to reply by text. I'll tell him to contact the clinic; recommend a colleague who can help. But I can't get the tone right, sometimes sounding too stiff, other times not quite formal enough, and before long I put my phone down, the message unsent.

I wake from the nightmare with a start. I've had this dream before – in the last ten months, it's split my sleep like a cleaver, more than a dozen times – but never quite like this. The streets outside are deathly silent. In darkness, I pull myself off the sofa and grope my way towards the sink to pour myself a glass of water.

The dream always starts the same way:

I'm standing on the bank of a frozen river – just like Dad was that day – and the girls are playing on the ice, just as Michael did. The riverbank is block-white, glittering as if scattered with fallen stars, and my breath forms solid clouds in the air. Everything is picture-perfect. Pillared pine trees, dusted with snow. A holiday cabin, snugly tucked on the horizon.

And the ice is thick – or so we believe.

A shout. Not Auntie Sue's, but Alfie's.

I turn to face the river, its frozen surface like a clouded mirror. *All the rivers run into the sea; yet the sea isn't full.* I glance down. Beneath the immaculate ice, its currents still flow, and flow fast.

Usually, the dream ends here: it ends as I glimpse the girls rushing past through the water, trapped beneath the thick ice – pitilessly dragged from where it broke, eyes staring in terror.

But this time, it's different. This time, it's Alfie I see, trapped at my feet – helplessly banging his fists against the river's lid – and I scream as the current sweeps him away.

I sip the glass of water as I pick up my phone. My eyes smart at the light from the screen. I've found the words, though it feels like they've found me; there's something automatic – irresistible – about them. I feel sick as I type them out.

I'll come round on Saturday and talk to the girls. I'll find out what's going on.

Four

Alfie

They say that grief numbs, but I still feel everything and mostly it hurts. So I try to savour small pleasures. It's Saturday, and the sun is shining. Shivering slightly in the early-morning air, I strip and step into the shower, yanking the lever. The water is tepid at first, then beautifully hot. I close my eyes as it runs over my head, across my shoulders, down my back.

I've always loved hot showers, the kind that leave your skin warm and glowing once dry. When Pippa was alive, she'd come into the bathroom after I'd finished, press her cool body against mine, and say something daft like, 'You're *definitely* a mammal.' Or, other times, she'd slip into the shower behind me while the water still flowed, and kiss my neck, my shoulders; take me in her hand.

The reverie lasts a few seconds, then I snap out of it, almost slipping. Searing pain is spreading like a rash across my stomach. The water is stinging me. Panicked, I tug the lever, stopping the flow, and look down. Four long, deep marks are scratched into my stomach – bright red, and growing redder. The suddenness of the pain surprises me; I didn't feel or see the marks when I got out of bed. It's as if the water carved them into my body.

I yank the lever again, and soap up, examining the scratches closely. I can't think where they've come from – what could have happened in the night. I start to feel uneasy, but then rebuke myself for being so childish; so irrational. I scratched myself in my sleep, I must have. The water just made the marks sting. Defiantly, I linger in the shower for even longer than usual, only leaving when the hot water runs out. I return to the bedroom and reach for my phone. Distractedly, only half looking, I type the words 'unexplained scratch marks appear in night' and search the web.

I get a range of results – from dermatitis to demon possession. I toss my phone aside, pull on some clothes.

Jogging down the spiral stairs, I sprint through sunbeams, scattering dust. The girls' bedroom door is closed; they must still be asleep. Whenever they're at school, or out with Marian, or in the land of Nod, I turn the days of the past inside out and wear them again, as I do when I run out of socks. Moments ago, Pip was in the en suite with me, naked and smiling. When I reach the bottom of the staircase, breathless, I see her again – drifting through the hallway in her old brown painting smock.

I stop on the bottom step and she looks at me quizzically – tubes of paint in hand and a brush tucked adroitly behind her left ear, as I saw her a thousand times. Her hair is a curate's egg, scraped back neatly in parts, otherwise falling chaotically; there's a smudge of black paint on her cheek. Prismatic light drifts through the air and settles on her pale, pinched face. Her smile is perfect.

'Come,' she says, before adding, with a burst of feeling: *'Alfie.'*

She claimed to love saying my name; the way it felt on her lips, the way it made her mouth move. These days, saying her name hurts – like I'm trying to breathe life back into her. I whisper it sometimes in the dark.

I long to reach out and touch her, to fold my hands under her smock, where it's warm; to follow her into the cellar.

'Five minutes,' I say, exactly as I used to: softly, teasingly. 'Just five.'

Her sister will be here soon.

Julia

I'm back. Not because I want to be, but because he's asked me to. And this visit will be the first of many. I've succumbed at last; I'm going to counsel the girls.

I ring the doorbell and rub my arms while I wait. It's a dazzling morning, but a cold one. An age passes before, at last, I hear movement inside Hart House.

Alfie opens the door with a sad smile.

'Thanks for coming,' he says, taking my coat.

'It's not a problem,' I lie, stepping inside. 'Are you okay?'

It's more than just a pleasantry; he looks a mess. He runs a hand through his unruly hair, which is still a little wet. 'Just tired. You?'

'Fine.'

He nods. His eyes are vacant; his mind's still somewhere else.

I lift my gaze to the spiral staircase, and lower my voice. 'And the girls?' It's gone nine, but I can hear that they're still in their room: the murmur of their voices filters through the floorboards.

Alfie chews over his answer. 'They're ... okay,' he says, waving a hand. He's talking generally, but at least I've brought him back to earth.

Has he even seen them this morning?

He takes my coat and cradles it in his arms for a moment, before turning to hang it up. 'Go through,' he says. 'Do you want some tea?'

'Please.'

I take a step down the hallway towards the kitchen. But as I get to the door, my hand, reaching out for the handle, is stilled in mid-air by what I see.

The cellar door is open.

'I thought ...'

'What?' Alfie turns and follows my gaze. 'Oh. Right.' He shrugs. 'I usually keep it locked. But I thought it could do with a clear-out.' He motions further down the hallway. I follow the arrow of his finger until my eye alights upon a large canvas frame resting against the wall. The canvas itself is hidden from view.

'One of Pippa's?' I say.

'Of course.'

Pippa's art was extraordinary. She painted human figures, but blurred, abstract ones, as eerie as Bacon's; figures that belonged to another world; who stood in dark, swirling fog, lit by shafts of ethereal colour – pinks, silvery-blues, off-yellows – the palette of El Greco. Her subjects were tricky to place. Sometimes, the figures seemed allegorical: the Seven Virtues, the Four Seasons, Death and the Maiden. In other works, I detected a classical theme: a portrait of a bathing girl with a voyeur crouched malignantly beside her – Diana and Actaeon possibly, or was it David and Bathsheba? Pippa stayed silent. Perhaps she wasn't always sure herself.

I pick at the hem of my sleeve. 'They were beautiful,' I say, quietly. 'The ones on display at her funeral.'

Alfie looks away sharply. *Her funeral.*

The service was a surreal affair, and not just because Pippa was dead. We were in a church, because where else would we be? But half the mourners didn't believe, and those who did rarely set foot inside a proper church. It was odd, seeing the congregants of the Lord's Servant – Sue, Sue's daughters, Mum of course, and more distant relatives – sitting awkwardly on the pews; just as awkwardly as Alfie and I, maybe more so. For all of us, the day was something to be endured. If anything would help us come to terms with Pippa's death, this wasn't it.

And there, in the midst of it all, were my sister's paintings – haunting in their beauty – hanging from every wall of the church. The Seven Virtues. The Four Seasons.

Death and the Maiden.

'Yeah, well,' Alfie says, rubbing his eyes, 'this wasn't one of them.' He tilts the canvas away from the wall and spins it around. 'She started it just before the accident.'

The light in the hallway is dim and large patches of the painting are either blank or underworked, so I have to step back to absorb the full picture: two shadowy figures, one male and one female, little more than silhouettes, and a large red halo, like a ring of scarlet smoke, curled above their heads. For a reason I can't quite place, the image disturbs me. The female figure is stretching out – her hand extended, like Eve reaching for the apple – towards the man who towers in the centre of the painting, right under the scarlet ring.

'What is it?' I ask, but as soon as I pose the question, I realise that I already know. I gasp, clapping my hand to my mouth. But Alfie's back is turned, and in any case, he's distracted by another thought.

'God knows,' he says, running a finger against the ridge of the canvas. 'I never even thought about displaying this one at the funeral. But now I wish I had. The ones on show were inappropriate. They sanitised things.' He smiles bitterly. 'Do you remember what the priest said in his sermon?'

I hesitate. I only vaguely remember the homily, which I'm certain rang as hollow for Alfie as it did for me – disjointed rambling about how Pippa had flown on to her new life, as if she were a bird; as if she now had wings.

Alfie's eyes narrow. 'Don't you remember what he called Pip's life?'

I shake my head.

'Brief. He called it brief.' His knuckles whiten as he grips the canvas frame. His mood swings are sudden, but subtle; I wonder if the girls spot them too.

'Pippa's life wasn't brief,' he says. 'It was . . .'

He breaks, and allows the picture to fall back against the wall, which it meets with a loud bang, like the strike of a gavel. The canvas ripples. Swathes of blank space buck against the confines of the frame.

'. . . unfinished.'

His voice is so flat, so miserable, I feel free to reach deeper into his grief than ever before. Right now, nothing I might say could make things worse.

'Did they ever find out?' I ask quietly. 'What killed her?'

He's silent for a moment, apparently unsure what I'm asking. 'You know what she died of. Anaphylactic shock.'

'Yes,' I say. 'But what was it that stung her?'

Alfie looks away from me and stares through the open mouth of the cellar door.

'Or bit her? Do you know?'

'Hm? Oh. No …' He's in another world again, walking on another plane, just like he was when he opened the door to me. In the ten months since Pippa's death, this is the first time we've spoken of the accident. Without thinking, I touch his stomach and he flinches.

'I'm sorry,' I say quickly, holding my hands up. 'I didn't mean to—'

'It's fine. It isn't you. It's just …'

'Yes?'

He hesitates for a second, then answers drily: 'Black Mamba.'

'Right,' I say, not understanding.

'Nine months,' he says quietly.

'I'm sorry?'

'Nine months after the accident. That's when they first saw him; that's when the dreams began. Like he'd been … *gestating* all that time.'

I nod slowly. 'Okay then. Call the girls downstairs, and I'll get started.'

Alfie

I watch them from the corner, keeping quiet, keeping still. Julia is sitting with the twins on the living-room floor. The girls' legs are crossed, like they're meditating, while Julia's are tucked beneath her body. She leans forward, her eyes searching. The bay window is wide open, bathing her in rainbow light. For the first time in my life, I think how much she looks like Pippa.

'When I was here last, you told me you'd made a friend. A snake. Black Mamba.'

The girls smile. Any reticence they had on the subject of their invisible friend has vanished. They enjoy talking about him. If I let them, they'd speak of nothing else.

'He can *turn* into a snake,' Sylvie clarifies, curving her arms above her head, like a ballerina.

'But he isn't one?'

'No.'

'He's a boy?'

'A *man*.'

'I see.' Julia runs a hand through her long dark hair – at once neat and chaotic – and smiles.

In life, she and her sister never presented as twins, at least not to me. Pippa was always buzzing; she'd wander from room to room, paintbrush in hand and a million things on her mind; she'd get upset and yell at me for no reason, then kiss me hungrily; she'd laugh until tears filled her eyes. Julia was everything she wasn't: steady, sensible – all sinew and dry wit. Attractive, certainly, though I never felt attracted to her. She was a closed book. If she minded being single, or childless, or Marian's keeper, she was too considerate to let us see it. She let us get on with our lives, and we were selfish enough to do just that. I liked her very much; I barely knew her.

'When he first came into our room, we didn't know who he was. But now he's our friend.'

'We want him to stay.'

'He's magical.'

'He can turn into anything he wants ...'

Julia's eyes widen – faux amazement, perfectly pitched. 'Oh, can he? Tell me more.'

And there it is: Pippa's ghost in Julia's face, and in her eyes.

'What else has he appeared to you as?'

The girls exchange a look, as if conferring psychically about how much to reveal.

'Well,' Cassia says eventually, 'last night he turned into a bird.'

'A bird?'

'Yes. A big black one, with soft feathers, like Grandma's coat.'

'We were trying to sleep,' Sylvie adds, 'but he wouldn't let us. He kept tapping the bed with his beak.'

Julia shakes her head. 'That's not good. You need your sleep.'

Sylvie throws her hands up in protest. 'But Black Mamba was bored. He wanted to take us flying.'

'*Flying?*'

I try not to laugh as scepticism strains her voice. There's the Julia I know – hard-headed, literal-minded – and briefly Pippa's spectre fades. Any scepticism that *she* displayed in life had merely rubbed off from me.

The girls seem undeterred.

'We told you,' says Sylvie. 'He wasn't a small bird. He

was enormous. We sat on his back, and he hopped out of the window.'

'We were frightened at first. It felt like—'

'Like falling down the stairs!'

'Yes!' Cassia grips her belly. 'My stomach left me.'

'Then we were outside, in the dark and the cold.'

'But Black Mamba flapped his wings, and we flew right over the park.'

Julia smiles. She's regained her composure now. Back to channelling Pippa. 'And where did you go?'

'All over London. He took us from roof to roof.'

'Then,' Cassia continues, coolly, matter-of-factly, 'he flew us to the moon.'

'Yes – *all the way to the moon.*' Sylvie's voice is a shriek now. She's jutting her chin out, bragging. She jumps up and mimes soaring through space.

Julia whistles. 'The moon? I'm jealous.' She settles Sylvie back down, then takes the girls' hands. 'I have to ask, though: weren't you even more scared then? It's okay if you were. It's normal to be scared of heights. To be scared of falling.'

I lean forward in my chair, remembering her probing about fear last time, when she put them to bed. *Aren't you scared of him?*

'We weren't,' Cassia says firmly.

Julia looks briefly surprised.

Sylvie nods in agreement. 'Not at all.'

'Of course you weren't.' Julia winks. 'You're big brave girls.'

'We weren't scared,' Cassia clarifies, 'because *he* was there. He'll always catch us if we fall.'

I get up, quietly, to leave the room. I can't bear to watch anymore. As I pass them, Julia, the spit of Pip – at least today, in this light – leans forward and hugs the girls. I feel vacant, somehow. Absent and detached. Like *I'm* the ghost.

I stumble into the kitchen, close my eyes. In the darkness I'm pummelled by memories. Sounds, scents, images – the last game of make-believe they ever played: Pippa and the girls, hunting for imaginary bugs in Peter's Park. Cooing over their invisible horns and feelers, their opalescent wings. Plopping them in empty jam jars.

The smell of freshly cut grass. A yelp. Confusion.

'Is this still pretend?'

'It's nothing.' Shimmering tears.

Blue lights. Blue fingers.

When Julia has finished with the girls, she comes to find me, closing the kitchen door behind her. For a few moments she leans against it, breathing deeply, her hands splayed across the paintwork. I start to worry that she's anxious, that the girls have revealed something awful, but then she shakes herself like a wet cat and unburdens the doorframe of her weight.

'Have you seen my mother?'

'Marian?' I stammer, caught off guard. 'No. Not since she came round with those tarts.'

'Have you told her? About all this. About Black Mamba.'

'I haven't said a word.'

Julia gnaws her bottom lip. 'Then don't.'

'Why not?'

She hesitates, then laughs, dispelling the tension. 'She'll tell you the girls need Jesus. You'll tell her that one imaginary friend is enough. I can't see it being productive.'

I wince, then smile, both in acknowledgment. 'My lips are sealed.'

She looks at me gratefully before sinking back into silence.

'So,' I continue. 'What do you think? In your professional opinion.' I smile again as she crimps an eyebrow. 'I'm not taking the Pips. I promise.' (It's a family joke.)

She takes a seat at the kitchen table, and gestures for me to do the same. 'It's like I told you. Lots of children have imaginary friends.'

'They do realise, then,' I ask, 'that he's imaginary?'

'I think so. Most kids do. And most will admit it, when pushed.'

'So they're just pretending?'

'More than likely. Imaginary friends can be a sign of a high IQ, you know. Divergent thinking. Creativity.'

'Mm?'

'Yeah. We sometimes call them woozles.'

'We?'

'In the field.' She reaches forward and clasps my wrist. It's a familiar movement of hers; intimate yet distant.

Something always prevents her from taking my hand. 'Almost all kids grow out of them. Before they reach adolescence.'

'Almost all?'

She shrugs. 'It's what normally happens.'

I withdraw my wrist: a familiar movement of mine. 'What's normal about any of this?'

Julia frowns. She doesn't quite know what I mean.

'Why is he male?' I ask. 'Isn't that strange? Shouldn't he be another girl?'

'It's actually more common than you'd think. Boys' woozles are almost always male, but for girls, they can be either sex. Honestly, the only thing that's—'

She halts; her brow furrows slightly. It's performative and that annoys me, but I take my cue.

'What?'

'The one thing that's unusual is his age. Typically, a made-up friend is the same age as the child in question, and the same height. As you'd expect of a playmate. Or sometimes they're smaller and younger. For girls especially, they can sometimes act as a surrogate baby. A proxy for a doll. Something to mother. But in this case, it's, well—'

'Not that.'

'No.' She hesitates, then says flatly, 'I still see no reason for concern.'

'All right then.'

'Alfie . . .' She chooses her words delicately. 'I have to ask you something, and please don't take offence.'

'It's fine,' I promise, impossibly. 'I won't.'

'Why is he getting under your skin?'

I flounder for a moment, then rise from the table and stretch my legs. The question is about the girls, I tell myself. About Black Mamba. It's not about me.

'I told you before. They've never had a proper friend. They've always been self-sufficient. That's why he bothers me. It's like they're ... I don't know. *Missing* something.'

Julia stares at me blankly. 'But they *are* missing something.'

'Yeah.' Leaning against the sink, I massage my temples. A feeling of resignation sweeps over me. 'So that's it then? He's a replacement for Pip.'

'These things are rarely so straightforward. But he might be helping them, in some way. A support mechanism of a kind. They first saw him at night-time, right?'

'Yes. They were scared of him. They came upstairs and asked to sleep in bed with me. I thought they were just having bad dreams.'

'Perhaps they were, at first,' Julia mused. 'Or perhaps he was always an invention, born of anxiety. A way to get close to you. A pretext to seek out some comfort.' She rises from her seat and sidles up beside me at the sink. 'Children don't grieve like us. Their neurology's different. They can't be sad for sustained periods. At times, when they're engaged, when they're active, they're okay. At other times, they're not. Bedtime's a pressure point. A stressor. It's dark. It's quiet. They have no task, no stimulation. All they have are their thoughts. Their feelings.'

I think back to the girls' night visits. Everything she says makes sense, but those visits seem distant. Black Mamba has changed shape since then.

As if reading my mind, she presses on. 'I know it seems different now, because of how they've embraced him. But I don't think it is, not at root. You heard what they said: last night they were trying to sleep, but they couldn't self-settle. So they lowered their stress levels with fantasy play. A big black bird, who offered adventure. A release of endorphins. Stimulation.'

'All right,' I say, with a reluctance I can't quite explain. 'What do we do?'

'I'll talk to them. Every week – twice if they need it. I'll find out what they're thinking. What they're feeling. There are techniques for reducing stress that I can teach them. Mindfulness. Breathing patterns. And CBT – talking therapy – should help to address the negative feelings that stress can trigger. Low self-worth, that sort of thing.'

'And what about me? What do I do?'

She weighs her words carefully. 'Don't stop being their father. Keep a routine in place. A structure. Discipline them if they misbehave. And ...' She hesitates. 'Keep playing with them too.'

My breathing slumps into a sigh, heavy as earth. 'I can't,' I start, trying not to let my voice crack. 'I know you said to play along, but I can't. Make-believe was Pippa's thing. Pippa and the girls. You remember?' *How they used to hang off the edge of the bed, pretending to fly. All her silly voices. How she'd lie on the floor, playing dead, then spring up when the girls got close, crying, 'I got you, I got you ...'*

Julia nods. 'I remember. You used to join in too, though,' she adds, gently, after a moment. 'I saw you. Can't you do that again? Can't you just ... pretend? As if she were still here.'

I run my hands through my hair, now just about dry. What can I say to that? That I pretend she's still here every day – every time I walk into a room; every time I want to tell her something; every time I need to hear her voice. That being with the girls, playing make-believe, only reminds me of the truth.

'All right,' I mutter. 'I promise I'll try.'

Julia

Back in the hallway, I gather my things. I've told him as much as I can. The rest, he wouldn't understand, at least not yet. I pass the half-painted canvas leaning by the cellar door, and shudder again at the swathes of dark paint, the streaks of smoky red. My eyes move from the male figure to the female; I examine her shadowy hair, the curvature of her nose. *The likeness is poor*, I think – not smugly, but with dispassion. Pippa never did master the art of a self-portrait.

Alfie shocks me by touching my arm.

'One last thing,' he says.

'Of course.'

'You're a psychotherapist.' (It's not a condemnation.) 'Does that mean you understand dreams?'

I tense immediately; I try not to glance at the canvas. 'Dreams?'

'Yes,' he says. 'I've been having a nightmare. About Pip. The same one, over and over.'

I relax slightly. *He doesn't know what the painting means.*

'Do they ... signify anything? Recurring dreams.'

I know immediately what Mum would say. Memories from childhood flash, abruptly, before my eyes: entire Sundays swallowed up at the Lord's Servant, poring over each other's dreams, weighing them like precious stones. *She can't hear about any of this.*

'Sometimes, yes,' I say. 'They can tell you something about yourself. But they aren't always easy to interpret.'

Without another word, Alfie lifts his top and jumper, bunched together in a single fold, revealing his chest: broad and firm, and lightly matted with blond hair. I go to look away, embarrassed, but then I see them. 'Oh my God,' I say, leaning in. 'What the hell ... ?'

Four scratch marks, dark red, almost purple, streak across his stomach. I touch them, lightly, and he winces. Once again, I feel relief. *That's* why he flinched from me earlier.

Alfie thrusts his top back down. Suddenly, he seems embarrassed too. He mumbles, red-faced, like a teenage boy: 'I must have done them in my sleep ... During the nightmare.'

I breathe in sharply. What should I say in response?

That I'm having nightmares too. That Pippa was, as well, before she died; she was painting them.

The words dry up in my throat, but Alfie spares me by continuing. 'The girls are in the dream too—'

'No they're not,' I say quickly, interrupting him. 'I mean, the girls in your dream aren't your daughters. Don't forget that, Alfie. Your daughters are in the next room. Flesh and bone. And they need you.'

He hesitates, then nods stiffly. 'Of course,' he mumbles. 'Flesh and bone.'

It was Dad who sparked Pippa's love of art, on the long winter nights they spent curled up on the sofa, leafing through old books, full of prints and paintings. Cranach, Holbein, Dürer: all the old German masters. Religious works, of course, but allegories too – the kind that would inspire her later; that she'd reimagine.

Like *Death and the Maiden*. I still remember the night Dad turned the page to Baldung Grien's painting of a naked girl, and the skeleton embracing her, gripping her hair. How Pippa shrieked. How she snatched the book from Dad's hands and threw it, in revulsion, to the floor.

She painted her version of it when she was pregnant with the twins. 'Facing my demons,' she told me with a grin, as she laboured on Death's neon bones, the Maid's pearly skin.

I was puzzled by the composition, and said so. 'The skeleton and the girl ... they're still so intimate. His arms, wrapped right around her. I can't believe you haven't changed that. I thought, when we were kids, his touch disturbed you.'

Pippa stared at me in disbelief. 'It wasn't the way he touched the girl,' she said. 'It was realising ... that the skeleton was *inside* the girl.' Her hands tremored as she rubbed her bump. 'And inside me.'

Five

Alfie

Spring is here. The world keeps turning. Weeds are sprouting in the back courtyard and, inside the house, the pattern of our days has slowly changed, as three has become four again. The girls wake beneath Black Mamba's gaze, we eat under his watchful eye, and he's there with us every moment in between.

For a second this morning – or half a second – I almost forgot he isn't real.

It happened first thing. I had woken, roughly, from the usual nightmare: the four of us at Collier Beach; the girls holding on to red balloons, Pippa and I holding on to each other. At first, it played out in the normal way. Sylvie lost her balloon to the wind, so Pippa brought her a shell, brimming with seaworms. But this time, when Sylvie spotted her sister floating away and threw the conch to the ground, it transformed the moment it smashed: from a smooth, pink shell to a black urn, filled not with seaworms, but with ash – like the jar the hospital gave us. And when Pippa returned to the sea to fill another shell, this time she seemed to know what was coming below the water. She waited, smiled – then was snatched.

I closed my eyes, unable to bear the sight of the sea, so vast and empty. But the dream didn't end there. Instead, I heard another sound, alongside the cry of gulls and the wind. Laughter. I opened my eyes in astonishment to the sight of Pippa, grinning and wading towards me, seaweed and wildflowers streaming in her hair.

I got you! she called, striding triumphantly through the waves. *I got you, I got you!*

And then I woke, falling so quickly and cleanly into the milky morning light I felt as though I'd never been asleep. I leaped out of bed, as if trying to shed the husk of the dream, but the tension remained in my body. I hurried to the twins' room, suddenly desperate to see and touch them, but I could tell that something was wrong even before I opened the door. There seemed to be an absence of sound – of life, even – on the other side. As I entered the room I immediately felt the drop in temperature. The window was wide open; the curtains, half drawn, were billowing gently in the early-morning breeze. I looked at their bed. The girls' quilt, with its sky-blue swirls, was crumpled and lifeless on the floor, and the sheets were nowhere to be seen. They'd been pulled clean off the mattress, exposing it as pale and discoloured, like something you might see in a skip.

The girls were gone.

'Sylvie? Cassia?'

Their names stuck in my throat as a single thought pounded, stupidly, round and round in my mind: *they're not in their bed, they're not in their bed, they're not in their bed.* And then, another idea – unwanted, unbidden. *They're with him. He came to them as a bird again. He stole them away in the night.* They were half-thoughts, non-thoughts, and I shook them off by focusing on the facts. The bed was empty. The house was silent. My daughters were missing.

I returned to the landing and rushed up and down the spiral staircase, throwing open doors. 'Cassia? Sylvie?' I forced their names out this time, loudly and clearly. Then I heard something from the bathroom on the second floor. Relief swept over me. It was the twins' voices, whispering through the wood.

I opened the door, blinking in the pearly light. The bathroom window is thick and textured, but the sun still streams in through the glass. It blinded me momentarily, rebounding off the bathroom mirror, which stretches from ceiling to floor. I glimpsed an unfamiliar figure in the reflection, dishevelled and panicked. For another half-second, I forgot that no man lives in this house but me.

Giggling wildly, splashing like naiads, the girls were sitting in the tub, which was half full, their missing bed-sheets wrapped around their wet bodies like togas. I stepped forward and slipped on water that had pooled on the porcelain floor. The girls stopped splashing as I caught myself on the sink, but seemingly couldn't drop their smiles.

'Why are you in here?' I asked. 'You scared me to death.'

Their smiles disappeared. It could have been my tone of voice. It was probably my choice of words. I exhaled deeply, and the whole room, white and glistening, finally came into focus. I grabbed a flannel from the basin and crouched down to mop up the water. As I lowered myself to the girls' height, my eyes met Cassia's. Cold, clear, unblinking. I bowed my head abruptly and pressed the flannel against the floor with the tips of my fingers.

(I was being ridiculous again; there was no reason to feel unnerved. I know she *saw* what happened in the bathroom all those years ago. But she's always said she can't remember.)

Leaving the flannel to soak, I rolled up my sleeve and dipped my elbow into the bathtub. The water was warm; freshly run. I drew a deep breath. 'I'm sorry,' I said. 'I didn't mean to shout. I was worried, that's all. What are you doing in here? And why's half your bed in the tub?'

They shared a glance.

'We were trying to sleep,' said Cassia, 'but Black Mamba wouldn't let us.'

'We could hear his voice in the walls, all muffled and strange.'

'He was in the pipes ...'

I nodded. I've heard them gurgling too, especially at night – sometimes, I hear a strange rattle as well. The house makes all sorts of sounds it never made when Pippa was alive.

'Come on,' I said, brandishing a towel. 'Out you get.'

'He told us to come here,' Sylvie insisted. 'To the bathroom.'

'We turned on the tap, and he fell straight out.'

'He'd turned into a fish. A black one, with hard, shiny fins.'

I swaddled the girls together in the folds of the towel, and dried their hair and skin. I was probably a little rough, my blood still pulsing with adrenaline, but they didn't seem to notice. They continued to speak in one voice – all smiles again, and breathless with excitement, tripping over each other's words.

'He told us to fetch the sheets and put them in the bath to make a raft,' Cassia said. 'We tied the sheet to his tail, sat on it, and he pulled us down the plughole.'

'It was so much fun,' said Sylvie.

I focused on the task in hand, towelling down my daughters.

'We were underwater then,' Cassia said, 'so we had to hold our breath.'

'The pipe took us all the way out to the sea. It was incredible.'

'We saw the sun rise, way above us, through the water.'

'It was amazing. There were sea creatures all around us. Dolphins and lobsters and turtles and—'

'All right, all right,' I snapped. I couldn't help it – or, if I could, I told myself I couldn't. Which in the end is the same thing. 'I get the idea.' I dredged their bedclothes out of the tub. 'I'll have to put a wash on. Another one. You realise that, don't you?'

Sylvie, who I'd interrupted, stared at me, half chastened, half incredulous. 'Are you angry?' she asked quietly.

I drew another breath, the deepest yet, and kissed her glistening cheek. 'No,' I said. 'Of course not. Not with you. Not in the least. Not ever.'

I gathered up the sopping bedsheets and carried them to the machine. I don't know why it got to me so much; the sheets are easily washed and the hieroglyphics on the dial are no longer an enigma. Still, it was another job that needed doing – or re-doing. And I felt guilty for missing their mother.

Cassia can't remember what she saw that night. I know she can't. She was only three years old. Why do I even question it?

She knows the story, though; they both do. We spun it for them so many times.

It was late, almost 1 a.m., and Pippa had just got home from a night out drinking with friends. The girls were sleeping soundly in their bed, entwined in each other's arms, and Pippa was trying to be quiet. In her drunkenness, she was failing beautifully.

I woke to the sound of her botched discretion. Echoing up and down the staircase was the clamour of the bathroom, at the heart of our house, coming alive with the clack of her heels; the clattering of shampoo bottles knocked

over; murmurs of 'Shit' and 'Christ' and 'Shh' to herself;
then giggles. And I thought, *for God's sake, Pip, don't wake
the girls*. And then I heard her burp, and 'Shh' herself again,
more insistently this time, whilst beating back laughter,
and I thought, *I love you, I love you*.

Then I heard another clatter, the sound of something
heavy hitting the floor, and then silence.

In an instant, I went from being at the bottom of an
ocean to gasping above the waves. I leaped out of bed and
ran down the spiral stairs to the bathroom. Undressing,
Pippa had stumbled and struck her head against the mirror.
A red streak glistened on its surface; her body, flat on the
floor, was perfectly still. If her eyes had been closed, I might
have been calmer. But they were open and staring – like a
fish in a shop window, lying on a bed of crushed ice – and
though Sylvie, somehow, miraculously, slept through it all,
Cassia was woken by my shouts.

'Is Mummy okay?'

Standing limply by the bathroom door, looking like
half a person, she chewed her hair and stared at her crumpled mother as I tried not to let the phone fall from my
shaking hand; as I tried, frantically, to follow the operator's
instructions.

'She'll be fine,' I think I said. And, mercifully, she was.
By the time the ambulance arrived, she was conscious and
sitting up, and after one night in hospital, as a precaution,
she was back with us the very next day. Pippa remembered
nothing. The trauma of that night belonged only to me.

'I keep feeling it, over and over,' I told her in bed, a few days later. 'The fear I might lose you …'

Pippa put her hand in mine and her mouth to the helix of my ear. 'That's one good thing about lightning,' she whispered. 'It never strikes in the same place twice.'

I strung that cliché round my neck and wore it like an amulet. And, like an amulet, in the end it preserved us from nothing.

Lightning. I stir our dinner and watch it through the kitchen window, veining the sky. A storm has been brewing all afternoon; dark clouds appeared in the air above Hart House at midday, and smatterings of rain soon followed. After this morning, I wanted a drink, but the bad weather worked as a pick-me-up. I watched it gather in the wet air as I remade the girls' bed, and it made me smile. It gave me the strength to put aside the tins and the ready meals, and to plunder the veg drawer and larder; to cook the kind of meal that the old me would make. Something we could eat, in the dining room, together.

Then the girls confront me with Black Mamba's latest request, and I rue that I went to the effort.

'A seat at the table … ?' I massage my temples, then go back to stirring the stew.

'Please, Daddy,' they say. 'Oh please, please, please. He wants to be with us.'

'Us' means them, not me, of course – so nodding takes effort, and smiling is a source of literal, physical pain. Hearing of their night-time adventures is bad enough; I never feel more excluded, though, than when we're all together.

The dining room is one of only three spaces in Hart House with no windows. The other two are the attic and the cellar. The dining table is long, but the room itself feels small. The walls are walnut-panelled, and the lights have no dimmer switch, so all the shadows are fixed in place. I set Black Mamba's mat, plate, napkin, knife, fork, spoon and glass without complaint.

'He doesn't want food?'

'Nuh-uh,' Cassia says. 'He'll bring his own.'

'You won't see it,' Sylvie adds, 'because he doesn't want you to.'

'Ah.'

I spoon chunks of sweet potato, thick and steaming, onto the girls' plates and onto mine, but leave Black Mamba's empty. My grip is steady, but the ladle still clatters against the rim of the dish. Asking for a jam tart was one thing. At least I could understand that request, and justify indulging it. *It's not for him*, I thought. *It's for the girls*. Yet asking for an empty plate is worse, somehow, than wanting something real.

A seat at the table: our table. He's making his presence felt.

'Black Mamba wants the pepper.'

I nod, and pass the silver pot into Cassia's outstretched palm. Silently, she powders his dish.

Sylvie swallows a spoonful of chopped carrot. 'Now he wants the salt.'

Since the day they learned to speak, the girls have been prone to ventriloquy – though, up until now, only of each other's thoughts. Pippa and I accepted it. Marian found it enthralling. Only Julia seemed, occasionally, to be unsettled. I remember her baulking at least once, when the girls were younger, upon asking Cassia a string of questions only for Sylvie to answer them, one by one.

She wants this. She wants that.

She thinks this. She thinks that.

'I wasn't asking you, Miss Mouth,' Julia had said, poking her tongue out. 'Let Cassia speak for herself.'

But Cassia had just smiled serenely, then stuck out her own tongue, like a puppet's limb. 'Sylvie thinks you're very rude,' she said.

And now? Like artists who've spent years honing their craft, the girls ventriloquise *his* thoughts and wishes with the same authority.

Black Mamba wants this. Black Mamba wants that.

Black Mamba thinks this. Black Mamba thinks that.

'He seems demanding.' That's what Julia said to them, the last time she was here. She put it more dispassionately than I would have. Julia's visits haven't helped. Or, I suppose I should say, they haven't helped me – at least not yet. She tells me I have to be patient.

'We need to keep him happy.' That was Cassia's response.

'So he doesn't leave,' Sylvie added.

'Should I keep playing along?' I whispered to Julia.

She nodded. 'I think that's best. For now at least. Let's see where we get to.'

Sylvie taps the salt cellar into the well of the plate. Then she jumps, as thunder rumbles suddenly overhead, and she drops it. It hits the tablecloth with a dull thud.

'What was that?'

I worry the food in my bowl, freeing some steam. 'It's only a storm.'

Sylvie and Cassia's eyes roll upwards, as if drawn magnetically to the ceiling. If they're expecting the lights to flicker, or shake in their fittings, they don't. Nor does any dust drift down onto the tablecloth. After a minute, the thunder picks up again – louder this time, more proximate.

'It sounds so close,' Sylvie says, her eyes widening.

I take her hand and squeeze it.

'Black Mamba says it isn't a storm,' Cassia murmurs. 'He says it's people. People, moving about upstairs ...'

I twitch and release Sylvie's hand to wipe my forehead. The thunder growls again. I know, instinctively, how Pippa would have described the sound if she were here: heavy beds and cabinets, being dragged about by angels in their heavenly boudoir.

But she isn't. Her seat at the table's been taken.

'It's definitely a storm, Cass,' I say, as gently as I can manage. I want to give her hand a squeeze of reassurance too, but she has hidden them both beneath the table. And my food is getting cold. 'I promise,' I say, speaking with my mouth full. 'There's nothing to be afraid of.'

Sylvie nods hesitantly, but then, after a moment's thought, lowers her cutlery, ashen-faced.

The twins refuse to take another bite. At least Black Mamba liked his dinner.

Once I've put the girls to bed, I have that drink. Then another. And I take the bottle up with me, where I lie alone in our room – my room – for what feels like hours, staring at the ceiling. Rain falls on the skylight. The blind is drawn over it, and flashes of lightning illuminate the fabric's edges. I should check on the girls, as the thunder grows louder and the lightning brighter, but I don't move. I stay where I am until, finally, I begin to drift, indifferently, into sleep. The last thing I see, or think I see, before the darkness swallows me, is something shadowy moving overhead, almost touching the ceiling – gliding noiselessly around the edge of the skylight, like a hawk in eerie, mechanical flight.

When I wake, to sunshine filtering steadily through the covered skylight, I feel the familiar sting of guilt. I left the girls alone, all night. If they'd needed me, I would have been too far gone. I indulge the feeling by imagining them huddling together beneath the quilt, the storm raging all around them. But then, from the corner of my eye, I spot the door handle beginning to turn. The door opens, just an inch, with a low creak, but no one enters. I'm being watched.

I groan loudly, ostentatiously. 'Too early,' I moan, and the twins laugh as they burst in. Shrieking, they bustle under the duvet and start to tickle me. Whatever I do, however neglectfully I treat them, their loveliness always seems to return the next morning, undiminished – blooming like the weeds in the courtyard, nourished not by me, but by the turn of spring.

'Why are you still in bed?' Sylvie asks. 'We were worried. We wondered where you were.'

The roles we played yesterday have been reversed, like we're actors swapping paper masks.

'I'm sorry. I'm just ... having a grumpy morning.'

'We were scared,' Sylvie said. 'We thought you might have gone.'

'Gone?' I screw up my nose, as though the idea is absurd. 'Where would I go?'

Sylvie shrugs, a little shyly. 'To be with the others?' she suggests.

'The others?'

Sylvie glances at her sister. 'You know,' she continues. 'The people we heard yesterday. Moving about upstairs.'

I hold them both close. 'That was only the storm,' I remind them.

'Oh yes,' Cassia murmurs. 'The storm. We heard it all night long. Couldn't you?'

'No. I missed it. Was it loud?'

'Loud? It was deafening!' Sylvie says – blasting the words in my ear to mimic its power.

'But you were brave girls. Right?'

'Of course,' Cassia says. 'We had Black Mamba.'

I knew it was coming, so I'm reasonably prepared. But not for her next words.

'He was in our bed.'

Before I can react, Sylvie throws her hands up in agreement. 'Yes, yes,' she cries with delight. 'In our bed. He clambered in as soon as it got dark, and put his arms around us.'

'We felt his heart thud and his body breathe.'

'He made the storm disappear. He made the thunder go all quiet, till all we could hear was his heartbeat. Ba-doom, ba-doom, ba-doom.'

I pull the girls even closer, until their heads are resting against my chest. Until they can't see my face. 'You should have come in here if you were scared,' I tell them.

'But we weren't,' they answer.

Six

Julia

Dad never explained what he was doing; he just set to work quietly one afternoon, shortly after we moved into Hart House, photographing the rooms. Not us, not Mum – just the rooms. Blank, yawning, empty. We couldn't understand it. Our belongings were barely unpacked and everything needed cleaning, or touching up. When we arrived, Hart House had been unoccupied for ages and was derelict. Abandoned furniture, draped in grubby white sheets and coats of dust, sat inelegantly all around, whilst paint peeled off the walls and ceilings – those, that is, that had survived the fire damage; those that weren't blackened and charred.

Susan Harris Estates had acquired it for a laughable price.

'It needs TLC,' my aunt had warned us, with a twinkling smile.

Mum set us to work, but Dad seemed in no hurry. He had other priorities. From our very first week in Hart

House, he was searching for something. Something in the very air, it seemed – invisible to the naked eye. Click. Click. Click.

Now I'm following in his footsteps. Now I, too, am searching, in my conversations with the girls, for something lurking in this house. Something hidden.

'Isn't it strange?' Alfie demands. 'He was *in their bed*.'

'As a bear.'

'What?'

'They told me he came to them as a bear – a big black bear. It's nothing to worry about. They just cuddled him until they fell asleep.'

'Well how touching.'

The girls look tired as they draw, and I don't think that schoolwork is to blame. Just speaking to Alfie has left me feeling tired too. He can't see the effect he's having on them. I think that's what concerns me most.

Sylvie is drawing Black Mamba as a bear, while Cassia draws him as a fish. I watch them shade and smudge, then blow on the paper. Their movements are exactly the same, just as every sparrow pecks and bobs its head identically, in arcs and parabolas that are pre-programmed. I admire the smooth motion of the girls' wrists as their pencils rotate, pressing lightly against the page.

Here and there, I break the silence.

'Do you like being twins?'

Even before they nod, I know the answer.

'I liked being one too.'

The girls' pencils halt, abruptly but in perfect unison. Specks of graphite fall haphazardly onto the paper.

I watch the girls carefully. 'What is it?'

They glance at each other. 'Why doesn't Dad have a twin?' Sylvie takes each word slowly, as if she's hearing the question spoken to her by another voice, deep in the cavern of her mind, and is merely repeating it.

'Well,' I say. 'Twins run in our family.'

She looks puzzled. 'But Dad's in our family.'

'No,' I say, and then correct myself. 'I mean, yes, of course he is. But he isn't on … *my* side of the family.' I swallow hard. It feels strange not to say *our*.

'Harris,' Cassia whispers.

'That's right.'

Pippa and Alfie never married, so she kept her maiden name, and gave it to the girls too. We were Sylvie Harris, Cassia Harris, Pippa Harris, Julia Harris and Marian Harris.

And Alfie Marvell.

'There are different kinds of twin. You know that, right?' The words *dizygotic* and *monozygotic* teeter on the tip of my tongue. I don't believe in patronising children, not as a rule, but I'm conscious that such a philosophy can be taken to extremes. 'There are non-identical twins, who are born at the same time but often look different. And identical twins, who always look exactly the same.'

'Like us.'

'Yes,' I say, and then correct myself. 'I mean, no. You do look similar. Very similar. But you're not identical.'

I always forget this; apparently they do too. Their bond has been so strong since birth, it's an easy mistake to make – and Mum had a hand in the confusion. This morning, the girls are wearing the matching polka-dot dresses she bought them last year for their birthday; pure white fabric speckled with circles and half-circles – bright blocks of primary colour – like children's hospital gowns. When the twins were very little, Mum was forever buying them the same clothes and fixing their hair in mirroring plaits or bunches. Just as she fixed Pippa's body and mine till we mirrored each other, on the floor of this very room, all those years ago.

'I had to,' Mum would insist, whenever Pippa queried why she'd bought the twins the same hairclip, or sandals, or toy. 'One mustn't have favourites.' In this respect, she treated her granddaughters much as she had her own children. If Mum had a favourite out of Pippa and me, she never showed it. Neither of us had the licence to escape her love.

'How do you know we're not?' Sylvie demands.

'Not what?'

'Identical.'

'Because ...' I pause, looking for the right words. 'Identical twins don't run in families. Identical twins ... are an accident. They come from a single egg that splits in their mummy's tummy to form two people. It's a random event that happens once in a blue moon. But non-identical twins come from two separate eggs in mummies that have ... well, a lot of eggs.'

Hyperovulation sounds better, of course, but I've no need to impress them. They aren't my clients.

'Does Grandma have a twin?' Cassia asks.

'No. But her father did.' They'd know this, I think, if Mum would only display some family photos – any photos. 'And his mother before that. And her mother before that.'

Cassia nods, and then both girls resume drawing, as if I've told them all they need to know. The twins have always had that veneer of confidence, that air of wisdom and precision. It comes from the way they mirror each other – not at their grandma's nagging insistence, but of their own volition. There's power in numbers.

I sit with Alfie in the kitchen and show him the drawings. Black Mamba the bear is standing on his hind-legs and turning, his furry limbs raised. He could be dancing. He could be about to attack.

'The bear's just another sign of regression,' I say. 'Normal in grieving kids. The twins imagine him coming to them at night, when they're struggling to settle. He's big and strong, and his fur is warm. He offers them comfort. Protection.'

Alfie's hands shake as they pass to the next drawing. The disconnect between his hands – their width and strength – and their tremulous movement strikes me. 'And the fish?'

Solid black scales; ephemeral, silvery fins; a fleck of gold in the eyeball.

'Yes. I've got a theory about that. I think they might've wet the bed. Or, at least, one of them did.'

Alfie looks up sharply from the drawing.

'Hear me out. They woke up and the sheets were soaking wet. So Black Mamba *told* them to dunk them in the bathtub. It's only a hypothesis. But it fits. They're seven years old. They were probably panicked, embarrassed—'

'Embarrassed?'

'Yes,' I say. 'Scared to tell you—'

'Scared?'

'Yes. I've said before: the girls are bound to be feeling shaken, unstable. It's not anything you've done. You're not to blame.'

He doesn't look like he believes me. I'm not sure I would, in his position.

'They're regressing, clinging on to whatever they can. Anything that keeps them steady.' I hesitate. 'Clinging on to each other.'

'What do you mean?'

I reach across the kitchen table for a clean sheet of paper, then draw for him: two large circles, intersecting to form a Venn diagram. The lines are wobbly, unpractised, but the intent is clear.

'I have another thought,' I say. 'A new perspective for you.'

In the left circle, I write Sylvie's name; in the other,

I write Cassia's. Then, in the intersection, I write: BLACK MAMBA.

Alfie brushes a finger across the overlapping region, the space between his girls. His eyelids flicker, but he says nothing.

'I think that's what he is,' I say. 'At least to a degree. A manifestation of the twinship. Or a device to bind each other into it more deeply. To give themselves that sense of connection. Of stability—' I break off, treading with care. 'You know, sometimes ...'

'Yes?'

I lay the pencil flat on the paper. 'Sometimes parents of twins try to parent each twin individually. They love the twins but, for some reason, they dislike the twinship.'

'I've never disliked it,' Alfie says. His eyes are wide with surprise. He's telling the truth. Or at least he thinks he is.

'You've never felt ... excluded by it? Not once, in any way? Even when Pippa was alive? Because it's not unusual, you know, for fathers in particular to feel cut out.'

Alfie frowns. 'I can't say it wasn't vexing at times. The way they'd challenge us, putting on a front. But we coped. Me and Pip, together. You know how we were. Strong, so strong.'

'Mm.'

'No,' he sighs, his head sinking into his palms. 'That's not the root of it. I know it isn't. There's something else. Something that isn't coming from the girls. There's something ... external. Shaping their behaviour. I can feel it.'

I nod my head, but only perfunctorily. I'm used to this pattern. Irritability and immense frustration when I first arrive, collapsing into lassitude and despair before I leave. But then Alfie pulls at his sandy hair and shakes his head, as if trying to dislodge something – water in his ear. When he looks up, I'm stunned to see his eyes are shot red.

'There are things happening in the house,' he whispers. 'Things I can't explain.'

'What things?'

'Noises. A rattling at night.'

'A rattling ... ?' I repeat, dazedly – trying to stay rational. Alfie looks exhausted; he can't have had a good night's sleep in weeks. And I noticed the empties, stacked around the bin, as soon as I entered the kitchen.

He's imagining things; he must be. And I'm seeing patterns that don't exist.

'I heard it last night,' he mutters. 'I've heard it on a few nights. And in the morning ... things are missing.'

'Like what?'

'Just stuff. Food. Cereal, things like that. I'm telling you – this isn't all coming from the girls. There's more to it than that ...'

I lean back in my chair. No words come, and I don't expect them to, not really. He's right, of course. Something else *is* influencing the girls. Distressing them. Damaging them, even.

Him.

*

Work is no longer a distraction; instead, I'm distracted at work.

My office is large, and painted in a soft sea-blue, which RCTs have shown can lower blood pressure, slow heart rate, improve mood. Pictures of sailing boats hang on the walls: colourful, childlike prints. The windows are wide; the sofas, plush. Everything in this room is perfectly tailored to relax my clients, to open them up. Everything, that is, except me. My 2 p.m. has only just begun, but already I'm checking my watch and thinking of the girls, who I'm picking up from school this afternoon and taking back to Hart House for, what – our sixth chat? Our seventh? I'm thinking of Alfie, too, waiting for us. And of what the girls might say.

I pull down my sleeve and battle to be in the moment – to focus on my clients. Simon and Ralf: the couple who can't decide whether they want kids. Or, more accurately, can't *agree*. Ralf wants them. Simon doesn't. And the conflict is pulling them apart.

This morning, Ralf is sitting in a lumpy knitted jumper with his body positioned towards Simon, and every time I ask Ralf a question, he looks at Simon pointedly as he answers. *Because Simon is the problem.* That's the subtext. *Simon is why they are here.*

'He says we're not a family,' Ralf informs me. He's German, I'd guess, by origin; his voice lightly accented. 'He says we're just … two individuals.'

'And he pretends,' says Simon, 'that that means I'm not committed. When he knows I am.'

They ventriloquise each other's thoughts and feelings – I think, not for the first time – with the same authority as the twins. The parallel unnerves me. Am I obsessed? Or is there truly some equivalence: an intimacy with someone who is, superficially at least, your mirror?

Simon adjusts the collar of his shirt, starched, buttoned up, and looks squarely at Ralf. 'If we had kids, whose name would they take?' he asks. 'Yours or mine?'

My eyes narrow. They've argued a lot about this sort of thing. Trivia – skirting around something bigger.

'What's in a name?' Ralf scoffs. 'It doesn't matter.'

'It matters,' says Simon, softly but with conviction. 'A family should have one name. And we're not married.'

'Well,' I interject, careful to keep my tone neutral – to make it clear this is a question, not advice. 'Why couldn't you marry?'

There's silence, and Ralf shifts awkwardly in his seat. 'We could. But I'm not changing my name,' he says at last.

'See what I mean?' Simon's tone contains only a hint of triumph. Mostly, it's full of sadness.

'Not really,' I say truthfully. 'Lots of women feel like that these days. And lots of families have more than one name. Why couldn't yours?'

'Because,' says Simon, 'it's not about the words; it's about their meaning. We *are* two individuals. Two men who love each other, yes. But not one flesh.'

The phrase catches me off guard. Perhaps it's my upbringing, but it has, to my ear at least, religious overtones – moralistic ones. Seemingly, that's not what he intends.

'There's nothing wrong with that,' Simon continues. 'Nothing at all. But it *is* who we are. It's no use pretending otherwise ...'

I need to speak to Simon on his own, I think, to get to the root of this. But before I can jot that thought down, my pencil falls slack in my hand. I'm thinking of the girls again, those motherless girls – and the loss of my own father. Don't all kids want two parents? I steeple my fingers, wondering, bleakly, if the girls will ever settle into their new life, alone in Hart House with Alfie.

And Black Mamba.

Ralf scoffs again. 'What are you really saying? That kids need one of each? A mum and a dad?' He turns to me, shaking his head in disbelief. 'Is that what you think, Julia?'

Normally, I avoid clients' questions, but this one I tackle head on.

'Of course not,' I say, as firmly as possible. 'Kids don't *need* a female parent. Or a male parent.' Without thinking, I pull my sleeve up again to check my watch. 'They just need good ones.'

'Where is Black Mamba? Where is he, right now?'

The twins smile, though they look a tad surprised; I'm seldom this direct. As soon as I brought them home, they changed out of their uniforms and into dungarees, and each put a ribbon in their hair – matching blue silk; gifts, again, from my mother. Once, the girls' blonde hair grew fairer every spring and summer until it glittered in the light, but over the past few years it's darkened with each equinox, and every day they look more like their mother. The one feature that links them to their father will soon have fled.

'He's here,' Cassia says.

'Where? In this room?'

'Yes.'

I glance around the lounge, at the open bay window and the hot patches of carpet where sunlight falls. It's late afternoon, but the sun is still strong. The nights are drawing out. I'm falling asleep and waking while it's light, and all the days are blurring into one.

'Can you be more specific?'

Sylvie grins. 'He's sitting right next to you.'

I glance, uneasily, into the empty air. 'Good,' I say firmly. 'What form is he in?'

Sylvie turns to her sister.

'He's a wolf,' she answers.

'Oh my,' I murmur. 'I bet he's hungry. All wolves get hungry.'

Cassia eyes me carefully, but gives a tight nod.

'Your dad's told me, a few times now, that food's gone missing. Cereal. He says there's never enough in the mornings. I wondered if Black Mamba might have eaten some. Is that what happened?'

The girls have gone quiet now, and very still.

'It's okay,' I say. 'You can tell me. Sylvie?'

I single her out because she's starting to twitch.

'Sylvie?' I say again, and slowly she nods her head. 'And when does he eat it, Sylvie? This is very important. What time of day does Black Mamba eat the cereal?'

She turns again to her sister. They say nothing; they just gaze into each other's eyes. But when Sylvie answers, it's with rediscovered poise. 'At night,' she says flatly.

'At night?'

'Yes. When it's dark. When Daddy's gone to sleep.'

I reach forward and squeeze her hand encouragingly. 'And does Daddy wake up if you prod him? Or is he too deeply asleep?'

Now, nothing. Silence. I've pushed too far. They are loyal to their father, by instinct if not conscious choice. But I don't need an answer. I smelled the drink on his breath when he opened the door, and I've suspected for at least a week now that he's passing out, sometimes in the early evening. The girls are having to feed themselves.

Alfie hasn't shared with me how much he's struggling. I'm sure he doesn't realise it himself. If this were a case at the clinic, I'd have to report it, but he's family. There's nothing wrong with my urge to protect him. It's only natural.

'All right,' I say, rubbing their arms. 'It's all right.' I know I should back off, leave them in peace, but a final question occurs to me, and I can't contain it. 'Tell me one last thing: what does Black Mamba look like when he isn't an animal?'

There's silence for a moment. Then, all at once, the mood lifts, like clouds dispersing after rain. The girls smile again, faintly, as though surprised for a second time.

'He looks a bit like Dad,' Cassia says.

'Yes,' Sylvie agrees, 'a *lot* like Dad. But his eyes are stranger, and he smiles more.'

Seven

Alfie

This morning, we must go outside; Julia has insisted on it. I don't like this development. Leaving the house always feels like a moment of danger. Over the past year, I've come to love its tomb-like solitude, the cool familiarity of its shaded rooms, the stillness. But she's given me no choice.

We abandon its dark interior, blinking in the sunlight, as though emerging slowly from a year's hibernation – from a year of dreams. The girls hold my hands, their small, unreal fingers squeezing mine. Julia isn't with us, but I feel her all the same at my back. She'll come round this evening with steaming food, and she'll check the kitchen cupboards, quietly, when she thinks I'm not looking, for evidence that I've done as promised. She no longer trusts me, but I don't blame her. I wouldn't in her position.

The three of us pass through Peter's Park, which is full of flowers beneath the spring light. The girls laugh and joke about Black Mamba, and fail to fall silent as we pass under the pink chestnuts, where Pippa was bitten or stung. And I can't fall silent, because I've been silent all the way, detached from it all, as if I'm watching another man walking through the park with my children.

We enter the supermarket, with its clean, cold aisles and gleaming floors and air that turns my skin to gooseflesh, and we wander through the labyrinth of shelves and crates and freezers. And I'm failing. Failing to find what I need, the items on Julia's list. Failing to control my temper. Domestic tasks expose me, just as surely as the bright supermarket lights that hang overhead.

Sylvie dumps it in the trolley, beaming with the pride of a master pâtissier. *Et voilà!*

'Take it out,' I say. 'Please.'

The chocolate cake sits, large and impassive, in the centre of the trolley, like an IED.

'But it's for—' Sylvie says, until I stop her.

'Enough.'

'But Dad—'

'No,' I say. 'You can't have it.'

Don't stop being their father, Julia had advised me. *Keep a routine in place. A structure. Discipline them if they misbehave ...*

Cassia is watching us closely, her hands behind her back. '*She* doesn't want it,' Cassia tells me, innocently. 'It's for Black Mamba.'

Playing along inside Hart House is one thing; in a public

space, it feels ludicrous, embarrassing – like remembering a night terror the morning after.

'Then *he* can't have it.'

Several heads turn at the sharpness of my tone. Heat rises to my face.

'For Christ's sake, Sylvie, just do as I say.'

I regret the words as soon as I hiss them. Never, when Pippa was alive, had we resorted to *do as I say*. We were never perfect parents, but we were usually patient. We asked the girls politely; we told them why. I turn away and breathe how Julia has taught me: as if blowing bubbles through a hoop. Gently enough to preserve the soapy membrane; slowly enough to yield a steady stream. More shoppers are pausing to look, but I try to block them out; to pretend it's just me and the girls, alone in Hart House.

I turn, just in time to see Cassia whispering, her hand cupped to Sylvie's ear. I don't catch what she says, but I witness its effect: how the embers of defiance, glinting in Sylvie's eyes, are stoked and kindled. She says nothing as Cassia removes her hand.

'Fine,' I say. 'I'll do it.'

I take the cake out of the trolley.

The effect is immediate, like the splitting of an atom. The second I lift the box, Sylvie screams. Loud enough to be shocking, but with enough control to keep it going on, and on: just as Julia has taught us to breathe. And all the while, Sylvie has her eyes trained on me, fixing me with a basilisk stare. Daring me to resist.

I look around and see shoppers appear at each end of the aisle, gathering as if in vigil. I know what they're thinking: *says more about the parent than it does the child.* But it doesn't matter. I grab Sylvie by the wrist, gripping tightly, and drag her, screaming all the way, towards the exit. The trolley stands abandoned in the aisle. Julia's list lies crumpled on the floor.

The screams continue all the way to the doorstep of Hart House, but I've tuned them out. I turn my key in the lock and the door swings open. A cool breeze issues from the dark hallway, and words come singing to me from the shadows of my mind, in a baritone voice.

Open thy marble jaws, O tomb, and hide me, earth, in thy dark womb ...

We saw *Jephtha* for the first time one evening when Pippa was pregnant, her stomach bulging beneath her black dress like an autumn vegetable; large as a pumpkin, smooth as a marrow. We loved it so much that we listened to the music for weeks afterwards, the four of us: me, Pippa and the girls. Its sound filled the rooms of Hart House as we redecorated. I painted the walls of his bedroom-to-be with eggshell white, wearing Pippa's old smock. The girls dipped their chubby fingers into pots and touched each other's noses, shrieking with pleasure; they gabbled in twin-speak about what it would be like to have a brother.

Pippa just sat with her feet up, rubbing the sacred dome of her belly, contentedly watching me paint.

All our joys to sorrow turning.

As soon as we step over the threshold, Sylvie's screams stop – as do the chorus of memories – and a chilly silence falls over the house. Sylvie flicks her hair, as if unmoved. I let go of her wrist. We stare at each other, locked briefly in a stand-off, until she strides into the living room, her eyes still crackling, and slams the door. For a moment the hall is still. Then, without warning, I feel Cassia's small, warm body pressing up against my side. She coils around me, until her head is flat against my soft belly. Where I'm most vulnerable.

'I tried to tell her, Daddy,' she murmurs. 'I whispered in her ear. To put it back. But she wouldn't listen.'

'Uh-huh?' The sound clots in my throat and no words come. I look down at my daughter, gripping my leg for dear life, and the sight of her is disturbing, like looking at an amputated limb. It's not just that the twins are physically separate, a sight that is always strange enough in itself, but for the first time since Black Mamba arrived, they're not *acting* in concert. Their moods – their motives – have come apart.

'Did you really?' I murmur at last. Flatly, not in belief or disbelief, but in exhaustion.

Cassia's chest distends a little and her body pulls away from mine. She nods coolly. Her eyes are icy, unreadable.

I kiss the top of her head. I need to decompress, so I gently separate us and head to the kitchen. I open the fridge, retrieve the wine and take a glass from the draining board. For a moment or two I sit silently at the table, rubbing my forehead. The ringing in my ears reminds me of the choir of voices that echoed through the house when Pippa was alive, and I want to hear them sing again. So I pour myself a drink. As the lip of the glass touches my own, I hear a smash from the living room, and a cry. I try to muster a sense of drama, of urgency, but nothing comes. I get up stiffly, then wander back up the hallway and push open the living-room door.

Cassia is standing in the centre of the room. At her feet lie the remnants of a large crimson vase, which used to sit on the mantel. Pippa sculpted it for me, three years ago, for Valentine's. I study its remains. One large piece, roughly a third of the vase, is sitting at Cassia's feet, propped up by its jagged edges – like a child resting on his elbows. The other two thirds are a belt of broken fragments across the floor.

'Who threw it?' I ask tonelessly.

I gaze at my daughters. Cassia is in prime position, standing over the shattered vase, but her face shows no trace of emotion. Sylvie, meanwhile, is crouched in the corner of the room, far away from the carnage, and she's shaking violently.

'It was him,' Cassia says simply. 'Black Mamba. He turned into a monkey. A skinny one, with bright eyes and spiky fur. He was dancing all around the room, swinging from the light. Look.' She points upwards to the art deco fitting, which is swaying gently. 'You tried to stop him, Sylvie. Didn't you? We both did. But he lost control, and ... and ...'

Sylvie says nothing; she offers her sister no help. She is staring at the broken pieces as though the enormity of what has happened to the vase – its permanence – has paralysed her. I bow my head, instinctively. I understand that paralysis.

Crouching down, simian myself now, I begin to sweep what's left of the vase into a small heap. I move carefully, but still I cut my hand. A drop of blood forms in my palm, like a glass bead, then tumbles to the floor.

I look up. Sylvie is crawling across the room towards me. When she reaches me, I put my arms around her and hold her tight.

'I'm sorry, Daddy,' she chokes out, tearfully. 'I'm so sorry ...'

It's time. I feel it like a tremor in my bones. I talk it through on the phone with Julia, and even she agrees.

She comes round, as expected, when evening falls, with a boxed-up stir-fry. But her smile drops when she sees the bruise on Sylvie's wrist, and the broken vase, and the tears still in Sylvie's eyes – and Cassia on her own in the courtyard, tracing shapes with a finger against the brickwork. We eat dinner with them in an eerie silence, and afterwards they drift about the house, hand in hand, like a pair of ghosts. When we put them to bed, they slink beneath the covers noiselessly, their eyes wide, their jaws set. As if they know what's coming.

'I'm sorry,' Sylvie mouths hoarsely.

'It's okay,' I say, holding her hand.

'She didn't break the vase,' Cassia repeats, eyeing me with cold astonishment. 'It was him.'

Julia strokes her downy hair. 'Black Mamba?'

Cassia nods.

'Yeah,' I say. 'About him ...' My gaze drops to the bed-covers, in nervous saccades, but I steel myself. 'You've loved having him to stay. I know that. You've had fun with him, and he's been a good friend to you. But what happened today can't happen again. I think you understand that, don't you?'

'Yes,' they say. Sylvie says it more loudly than her sister. 'We'll make him listen,' she adds, her eyes still red and puffy. 'He'll do as he's told. We promise. He won't—'

Julia lifts a finger to Sylvie's lips. 'Let your dad finish,' she murmurs.

'He needs to leave.' There's no gentle way to say it, so I opt for firmness instead. 'It's been nice having him, but the time has come. From now on ... it has to be just the three of us.'

The girls are dumbstruck. I was wrong: they hadn't seen it coming.

'He doesn't want to go,' they say in unison.

'He doesn't have a choice,' I answer. 'Tonight, you say goodbye. Tomorrow morning, he'd best be gone. Understood?'

For a moment, I expect more tears. But then they nod slowly, and my chest heaves a powerful sigh.

'I love you,' I say, 'very much.'

And the nodding stops.

*

'Is that it?' I ask, closing their bedroom door.

Julia leans against the bannister and glances up, towards the attic. 'Mm?'

'I think it is,' I say, declining to repeat the question. 'I think we're through it.'

She says nothing, as together we descend the spiral staircase.

'Would you like a drink?' I ask. I know I would.

'I'd better not.'

She stays in the stairwell while I gather her belongings. 'That went better than expected,' she says abruptly.

'I suppose. What did you think might happen?'

She puts on her coat, not answering. I stifle a yawn, suddenly tired. She touches my arm. 'Are you sleeping okay? Or still having the nightmare?'

'I'm fine. I'll sleep better tonight.'

'How come?'

'How come?' I laugh. 'You saw them. They listened. I really think he'll go.'

'By morning.'

'Yeah. That's what they promised.'

Julia pauses at the front door, her fingers resting lightly on the handle. 'They promised they'd *tell* him to go.'

I nod defiantly. 'It's the same thing.'

*

Alone in my bedroom, swaddled in sheets, I stare at the ceiling, its contours barely visible in the dark, and begin, at last, to feel at peace. The mark on Sylvie's wrist comes momentarily to mind, and I feel a flicker of guilt. But things have worked out for the best.

I roll beneath the cold cover and must fall asleep, because the next thing I know I'm rising sharply. I heard a noise, or thought I did – the sound of two hands, clapping – but when I sit up, I'm met with total silence. I listen for a bit, wondering if it could have been the rattling that I've heard on other nights. But that noise has always been faint and distant, never so intimate. Never, before, in the room with me.

Two hands, clapping. I chide myself. What a thing to imagine. *Round of applause, Alfie Marvell, Dad of the Year. Take a bow.* I smile in the dark. Even my delusions are sarcastic.

I sink back into the mattress, while it still holds the mould of my body. Feeling awake now, I touch myself beneath the covers, and as I do, I sink even deeper into bed; *through* the bed, down through the house – to the place in my mind where I feel unseen. I think about Julia, earlier this evening, putting on her coat, the white line of her underwear just visible above her jeans.

Deep in the cellar now, she touches my hips, pulls me towards her. She's the nearest thing I have to Pip; in a sense, I'm still faithful to Pip. Kissing her neck, her breasts. Moaning softly in the dark.

*

When I wake, a man is standing by my bed.

I don't know what time it is – after coming, I must have slipped back into sleep – but I see his outline clearly in the blackness. My heart pounds behind my ribs. He's standing perfectly still, just inches away from the mattress edge. I can't see his face, or the whites of his eyes – only his body, immense and immovable in the dark – but I feel the weight of his presence bearing down on me, and the throb of an emotion pulsing from him, so tangible it thickens the air between us.

Anger.

I extend my left arm slowly, half expecting him to pounce, to scream, anything to puncture the stillness. But he doesn't move. He just stands there, large and motionless, radiating an unspeakable rage. My fingers travel silently up the cord of my bedside lamp and lock around the switch. I keep my eyes fixed dead on him.

Flick. Instant brilliance, clarity, colour. The room is empty.

My heart is still racing, jockeying with pure, animalistic fear, as I stare into the space where he stood just seconds earlier. I look all around the room, skimming over the contours of the furniture, halting momentarily in empty corners. There *is* no one here.

I check in the en suite, then out on the landing. I pace down the spiral stairs and towards the girls' room. Something has awoken inside me: a primal instinct to protect my daughters. The fear I felt at the sight of him by my bed – at the weight of his anger – hasn't left me, even if he has. I sweep into their room, hurrying to switch on their bedside lamp, but then I stop. For the first time since I woke, something is slowing me, making me think. It's not quite embarrassment, but something like it, a distant cousin. Incipient realisation. The return of reason. I quietly open the wardrobe doors, then check under their bed. And only then, as my pulse slows and my vision adjusts to the gloom, do I spot something in the shadows. Cassia's eyes are open, and moving with me. She's awake.

Sylvie isn't. The girls are spooning beneath the duvet. Cassia's arms and legs are wrapped around the curved body of her sleeping sister. And she's watching me silently in the dark.

I walk backwards, out onto the landing, and close the door without a word to her. What would I possibly say?

Cass, there's a man in my room?

Eight

Julia

Crescent Place looks so peaceful, I'm loath to disturb it. Clouds hang motionless above No. 2 like piled snow, and the net curtains barely twitch when I tap the knocker.

Auntie Sue answers the door. She smiles at the sight of me, but it's a fleeting smile, which quickly sinks back into a lattice of worried lines. 'Come in, love,' she says breathlessly, glancing up and down the street as though she thinks someone's watching – which I suppose she always does. Her crucifix is dangling from the tawny folds of her blouse, and it sparkles in the morning light. Once the door is closed, she shakes her head darkly. 'Your mother's having a bad day.'

'Thanks for the warning,' I say, girding myself – and trying to suppress the same cynical thought that I always have on one of Mum's bad days: *that I'm being punished.* Mum suffered her stroke three days after I finally moved out of Hart House, leaving her to live alone. She managed to call an ambulance after twenty minutes, prone on the floor in pain. By that point, permanent damage had been done: to her mobility, her energy levels, her frame of mind. She's never blamed me explicitly, of course. She's never had to.

'Downstairs?'

'Yes.' Sue opens the door that leads to Mum's quarters in the basement, and motions for me to walk ahead of her. 'Barely had a thing for breakfast. Struggling to chew and swallow.'

I nod as I pass. 'Poor thing.'

The staircase that leads down to Mum's rooms is dark and narrow, and the scent of Sue's perfume is cloying in the tight space. I hear Mum's moans long before we reach the bottom stair.

'Julia?' She's sitting, scarcely upright, on a velvet sofa; waving a hand limply through the air. 'Is that you?' she asks, as though the pain in her body is overwhelming her sight.

'It's me,' I say. 'It's Wednesday.'

She sighs. Her half-closed eyes are baggy and panda-like, her mascara having run with her tears. 'I didn't think you were coming.'

'I always come.'

Mum's basement flat is perfectly comfortable, if a little dingy. No surface is bare; everything is carpeted or wall-papered. The windows are high up in the walls ('like a prison cell,' she sometimes says) and the light they let in is broken at regular intervals ('also like a prison cell') by a series of iron bars: the railings that run up and down Crescent Place. My eyes take a while to adjust.

'How are your *bones*, Marian?' Sue asks earnestly, and Mum clasps a hand to her ribcage and groans, as though the question itself has pierced her sides. 'Do you think you can manage some tea?'

I turn. Sue is wavering at the bottom of the staircase, one foot on the final step, the other hovering just above the basement floor, as if she's reluctant to intrude fully on Mum's domain.

'Yes, please,' I say, answering for her. I drag a high-backed wooden chair from its position against the far wall and sit opposite my mother. We scowl at each other in silence as Sue makes her slow ascent back towards the kitchen.

Steadily, my eyes begin to pick out more details from the gloom: a short bookshelf along the back wall (there are only ever two books on it: the church's sacred texts) and, just below, a series of grisaille icons – woodcuts, I think – in tiny black frames. Each one depicts a scene from scripture: the archangel Michael, with a demon underfoot; Christ, exorcising the man at Gerasa; Paul, casting a demon out of a slave girl; and, of course, the holy woman at Endor, listening solemnly to King Saul's request. If I lean forward in my seat, I can just about read Saul's words, written in florid script beneath the woodcut – 1 Samuel 28:8.

Harness for me the power of that demon, and use it to contact the soul I name to you ...

Demons. The things that haunt us, the things that tempt us. To be a Christian is to be in control of your demons; that's what we were taught, growing up, though Mum's mastery of hers has always felt, to me at least, unstable – a preserve of occasional days and certain curated moments.

This isn't one of them.

The click of the door closing, as Sue reaches the top of the stairs, reminds me I'm not here to look at pictures.

'How are you?' I ask, as tenderly as possible.

'Oh, I can't complain.' She shifts a little on the sofa, and winces. 'Or maybe I can. After all, everyone who's ever loved me is dead.'

I try not to roll my eyes. She's straight in there with the melodrama – and trying to hurt me, too. It's a standard blow (at least by Mum's standards), familiar in every respect, even down to the architecture of it: the fleeting moment of false stoicism, followed by the gut punch. One, two – crack!

Mum's eyes are mostly closed, as though weighed down by suffering, but I still see their lids peeking open, just a sliver, as she gauges my response. Not for the first time, I imagine my mother as an over-sized child. It's an uncomfortable thought, but apposite. The children I treat at the clinic display many of her attributes: depression, hypochondria, anxiety, demand avoidance, low self-worth. And, of course – I glance again at the winged, fanged demons that adorn the wall – a penchant for fantasy, delusion.

'That's not true,' I say flatly. 'The twins love you. At least, I think they do.'

(The one-two punch is not my Mum's preserve.)

She grunts and touches her head. Then, after a moment, she says in a low, cold voice: 'They may as well be dead to me.'

'What are you talking about?'

Mum sighs again. Her sighs have a musical tone, as if she wants to turn them into full-blown wails, but – like an ageing contralto – lacks the lung power. 'They're not mine anymore. I'm losing them.'

'That's not true either.'

'Oh, it is. Alfie despises me. Always has. He wishes I'd leave him alone.'

So did Pippa, I think acidly, but I don't say it. There are unspoken rules when I spar with my mother; we can needle each other, but only with falsehoods. The truth is always off limits.

In the early days, Mum was barely permitted access to Pippa and Alfie's lives, and she remained excluded until Pippa fell pregnant with the twins. That's when she slithered back in. Pippa needed help, and Alfie was busy with work. Mum had a right to know her granddaughters, and the girls had a right to know her too. Once she'd given them the house, there was practically no way of stopping her.

Of course, they tried to loosen her coils, but it wasn't easy, especially given how happy she was, how giddy, at the prospect of twins. Her joy was so great – reaching heights unheard of since Dad had died – that at first Pippa even tolerated the odd verse of scripture.

'*Two are better than one*,' I heard her say, massaging Pip's swollen belly at six months. '*For if they fall, one will lift the other up.*' And then, on the day the girls were born, shell-pink, shrieking and perfect: '*If two lie together, they keep warm ... And though one might prevail against another, two will withstand one.*' But then she pushed too far, on the twins' first birthday, when she twinkled: '*A cord of three strands is not soon broken ...*' and Pippa – who knew the third strand to be God – announced that reciting scripture was forbidden, thereafter, in her daughters' presence.

Pippa stayed a believer till the end, I think, just not in organised religion; Alfie's derision for it saw to that, and, in the process, poisoned his relations with Mum. Now would be the perfect time to share with her my worries about his drinking, my criticisms of his parenting – or lack thereof. But I resist the temptation.

'He's been wonderful to you,' I say instead. 'Since the accident.' (It's sort of true. He's been patient, at least. Nothing like how he treated her when Pippa was alive.) 'He lets you see the girls whenever you want. He's allowed you to stay part of their lives.'

Mum laughs – a rasping, hollow laugh. 'Exactly. He doesn't fight me anymore. Because he doesn't have to. I'm at his mercy.' She pauses, for a pinched moment. 'And yours.'

Mine? Momentarily I freeze, certain that she's heard about Black Mamba – that she knows I've been keeping the news of him from her – but then I think, *Relax. She can't have. She only sees the girls when Alfie's there. And he'd have told me.*

'What does that mean?'

Mum shrugs despondently. 'Nothing,' she says eventually.

I don't rise to it. Would you scream at rainclouds? Mum's bad days are like bad weather; they come, they go, they can't be helped. And they're not my fault.

'I wish I could help you,' I say, and I mean it.

'Me too,' she answers glumly. For a second, she seems so sad I'm almost moved to touch her, but then she pulls herself up. 'If you want to help,' she says, 'don't let me die of thirst. Go on: see what Fruit Cake's up to. Help her find the kitchen.'

Upstairs, the kettle is untouched, the mugs still sitting neatly on the shelf. My aunt has been distracted by something – or nothing. I walk back down the hallway, following the sound of a voice, faint and disembodied. I strain to listen. At first, I think it's the radio, but then I realise that it's Sue. Puzzled, I push open the door to the sitting room and find my aunt, talking to empty space.

'All right,' she whispers, 'but afterwards, you're going straight to bed—'

'Auntie?'

Sue turns, slowly, and straightens up, to the extent she still can. She smiles brightly. 'Is everything all right, dear?'

'It's – yes. Everything's . . .' I frown. She's good at masking her confusion, sometimes disarmingly so. 'Are you okay?'

Sue sucks air in sharply through her front teeth. 'Oh, you should have seen this room on Sunday. Crumbs everywhere!' She laughs, a loud, braying laugh, then steps forward and clasps my hands in hers. 'You should come to church again, Julia.' Her hazel eyes are unspeakably earnest.

I pull away.

'You loved it as a child,' she presses. 'Don't you remember?'

I do – so clearly. If I close my eyes, the sensation envelops me still: that feeling of perfect belonging, tucked away behind the walls of this faceless house. The imprint of a thousand hours spent communing with His people. My family.

Slowly, reluctantly, I nod.

'Well?' she says gently, nonplussed. 'What changed?'

I don't know what to say. That my faith fell away. That it peeled off the walls of my mind like old paper as soon as I could think for myself. That its particulars – the existence of God, and of demons – collapsed, first into metaphor, then into irrelevance as I reached my teens.

They're the usual clichés, but not the whole truth. I never had faith, not really. Not even when I believed in God.

Suddenly, Sue gasps, and I'm spared by a flash of memory. 'Tea!'

'It's all right,' I say. 'Honestly. I'll do it.'

But she covers her ears cheerfully, and shakes her head.

'Let me help at least.' I follow my aunt into the hallway. As I close the door behind us, I catch a final glimpse of the pencil sketch of Michael above the mantelpiece, shimmering in the morning light.

Back in the kitchen, Sue busies herself with teabags, and taps her nails distractedly against the steel cylinder of the kettle. I lift the spotted mugs off the top shelf.

'Are you still going to Redd Hall?' I ask. But she's turned on the tap and can't speak over the heavy jet of water thundering into the kettle. Redd Hall is the community centre. Once a week, a meeting is held there for people in the early stages of dementia – an activity group, of sorts. I know her daughters have been taking her.

She tightens the tap shut. 'No, love. I can't. It's a beautiful thing they're doing, but I don't have the time to keep helping. What with your mother, and all the church stuff to take care of.'

'Oh,' I say. 'Right.' *She thinks she's going as a volunteer.*

Sue flicks the kettle switch and falls silent as it starts to heat up. 'I'm sorry,' she says after a minute, 'for pressuring you. About the church. It was wrong of me.'

'It's fine.'

'I was just thinking, about what you asked me the other day. Do you remember?'

I bend down to fetch milk from the fridge. 'What?'

'You asked if He comforts me. The Lord.'

'Oh.' I place the carton carefully on the counter. 'That was weeks ago. But yes, I remember.' In truth, I'm surprised that she does.

My aunt goes quiet again. She runs her fingers up and down the height of the mugs, and adjusts their positions on the kitchen counter until the handles are parallel with one another. 'It upset me,' she says, in a small voice.

'Oh,' I say. 'I didn't mean—'

She looks up and smiles. 'Not like that. It upset me that you even had to ask.' She draws back a dark strand of hair that has fallen over my eyes, tucking it behind my ear. 'How is your faith, my dear?'

'Oh,' I say, looking at my feet. 'You know. It comes and goes.'

Sue looks doubtful. 'Yes?'

No.

'Because I wouldn't be without mine,' she says. 'Not on any day.'

She smiles, and I can see she expects me to reply, to acknowledge the truth in what she's said. But I can't. From a very young age, I knew that I was different. I wasn't like Pippa, with her drawings, and feelings, and dreams. I never felt God's spirit. I believed He was real, of course, but I never felt His eyes upon me; I never felt *seen*. Before it occurred to me that He might not be there at all, I used to think there was something wrong with me – something missing, or defective.

Part of me sometimes still does.

The kettle begins to whistle and Sue lifts it up to fill the teapot. Steam rises in a perfect, vertical column. 'You know our family wasn't always religious?'

I didn't, though it isn't a complete surprise. Sue fell pregnant at sixteen, but never married – never even knew the father's name.

She leans in to whisper, solemnly: 'We found the Lord when Michael died ...'

The kitchen seems airless, suddenly, and I realise I'm holding my breath. I've never heard her say his name aloud before.

'You know what happened to my son? Your cousin.'

I nod dumbly. It happened before I was born, of course – before Dad met Mum, even. But I know the story. Dad and Sue were on holiday together, in the Black Forest, and Dad was supposed to be watching Michael, his only nephew, but he left him alone, playing on the Danube. The ice broke.

'Everything's in His hands,' Sue says. 'Everything. If you don't have that, what are you left with? Thinking: if we hadn't gone to Germany. Or: if I hadn't left him alone with Eric ...'

Her phrasing is disjointed and I realise she's getting upset, but I know what she's trying to say. I rub her arm and she grasps my hand again, gripping this time with surprising strength.

'Your father was the same,' she says grimly. 'His faith came and went. Just like yours. Just like your mother's.'

I'm surprised and unsurprised at once. In the blur of my memories, Dad is always fervent in belief. But then I think of how he died.

'Remember Thomas? The disciple who had to feel Christ's wounds before he would believe He'd risen? That was your father.' She lets go of my arm, shaking her head. 'He couldn't just accept that Michael was okay. That everything had happened as it should. He needed proof.'

'Proof ... ?'

Sue nods mournfully. Her eyes meet mine, and as they do, a chill spreads rapidly across my chest. 'What kind of proof?'

Suddenly, her distress mounts. Muttering, she punches her forehead with a frail fist. 'We shouldn't have done it,' she whimpers. 'We knew it was dangerous. His faith was too weak. He wasn't ready. Oh, God, Julia, he wasn't *ready* ...'

'Sue,' I say, trying to calm her, 'what kind of proof?'

But she's too distraught to speak. I put my arms around her and feel her thin limbs trembling – a cadaver brought to life.

'It's all right,' I say quickly. 'It's all right.'

Her daughters' phone numbers are taped to the fridge for exactly this kind of occasion. Once I've soothed my aunt as best I can, I dial them both. In any other house their photographs would be there too – especially as her memory starts to give way. But no photographs have ever been displayed at No. 2.

140

Nine

Alfie

I'm holding the flowers that we're going to lay on Pippa's grave – blue and white irises, tied with a silver bow – and Cassia is staring at me, sphinx-like, seated at the foot of the spiral stairs, her shoes placed neatly beside her.

'She won't move,' Sylvie explains, 'until he says she can.'

Today is Pippa's birthday. She would have been thirty-three. Reason tells me that it's just another day now, and marking it in any way is pointless – that in some profound sense, today is no longer her birthday, and to pretend otherwise, as if she's interned somewhere or stranded abroad, is delusional. The kind of thing the girls would do, or Marian. But I can't just let it pass. I've been dreading this day for weeks, reminded of it each time I look at the calendar that hangs in the kitchen; resenting the way it lurked, innocently, between all the other days, preparing to wound me with its uneventfulness, its lack of consequence. I've felt it staring back at me, daring me to ignore it, to let it slip into quiet anonymity among its peers. But I can't. Whether out of weakness or strength, I have to turn it into something it's not; I have to mark it, somehow.

The girls had no idea what day it was until I told them a moment ago, stumbling over my words, cradling the flowers pathetically in my arms. They didn't reply. They didn't look happy or sad, just blank. So I said, 'Put your shoes on,' taking their lack of expression as a sign of consent. But only Sylvie obliged.

'Please, Cass,' I say. 'Please, not today ...'

Slowly, almost imperceptibly, she shakes her head. 'I can't,' she whispers hoarsely. 'He says I can't. He says we've got to stay.'

The tips of my fingers prickle as Sylvie sits down next to her sister and wraps an arm around her shoulders.

'He?' I ask.

'Black Mamba,' Sylvie tells me solemnly.

'But ... he's gone.'

'No,' Cassia says. 'He hasn't.'

'Look at me,' I say to the girls – redundantly, since they're already looking. 'I told you he had to go. Remember? And he did.'

I almost believed it. The girls hadn't mentioned him since the night of his eviction. An uneasy hush had settled over the matter as if, somewhere in the space between us, the lines of a truce had been drawn, chalked invisibly on troubled ground.

'It's not our fault,' says Sylvie, sensing my anger. 'We

asked him to go. We told him to. I promise. But he just won't leave.'

'Black Mamba says that you can't make him.' Cassia's voice differs from her sister's. It's hard and cold, yet there's no edge to it, at least none that I can detect.

'Cassia,' I say. 'Please stop.'

Sylvie reaches up and pulls beseechingly at my arm. 'It's not our fault. He doesn't want to leave.'

Cassia nods stiffly again, her eyes vague, as if she's in a trance. 'Black Mamba says he wants to stay forever …'

I take a breath. Unclench my fists. 'We'll talk about this later. Let's just go. It's Mummy's birthday. Come on. We have to go.'

I begin to turn, but Cassia's voice, rising now, harsh and insistent (there's the edge), halts me. 'He doesn't want to.'

'Cass—'

'She's not *his* mum.'

The flowers droop as my wrist goes slack. I grip the bannister with my free hand to steady myself, my knuckles whitening. 'What did you say?'

'She's not his mum. She's nothing to him. He doesn't want to go. He wants to stay here with us and play. Black Mamba says that you can go on your own.'

I feel my head shaking, and I hear my voice crack in disbelief. Not at what Cassia's saying; at what I'm saying. 'No he didn't.'

'Didn't what?'

'He didn't say that.'

143

'He did.'

'No, Cassia, he didn't.'

'You can't hear him,' she says, her voice rising higher still. 'You can't hear him because he doesn't want—'

'He didn't say it,' I shout, cutting down her voice like a stem, 'because he isn't real!'

And then, silence. Silence of a kind I've never heard before. It's as if the girls' breathing has stopped; as if the birds outside have been struck dumb; as if the traffic has vanished, and the wind has dropped. They stare at me, their mouths closing and opening, like landed fish.

'He is real,' Sylvie gasps. 'He is.'

'No,' I say, still shaking, though speaking now as gently as I can. 'He's just a story. You imagined—'

'Stop it.' Cassia lunges forward and tries to force her hand over my mouth. 'Stop it, stop it, stop it!'

I push away her fingers. 'No, I won't. This has gone on long enough. Too long. Black Mamba isn't real. He never has been. You invented him. It's all pretend.'

Sylvie starts to cry. 'Daddy, please,' she whimpers. 'Please, don't ...'

'He was a game. That's all. A way of coping ... with everything that's happened to us.' I stop short, unbalanced suddenly. I'm crying too, I realise. 'For Christ's sake,' I hear myself say. 'It's Mummy we're talking about. Mummy. Please. This has got to stop. It's got to stop—'

Sylvie lets out a cry. Not the noise she made in the supermarket – a controlled and calculated scream –

144

but something guttural, animalistic. She stands bolt upright on the steps, then begins to hunch over, clutching her stomach.

'Sylvie? What's wrong?'

'I feel bad,' she whispers. 'Really bad.' She breathes deeply, rubbing her legs in agitation.

'Sylvie?'

She ignores me. I reach to touch her shoulder and she shakes me off, losing her footing on the stairs. I catch her, steadying her on her feet. 'You're all right,' I say, hopefully. 'You're all right.'

She looks at me, barely focusing, then retches. Nothing comes out, but it's a violent convulsion, as if something in her lungs, her throat, is trying to work its way free.

I look up at Cassia, still sitting on the stairs.

'Now you've done it,' she says to me softly. Fury smoulders in her eyes. But her tone is fearful.

Sylvie retches again.

I scoop her up into my arms. 'We need to get her to the bathroom,' I say. 'Help me.'

Cassia noses up the stairs in front of me. She opens the door, and I carry her sister inside.

'Sylvie? Sylvie?'

I put her down. She can stand, just about. I grab a flannel, douse it in cold water, pat her head. She's still wearing her shoes and coat.

'Help me get—' I start to say, but Cassia's already unlacing her sister's boots.

'Breathe,' I say. 'Just breathe. You're fine.'

She's not. Sylvie drops to the floor, still clutching her stomach. 'It hurts,' she whimpers. 'Daddy, it hurts!'

I crouch down and prop her against the side of the bath, trying to steady her – desperate not to see her lying flat, outstretched on the bathroom floor. *Like Pippa, the night she fell.* But it's no use. She keeps rolling onto her side, tears streaming.

'Sylvie, talk to me. Tell Daddy what's wrong.'

'It's *him*!' she screams. 'He's doing this. Black Mamba. It's him!'

I stand up, trembling, using my height to put distance between us. 'Are you pretending?' My voice is cool, but my hands are shaking. 'Sylvie, are you pretending?'

She doesn't even reply. She's curled up in a tight, tiny ball, hugging her knees. Then she lurches forward, towards the toilet. Without a sound – almost calmly – she vomits cleanly into the bowl.

This is beyond my comprehension.

'I'm calling Julia,' I say, pulling my phone from my pocket.

'But what about Mum?'

Cassia's voice catches me off guard. I turn. She's standing quietly beside her sister, her hands folded neatly behind her back, her face inscrutable.

'What?'

'It's Mum's birthday,' she continues. 'What about the visit? The flowers?'

'Forget it,' I say, scrolling for Julia's name. 'It doesn't matter.' And, as I speak, Sylvie gasps, collapsing back onto the bathroom floor, spent; as though whatever was afflicting her stomach has, at last, released its grip.

'Sylvie?' I crouch down again, put my phone aside and begin to massage her back.

Warily, her limbs shaking, she props herself up and coughs and spits into the bowl. 'They've gone,' she says, her voice quivering, awestruck almost; as though she can't quite believe it. 'The stomach pains ... they've gone.'

'You're sure?'

She nods, reaching meekly to pull the flush, her arms still trembling.

I scrape back her hair. 'Shh. It's all right. You're all right.' I pick her up and hold her gently. 'I'm here.'

'Please,' she rasps in my ear. 'Don't do that again.'

'Do what?'

Her hot, sour breath tickles my skin. 'Don't say he isn't real.'

I keep stroking her back.

'You made him so cross. So cross. Please, don't let him hurt me again.'

'Let's get you downstairs,' I murmur. 'We'll make you a bed on the sofa, in front of the telly.'

'Promise me,' says Sylvie insistently, wrapping her arms around my neck. *'Promise.'*

I draw breath sharply as, in the distance, I hear the penny drop.

Julia was wrong. They aren't pretending. *They think he's real.*

'All right,' I say, defeated. 'I promise.'

'Thank you.' There's nothing jubilant in Sylvie's tone; she sounds defeated too. I hold her tightly to my body and she softens. My touch seems soothing at last, and I feel useful. I scoop her off the bathroom floor and carry her downstairs. In the kitchen, I brew her a hot chocolate, her favourite drink, and a coffee for me – spiked with a little something. Then, as promised, I lay pillows and blankets on the sofa and switch on the telly.

'You're all right,' I say once more, kissing her forehead, and this time, for the first time, those words feel true. 'Daddy loves you very much.'

We lie there together for five minutes, then ten, just watching the telly – breathing in harmony, allowing our pulses to settle. Cassia didn't want a hot chocolate, and she didn't want to watch cartoons. I call out her name a couple of times, but she doesn't respond or enter the room. Exhaustion and Sylvie's weight pin me to the sofa. I don't hear Cassia again until a creak in the hallway, which Sylvie doesn't seem to hear, alerts me to her presence. I crane my neck and watch her through the half-open door, walking into the kitchen, carrying something in her arms. A feeling of unease spreads over me as I glimpse what she's doing: dumping the blue and white flowers, two fistfuls at a time, into the bin.

Ten

Julia

I'm dreaming of Dad. We're curled up together in a warm, dark bedroom, his right arm weighing on my tiny shoulder blade. I'm breathing in the warmth of his body, the musk of his jumper. If I lean back to look into his eyes, my forehead brushes against his beard. It looks wiry, but feels soft.

Pippa is here too, on his left, but that's okay. We're infants, and this dream – this memory – is from before our characters emerged and crystallised; before she became his favourite. Right now, everything is even. Dad has an arm around each of us, and we both have a book in our lap. The Bible rests in mine, hardback black, bound in creased leather, a silver crucifix engraved on the front. And in Pippa's lap ...

The Book of the Princes. I can't quite see it in the dream, but I can sense its presence, feel its weight and proportions, as though it lies in my lap, not my sister's. I haven't looked at it properly in years, but I remember the cover:

black ridged leather with a silver serpent engraved on the front. I remember the smell of the pages – old and dusty, like dried lavender – and I remember the markings upon them. English and Hebrew letters, combining to list the princes' names and their abilities: sorcery, telepathy, prescience, therianthropy, necromancy ...

Dad is speaking of the princes. I hear his voice and it's exactly right – the rhythm, the oaky timbre, the West Country lilt. My brain has preserved the memory of it, locked it away safely all these years, and is now reproducing it perfectly.

'They were angels once,' he says. 'Princes of Heaven. But they rebelled against God, so He banished them, cast them down into the pit. *Sheol* ... the place of shadows. After that, they were known as demons.'

I reach across my father's waist and take my sister's hand, which is hot and sweaty. This story is familiar; we've heard it a hundred times.

Tell us again.

'God made Man, but a prince of shadows crept into the Garden and led him astray. Then Man was banished too, out of Eden, to wander the Earth, to live among demons, to be preyed on by them. But God didn't abandon His creation. All those who worshipped Him could make those demons cower and flee. All those who served Him could bend those demons to their will. All those who kissed the Son could control those demons – and use their heavenly abilities ...'

I wake cleanly from the dream, Dad's rhythmic voice still thrumming in my ears. I'm alone in the darkness of my flat. For a split second, I still feel the curve of his arm and the shape of Pippa's fingers; I still feel the weight of their bodies. But they're ice cold.

It's late afternoon, and I'm still at the clinic. Everything I'm doing for the twins and Alfie is taking its toll, so I've decided to cut back, to palm off clients onto my colleagues, only retaining those cases which, for some reason, I can't let go of.

Like Simon and Ralf. I'm seeing them separately now. Ralf today, Simon tomorrow.

Ralf is tall and bearded, with an accent that seems to grow stronger each time we speak, and when he greets me I think of my dream last night with a cold pang. He lies down on the sofa and closes his eyes – both ironically, I reckon. He still thinks that Simon's the problem; that Simon, with his reticence to start a family, is the one who needs therapy.

All the same, I feel awkward in Ralf's presence. A desire for kids is natural, of course, but not when it becomes all-consuming. I want to ask him questions, like whether he's satisfied with his career, but it feels rude somehow, which only heightens my discomfort. I'm second guessing myself; if he were a woman, I think, with irritation, I'd ask him that question, no problem.

'Are there kids in your family?' I say instead.

'Yes. I have a sister. She and her husband have just had a baby girl.' He opens his chestnut eyes and smiles. 'I'm not sure they even thought about it – whether or not to have kids. Imagine that ...'

I hesitate again. Afraid, perhaps, of what he might say next.

That nieces aren't enough, and never will be.

I draw a breath, trying to stay detached.

Perhaps he misinterprets my silence, because he speaks again, quickly. 'Don't get me wrong. I'm happy for her. Truly.' He exhales deeply. 'Simon thinks I'm in denial about who I am ... who we are. But he's wrong. I know I can't have my sister's life. I know we have limits.'

'Limits?'

He shrugs, a little too lightly. 'Any child wouldn't have our blood.'

'There are options, these days,' I say.

He shakes his head. 'Even if we use a surrogate, the child won't be mine and his. There'll be this ... other element. My blood, mixed with another's. It can't be simple. It won't be easy.'

I nod sympathetically, trying to stay in the room; to stop the walls of Hart House closing in on me. But I can't. His frankness is flustering me. Somehow, it feels exposing.

'No,' he says quietly, 'I can't have my sister's life. But I could have something like it. Something close.' He closes his eyes again. 'And that's what I want. I'm sorry,' he adds, shrugging – not sounding sorry at all. 'It's what I want.'

*

By four o'clock, the session's over, and I'm heading towards my sister's family – my sister's life.

The weather recently has been so fine that I'm walking everywhere rather than driving, and my route from the office to Hart House takes me through some of the more scenic parts of London, including an old graveyard that I've always loved. When I say old, what I really mean is disused – though not, I suppose, by the people buried in it. The gates are busted from their hinges, and the graves themselves are sunken and weathered, palled by unruly grass. Most graveyards belong to the living, but no one has been buried here since the 1800s, and the people who once grieved for them are long dead too – and so, unlike most graveyards, it's not a place of pain but a place of peace. I can walk alone among its winged stone seraphim, happily without religion; without feeling hollow.

The streets get busier as I approach Hart House. Peter's Park is beginning to fill up with young families, and teen-agers who've escaped from their families. One or two groups are loitering beneath the red horse chestnuts, whose blooms are beginning to flourish now in bloody splashes. The petals were only just emerging the day that Pippa died; this is the first time they've blossomed again since the accident.

I step out of the undergrowth into Allington Square, and the house rises suddenly before me, a tidal wave of peeling white paint. The gaping square windows, cut into the façade, let you see clearly inside, but I don't spot Alfie or the girls. The front door is painted a vine-green, also peeling. I go to ring the bell but pause when I notice something strange: the door is ajar. I push it open, uneasily, and step over the threshold.

'Alfie?' I freeze in the cool, dark hallway. A peculiar smell is hanging faintly in the air – the smell of incense and charring – and it makes my stomach turn. I haven't smelled it in decades, but I recognise it instantly; another memory that's been locked away inside my head, out of reach, yet somehow still in pristine condition.

It's the scent that hung around Hart House for days after Dad died.

Could I be imagining it? That seems the only logical explanation. Phantosmia is unusual, but not unheard of; we've treated cases of it before at the clinic. I touch my temples, shakily. The thought that last night's dream is still lingering inside my head, now warping my perception, disturbs me.

Voices coming from the living room refocus my attention. First, a woman's, honeyed and smooth. Then a man's, high-pitched and nasal.

'. . . just to get an idea,' the man is saying, 'of how the girls are doing.'

'We haven't noticed any tension at school—'

I turn the handle of the living-room door and gently push it open. The woman, who's standing in the centre of the room, looks up and instantly closes her mouth, neatly, like she's shutting a book. She's tall, with dark, frizzy hair, and her slim body is swaddled in a grey trench coat. I've never seen her before. The man is sitting on the sofa with his back to me. As I enter, he doesn't turn, so I don't see his face. But I'm pretty sure he's a stranger too, just like the woman. For a moment or two, I simply stare in surprise while the pale walls of the living room shimmer in the summer light as if they're shaking; as if they're trying to dispel this alien presence.

Only then do I spot Alfie, standing in the corner like a naughty schoolboy. His burly arms are clenched across his chest defensively, but his eyes are wide, and he's chewing his bottom lip. 'Julia. You're here.' He sounds relieved.

The woman smiles. 'Hi there.'

'Hi,' I echo uncertainly, taking off my jacket and draping it over the sideboard. Staking out some territory.

Alfie turns to the visitors. 'This is Julia Harris, the girls' auntie. Pippa's sister.' Then, to me: 'This is Miss Addison.'

The name is familiar, but I can't quite place it.

'Call me Bella,' she says, extending a hand. Her fingers are jewelled and slender, and her palm is cool to touch.

'And this is Mr Lewer.' Alfie swallows, his Adam's apple bobbing. 'From social services.'

'Social ... ?' I trail off. A dozen thoughts spring to mind, everything I've witnessed these past few months. Alfie's drinking, his lapses, his neglect – I hate to call it that, but it's the word a court would use – his depression. His *unfitness*.

At least now I understand his nerves, and his relief at the sight of me. He's cornered, in more senses than one.

Mr Lewer, sitting on the sofa, still has his back to me. I step forward into the middle of the room, and at last he tilts his head. Our eyes meet. He is bald and bespectacled, his body sagging in a drab suit. His mouth is naturally downturned, but it lifts sleepily to greet me with a reassuring smile. *It can't be him*, I think, heart thumping. *That was decades ago.* My mind is betraying me again ...

I stare at the man, with his thick-rimmed glasses and inscrutable eyes that are so painfully familiar. I open my mouth and stutter.

I shouldn't say it. It's crazy.

'I've seen you before.'

He frowns. 'I don't think so,' he says politely. 'No, no. I don't think so.' And he shakes his head.

'No, I have. Definitely. You were—' I break off, sensing Alfie's eyes boring into the back of my skull.

'I think,' Mr Lewer says, firmly but not unpleasantly, 'you have me mixed up with someone else.'

And he's right: I must do. It's the *parallel* that's plaguing me, confounding my thoughts. Two strangers – two officials – suddenly present in Hart House. *Just like after Dad died.* I close my eyes and try to picture the man who spoke to us as little girls – to see beyond his briefcase, and glasses, and cold gaze that gave nothing away. But his face eludes me. All I can see is Mr Lewer, who is staring quizzically at me when I open my eyes.

'You're confused,' Alfie says. 'You must be.' He sounds confused himself.

'Not necessarily.' Miss Addison smiles gently as she intervenes. 'Ms Harris is a psychotherapist, isn't that right? Alfie said you've been counselling the girls?'

'That's right.'

'Perhaps your paths have crossed professionally, then?'

'Perhaps,' Mr Lewer admits. He shifts gracelessly on the sofa – uncertain, in the face of my silence, of where to go from here.

I clear my throat, conscious of the blood rushing to my face, and attempt to regain my composure. 'Where are the girls?' I ask Alfie.

'Upstairs.' He places a hand on my shoulder. 'They're fine.' A moment of taut silence follows as he begins to look uncomfortable with what he's said. He jams his hands into his pockets. 'Well ...'

I turn to Mr Lewer. 'Why are you here?' I don't mean to be so blunt. Fortunately, he doesn't seem fazed.

'There's been an incident,' he says.

'An incident?'

'Yes,' says Miss Addison. 'At school.'

'Bella is the girls' teacher,' Alfie explains.

'Right,' I say. *That's why I recognised her name.*

'I know it's unorthodox,' she continues, raising her palms, as if feeling guilty for her presence, 'but I wanted to come with Mr Lewer, to explain what happened. To Alfie. To you.'

'What *has* happened?'

She glances at Mr Lewer, apparently unwilling to over-step the bounds of her authority.

'Ms Harris,' he says, 'we know it's been a tough year for the girls. For all of you. From your sessions with the girls, how would you say they're coping?'

I take a deep breath, and speak quickly. 'Okay, all things considered. They're both suffering from stress and anxiety, which they're struggling to regulate. They've always had a close twin bond, but they've become even more co-dependent. I'm seeing them several times a week, though, and we're working through it.' I turn back to Miss Addison. 'What kind of incident?'

'Has there been any tension between the girls?' Mr Lewer says.

'Between them?'

'Yes. Have they been fighting?'

'Not that I've witnessed,' I say carefully. 'Not that I'm aware of.'

He fiddles briefly with his spectacles, and I notice, with a spasm of apprehension, that a plastic folder is lying in his lap. He taps the edge of it lightly against his knee and leans forward, his mouth twitching as he mulls his words. 'Sorry, but I've got to press you. Are you saying you haven't witnessed any problem behaviours? Any violence? Non-compliance?'

I think immediately of what Alfie told me on the night we agreed that Black Mamba should leave – of Sylvie's tantrum in the supermarket, and Alfie's furious response.

'I suppose,' I begin, 'there was—'

'We've had problems with Cassia,' Alfie says, cutting across me.

I stare at him, but he doesn't look back.

'Go on,' says Mr Lewer.

'It was Pippa's birthday this week and Cassia refused to leave the house, to lay some flowers for her.'

'But she didn't become violent?' Mr Lewer presses. 'Towards her sister?'

There's a look in Alfie's eyes that I can't quite place. 'No,' he says quietly, then after a moment, adds: 'Sylvie became distressed when I tried to discipline Cassia. Very distressed. But Cassia didn't do anything to her, per se. She didn't even say anything. She just ... Well. It was odd.' He shrugs weakly.

A moment of silence ensues, which I fill with repetition. 'What kind of incident?' I face Mr Lewer squarely, and fold my arms. 'I'm sorry ... but I'm not saying any more about the girls' behaviour, or our sessions, until you tell me what happened, and why you're here.'

He nods. He doesn't even look offended. As a social worker, I guess he's used to worse.

My hostility is surprising even to myself. I'm trying to keep my tone neutral, but animosity keeps seeping out. It's a primal feeling, coming from deep in my gut – braided with those memories that I can't quite shake.

At last, Mr Lewer opens his folder and passes me a photograph. 'A few weeks ago, Miss Addison—'

'Bella, please ...'

'—noticed a mark on Sylvie's wrist.'

I take the photograph and recognise it instantly. It's the bruise that Alfie gave Sylvie when he dragged her home from the shops, after her meltdown.

'It looked to me like someone had gripped her wrist,' Miss Addison says, shaking her curls unhappily. 'Very tightly.'

'Christ.' I try to look shocked, playing for time.

'Sometimes,' Alfie interjects, carefully and with surprising coolness, 'kids can be rough when they play. Perhaps Cassia ...'

I grit my teeth. I understand how it happened, of course. He was angry, embarrassed, sleep-deprived and – as now – still grief-stricken. I understand why he's lying, too. All the same, a small part of me bristles on Cassia's behalf as he lays the blame, albeit implicitly, at her door.

Miss Addison nods fervently. 'That's what I thought too. Cassia wouldn't hurt her sister on purpose. She's a sweet girl. They both are. But perhaps an accident of some kind ... ?'

'Did you ask Sylvie what happened?' I say. Mr Lewer's poise unsettles me. Best to get all the facts, I think, before going too far. We don't want to get tangled in our words.

Miss Addison nods gravely. 'But she wouldn't say a peep about it. I assumed she was protecting her sister.' Her eyes drop to the image in my hand. 'Honestly, it faded quickly. I had to report it, you understand. It's a safeguarding issue. But it wasn't *that* bad ...'

Mr Lewer clears his throat, a little testily. 'Which,' he says grimly, his spindly fingers dipping into the folder again, 'is more than we can say for these ...'

He passes me a second image: this time, of my niece's arm.

'I'm so sorry,' Miss Addison whispers. 'I know this is upsetting.'

I stare at the picture in blank incomprehension. Alabaster skin, covered in a rash of bruises – injuries that put the wrist-mark in the shade. Blotches, red and blue and purple, up and down the arm. Everywhere.

'Jesus.' I feel sick. 'This is Sylvie?'

Mr Lewer shakes his head. 'Cassia. It seems both girls have been sustaining bruises. Though Cassia's, as you can see, are far more severe ...'

It's a hideous picture, but if there's one chink of light, it lies – weirdly – in quite how hideous it is. For I know, instinctively, down to the marrow of my bones, that Alfie could never have done this. Not to Sylvie; not to Cassia. It's impossible.

I take a moment to gather my thoughts. Alfie is beside me, but I can't quite bring myself to look in his eyes. 'Listen. I'm not sure what you know, or think you do. But I must state, from the outset ...' I stop to take a punishing breath. 'If there's any suspicion that their dad might be responsible for this, he isn't. I'd swear to that in court – and will if I have to. I say that as a professional, and as the girls' aunt. They're my family. All I have left of my sister. I'd never take a risk with their safety.'

'Ms Harris—' Mr Lewer begins. But I'm not finished.

'You're right: this past year has been hard for all of us. Alfie's been struggling. We both have, in our own ways. But I've known him for almost a decade. And he's a good man. A good dad. If you doubt that—'

I jump. A hand on my shoulder, silencing me. But not Alfie's. 'We don't,' Miss Addison says swiftly. 'Don't worry. We know Cassia didn't get injured at home. That's why I'm here.' She swallows. 'Cassia got these bruises yesterday, at school.'

I glance at Mr Lewer. 'You're sure?'

His stare remains impenetrable, but he gives a stiff nod.

My face goes red. I feel Alfie's eyes upon me, but I still can't meet them.

'Cassia spilled water down her top at break time, so we had to change it,' Miss Addison explains. 'I helped her take it off, with my assistant. Cassia's arms were bare. I promise you, there were no marks. She wore a spare blouse whilst her own dried out. But then, after lunch, when she got hers back, she refused to get changed.' Miss Addison chews her lip guiltily. 'I'll admit, I was cross at first. I told her it was the school's property. That she couldn't keep wearing it. That she shouldn't have been so clumsy in the first place.' She presses a hand to her mouth. 'I can't tell you how mortified I felt when she took it off. When I saw the bruising underneath.'

I pass the photo back to Mr Lewer, who slides it delicately back into the plastic folder. 'So how did it happen? Who gave her those bruises?'

Alfie laughs, hollowly. It's an incongruous sound, inappropriate. But at least it girds me for what's coming next.

'She said it was Black Mamba.' Alfie shrugs again. 'He's back. In fact, he never left.'

I take a moment to process it all – to be sure of what I think. Then I say: 'It was Sylvie.' Not cold-heartedly, I hope, but with purpose. 'It must have been. She's always been the more aggressive one. And Cassia wouldn't lie for anyone else.' I turn to Mr Lewer. 'Have you spoken to the girls yourself?'

'Not yet,' he answers. 'I want to, though.'

'Now?'

'Well, if you wouldn't mind ...'

He had questions too, I think. *The man who came round after Dad died.* An instinct rises up within me to tell him no, but I master it. The past is the past. I will not be forced to relive it.

'Of course. And while you do that,' I say, turning and pointing, 'I'd like to speak to *you*.'

Miss Addison blinks. 'Me?'

'Yes,' I answer.

She's bound to know more. She's their teacher, after all – and her nervous glances at Mr Lewer have suggested to me, all along, that she didn't come here solely out of guilt. *There's something on her mind. Something else she wants to tell us.*

*

'This is a beautiful house,' Bella says (she insists I stop calling her 'Miss Addison'). Sitting alone with me at the kitchen table, she warms her fingers by folding them around the cup of tea I've made her. I've given her my mug of stars – why, I'm not quite sure. For some unfathomable reason, I find it reassuring to watch her sip from it, not knowing that it's mine. Not knowing that the house is mine, too – or used to be – and that I still belong to it.

'Yes,' I say. 'It has a lot of history.'

Bella nods. 'The girls are lucky to live here. To have Alfie. To have you.'

'To have each other?'

She looks away, seemingly embarrassed, though whether for my sake or hers I can't tell. A vague memory stirs within me, suddenly, of a conflict that took place last September between my family and the school. This was back when I was holding Alfie and the girls at arm's length, so I remember it only in outline – snippets of detail passed on, gnomically, by Mum. The girls had never been in the same class. Ever since reception, the school had kept them apart: a deliberate strategy to foster the girls' individual identities, to teach them independence. But after the accident, Alfie insisted that they needed each other. So he went to see the headteacher to fight their corner. Mum came too and, for the first and only time in their lives, she and Alfie worked in tandem. She, too, thought the girls should be together. Even before the accident, she'd never understood the case for separation.

The headteacher pushed back. Mum won.

Bella lifts the mug, a belt of stars still bright. She sips and winces. Too hot. (I could have told her that.)

I wonder where she stood on the question of the twins' reunion, and where she stands now. All this time, I've treated my nieces as a single unit, and seen Black Mamba as a child of the twinship; of how they feel about Alfie; of how they felt about Pippa. But the bruises on Cassia's arm speak to something else: a change in the power dynamic; a sawtooth crack between them.

'Tell me,' I say, when she's regained her composure. 'How are they doing at school?'

'They've struggled,' Bella replies, without hesitation. 'But that's not surprising.'

'Both of them?'

She nods firmly, almost dismissively, then stops and thinks for a moment. 'Especially Cassia. She seems to have gone backwards slightly.'

'Backwards?'

'Yes.'

'In everything?'

She pauses, thinks again. 'In maths in particular. But you mustn't worry. It's not uncommon, after a bereavement, for children to have trouble focusing at school. For their progress to falter a bit. Cassia will be fine, in time.'

'I know she will.'

'Of course.' Bella smiles. 'Besides, Sylvie's *always* struggled with maths. It's just one of those things.'

'Mm.'

A hypothesis begins to form, but before I'm able to voice it, I notice that Bella's smile has subsided and her lips have come apart slightly, revealing her teeth.

'Why did you come here, Bella?'

She sits stock still, as if making a decision.

'What else have the girls done? Tell me.'

She reaches down into her handbag. 'I haven't shown these to anyone,' she whispers. 'Not Alfie. Not Mr Lewer. I just didn't know what to make of them ...'

She places two dainty, salmon-coloured workbooks on the kitchen table. The girls' names are scrawled on their respective covers.

'A week ago, in English, I asked all the kids to write about their best friend. The twins wanted to write about each other, of course, but I said it couldn't be a sibling.' Bella tugs her trench coat even more tightly around her chest. 'That's when I found out about *him*.' She slides the books across the table. 'Open them,' she says. 'Read what they put.'

I open Sylvie's workbook first and flick through the lined pages, until I find the relevant entry. I hold my breath, and read:

My best frends BLACK MAMBA. Hes a wunder. Hes a marvell. He can speek withowt moving his lips. He can turn into any animal he wants. My faverits the big black bear. Nobody can see him apart from me and my twin

*Black Mamba says he loves us but sumtimes he gets
angry and Im scared of his teeth. Wunce he flew us to the
moon and back. Another time he took us out to sea Black
Mamba lives with us but Heart House isnt his home, his
home is sumwhere else. We want him to take us there but
he says it isnt time.*

*When the time comes hell take us but we wont be able
to come back to Heart House. Im wurried Ill miss my dad*

I close the book, my mind spinning. Of course, the girls
have already shared some of those fantasies. The idea of
Black Mamba carting them off for a night of play, in the
guise of a bird or fish, isn't new to me – but the prospect
of permanent removal is. I know from the literature that
it's not unusual, after a bereavement, for children to fear
being kidnapped.

But, I think uneasily, there isn't just fear in the girls'
fantasies. Desire is mixed in there too. They *want* to go.

'Can I take a picture?' I ask. 'For my records.'

Bella nods, and waits as I fish out my phone. 'Now read
Cassia's,' she says, the moment I'm done.

I pick up the second book and flick to the right page.
Cassia's description is shorter than Sylvie's, but it takes me
longer to digest. I read it once, then again, and again:

*I cant write about Sylvie but black Mamba is my second best
freind. He was with us before we were born, in our Mummys
tummy. He told us storys in the dark We forgot about him,*

but when mummy left he came back to protect us. He likes me and Sylvie because were speishal and black Mambas speshial to. No ones stronger than him or more clever.

When daddy gets angry and bad things happen Black Mamba makes us feel so safe!

I read the last sentence repeatedly, still struggling to accept that Cassia wrote it. I try to hear those words in her voice, and I can't imagine it. I look up at Bella.

'What does this mean?'

'I've no idea.' She shifts in her seat. 'I know Alfie a little. He's always seemed like a wonderful dad.' She stiffens slightly as she puts the workbooks back in her bag. 'I think he should be careful.'

'Why?' I ask. 'What are you saying?' But before Bella can respond, Alfie opens the kitchen door.

'Mr Lewer is leaving,' he tells us with a shrug. 'They wouldn't talk to him.' I slip back into the living room. The girls are sitting cross-legged on the floor – just as Pippa and I were that day – but they spring up in perfect unison, like a single living thing, and embrace me. Surreptitiously, I study Cassia's arm. The marks are mottling, and will soon fade, but for now they look no better in the flesh than in the picture.

I rub the girls' backs, massaging their warm skin. My head between their shoulders, I catch a glimpse of Mr Lewer through the bay window, standing alone and writing in his folder, occasionally frowning up at the house.

*

At last, his face returns to me. Until now, it's been melded with Mr Lewer's: a blur of over-sized spectacles, crow's feet, and reassuring smiles. But now the images come apart, like shapes estranging in a kaleidoscope, and I remember the dirt under his fingernails; the gingery hue of the hair that swept around the base of his head; his vulpine stare.

It was a week after Dad died, or thereabouts – I can't be sure exactly, though I remember the smell was still here: the strange, sweet, charring smell that clung in the air for days, as if seeping from the very walls of the house. The visit was unexpected. One sunny afternoon, two bland, blank bodies from social services rang the bell. I don't remember the woman's face; she asked to speak to Mum alone in the kitchen. I only remember *him*. Nowadays, I don't suppose you'd let a perfect stranger speak to your children unaccompanied, even if he did come armed with official papers and a briefcase. But Mum was still in bits – still wandering the house at night and staring blankly at walls – so perhaps her judgment was impaired.

'I'm so sorry,' he said, 'for your loss.'

His words echoed in the silence. Even now, I can't think what he expected us to say. We were too young to offer him thanks; too old to be trusting of a stranger.

Pippa and I glanced at each other, then down at the floor. We picked at the black tulle of our matching dresses and tried to avoid his eyes.

'You were at church – is that right? When it happened?'

When Dad hanged himself, I wanted to say, to force the words into his ugly, downturned mouth, but we kept silent; confined ourselves to nodding.

'At church,' he repeated, 'with your mother and auntie … ?'

The sound of Mum's voice, angry and strained, floated down the hallway from the kitchen as she faced pointed questions of her own.

(The answer to his last question was no – though somehow we knew better than to say it. Pippa and I *were* at Crescent Place when Dad died. But not every member of our congregation was. And Mum and Sue were nowhere to be seen.)

'The coroner,' he continued, hearing Mum's anger and perhaps sensing that his time with us would be cut short, 'recorded an open verdict at the inquest. Do you know what that means?'

We shook our heads.

'What do they teach, at your church, about people who die? Where do they go?'

I glanced up, then recoiled again from his gaze.

'Can they see us, the living, here on Earth? Can they be reached … ?' He leaned forward and touched our shoulders. 'Do you know why you moved to this house?'

His voice was pressing, insistent, but Mum's footsteps were hurrying down the hallway now, and we knew that rescue was close. I squeezed Pippa's hand. *Just a few more seconds.*

'Do you know,' he whispered, 'about what happened here ... ?'

She burst in, her whole body shaking, and before the man could ask another question, Pippa and I jumped up and fled. We pushed past our mother, out into the hallway then up the spiral staircase, all the way to the top floor. When we reached the attic door, we baulked and lay down in front of it, on the landing. We stuck our heads through the bannisters and listened.

'We're sorry,' the man was saying, three floors below us. The woman was apologising too.

'It's our job,' they insisted. 'You understand. We have to ask.'

But Mum just shouted, 'Get out, get out!' until they left, and Hart House was silent again but for the sound of her sobbing, alone in the hallway, and the wind whistling through the wooden slats of the room above our heads.

Eleven

Alfie

She spent an hour with them, maybe longer, asking questions, each a variant of: *why are you lying to me?* But they yielded nothing. So we're on a stake-out, in the bedroom I once shared with her sister. The blinds are half drawn, swaying in the breezy heat. Julia and I are kneeling on the soft carpet. She's resting her head against the windowsill, strands of her dark hair dancing on her shoulders.

Hart House has no garden, only a square stone courtyard dotted with weeds and pot plants and surrounded by three other houses, each one as tall as ours. From my bedroom, on the top floor, we can hear the trickle of water as the girls tend to the plants, and the clap of their Crocs, carried on the humid air. We can see the girls too, albeit in miniature from this height – like Lilliputians going quietly about their business, unaware of the giants observing from their seats in the sky.

Julia is watching more closely than I am, though occasionally she looks back at the double bed with a curious expression. This was her parents' room, decades ago, so I guess she's thinking of them, not of me and Pip. Other times, she turns her head towards the doorway, inclining her head subtly, as if she hopes I won't notice, up to the attic. Her expression is hard to read, but I hear the gentle catch of her breath.

Then she turns back to the window, as if I'm not even present.

'Why are we doing this?' I ask, after clearing my throat pointedly to no effect.

'You *know* why.' The words come out in one great, melancholy breath, as she continues to stare at the courtyard.

'Why are you sure it was Sylvie? It could have been another kid at school.'

'It wasn't,' she murmurs.

I snort, but not aggressively; I'm too anxious for that. I'm craving Julia's attention in a way I never have before, and it's an awful, clawing feeling. I preferred it when she was actively trying to placate me; holding my wrist, treading on eggshells. Now, it's like I need her reassurance. The balance has shifted.

Julia's eyes don't leave the girls. 'Like I said, Cassia wouldn't lie for anyone else.'

'What makes you so sure that she's lying?'

Now I have her attention. Julia looks at me dead on; her face is so close to mine, I see her pupils dilate as she turns from the bright window. 'What do you mean?'

'Lying is a conscious act. Deliberate.'

'Yes?'

I shrug, a little embarrassed – it's the first time I've said this aloud: 'I think the girls believe Black Mamba's real.'

'That would be psychosis,' Julia says, after a moment. 'A *folie à deux*. What makes you think that?'

'It's just …' I pause, mulling over my words, desperate not to sound stupid. Or at least not *too* stupid. 'The way Sylvie was on Pippa's birthday, when Cassia was playing up … The pain on her face … The vomiting. It all felt so real.'

Julia weighs the possibility, then she shakes her head and returns to her watch duty. 'No. No, I don't think so.' She exhales deeply and steeples her fingers: a clear sign she's going into psych mode. 'All along, this *thing* has been a coping mechanism. A way of relieving their stress, which is caused, I think, by a lack of control. An inability to manage their grief; to express their emotions verbally. Sylvie may well have felt pain on Pip's birthday. She may well have made herself sick. But she's always been vola-tile. Violence towards Cassia wouldn't be out of character, given the circumstances.'

I say nothing, and she begins to pick at the carpet.

'Any violence is on her, Alfie. It's on *her*. She can't just blame it on an imaginary friend.' Julia looks at me sharply, and I nod – of course I do. What else does she expect? 'And,' she mutters, turning away again, 'neither can you.'

'What does that mean?'

A moment's rumination, then out with it: 'Sylvie's always been your favourite.'

The words hit me like a slap. 'That isn't true.'

Now it's her turn to snort.

'It *isn't*,' I insist. 'I don't prefer Sylvie. I never have. Sylvie's just ... always preferred me. And Cassia preferred Pip, too, you know? Are such things unheard of?'

Julia doesn't answer straight away. She looks over at the bed again, combing the hair out of her eyes. 'Sometimes that can happen with twins. A phenomenon where they ... show a preference. A mother's twin, and a father's twin.'

My irritation subsides a little, dampened by intrigue. 'And is it real? That preference?'

'Sometimes not,' she says softly, almost dreamily. 'Sometimes it's just ... a creation of the twin dynamic. A way to secure undivided attention. But sometimes it is real, I believe. On the child's part, and the parent's.' Julia picks roughly at the carpet again, staring hard at the floor, then says flatly: 'My dad always preferred Pippa and that felt very real to me.'

'Oh.'

She smiles darkly. 'I say *always*. Really, it was as we got older. As he got to know us.' Her voice is more toneless than bitter.

I shift uncomfortably on the floor, thudding my back against the wall, stretching my legs out to relieve my knees. Throughout the past year, Julia must have wanted to say, *We're both grieving* and *I loved her too*, whenever I've been unbearable. But beneath her grief, something else has been present, too – a skein of unhappiness that was always there, even when Pippa was alive.

Of course, Pippa felt low now and then, but they were moods, which came and went. She'd get angry, and paranoid, and despondent. And then she'd rise again. Marian was the same. They were people of passions.

Julia's been different for as long as I've known her. Ever calm and collected, smiling – with a darkness just below the surface.

'You're more like her than I am,' Pippa mused to me on occasion, whenever Julia and I shared a wry joke, or a cynical one – or kept our heads when Pip was spinning with joy, or spiralling down into despair. And it was true: we were alike, Julia and I – except for that sadness. Where it sprang from, I couldn't say. Before this moment, I'd never thought to ask.

I watch her for a little longer, wishing that she'd open up to me. I feel a strong urge to hold her, and feel her against me. But something stops me reaching out. I'm still thinking of the defence she made of me to Mr Lewer. Assured, passionate – and wholly undeserved. 'Julia,' I say eventually, 'd'you think—'

But before I can finish the sentence, she cuts me off: 'Alfie, look.'

An eerie silence has fallen over the courtyard, despite the girls' continued presence. The trickle of water has ceased, as has the clap of their Crocs.

'What?' I whisper.

'Just look.'

The girls have finished tending to the plants. Cassia is crouched on the patio, and Sylvie is standing over her. Their hands are linked and they're both swaying, as though in a dance. No, I realise suddenly, they're struggling; trying to overpower each other. They're speaking to each other too, but not loudly enough for us to hear.

'Are they fighting? Shouldn't we—'

Julia hushes me, staring intently.

They continue to struggle, until suddenly, Sylvie pulls back her right foot. I see what's coming, but don't have time to shout. With all her might, Sylvie kicks her sister in the stomach. Cassia yelps, falling hard against the stonework.

Jesus. I scramble to my feet, head swimming.

'Alfie? Alfie, try to stay calm,' Julia says, but I'm already gone, out of the bedroom, pounding down the spiral stairs, then out into the courtyard.

'We saw,' I gasp, as I approach Sylvie. 'We saw everything.'

Her face is hard, stiff with violent purpose, but she trembles as I approach.

'What the hell were you doing?'

'It was him,' Cassia moans, already sitting up dazedly. 'Black Mamba. He made her do it ...'

'Alfie, take Sylvie upstairs.' I didn't hear Julia follow me, but she's at my elbow.

I react with unthinking obedience. I reach forward and seize Sylvie by the wrist, just as I did in the supermarket.

As soon as I touch her, she screams, so loudly I half expect the walls to fall on our heads.

'Alfie, remove her,' Julia says, more firmly still.

I drag Sylvie inside. 'Stop it! Just stop it!' But it's like she can't hear me; like she can't control her body. She bucks and kicks me as I drag her upstairs, her face contorted in fury. When we reach the second-floor landing, I push her into the bathroom – the only lockable room in Hart House – and turn the key. I stand on the other side of the door and try to steady my breathing. My hands are pressed against the wood, which I can feel her punching; it judders against my palms.

'Stay in there,' I bark. Redundantly: the key is in my hand. 'Stay in there and think about what you've done.'

Her fury only swells at that, but the bathroom contains it. Her shouts echo off the tiles and fold in upon themselves. I hurry back down to the courtyard. Julia, disarmingly composed, is sitting next to Cassia, who's still hunched over, winded, on the paved ground. I gently take her arm – the one that isn't covered in bruises – and help her to her feet.

'Oh, God,' I say, hugging her tightly. 'I'm so sorry.'

But Cassia seems more irritated than upset. 'She won't listen,' she complains.

'Who won't?' I ask. 'Your auntie?'

Cassia feels unsteady in my arms. She must still be dizzy from the fall. 'Yes! Tell her, Daddy.' She wriggles away from me. 'Tell her it was him. *He* made Sylvie do it.'

'No, my love,' Julia says, reaching to touch her cheek. 'It wasn't. Sylvie's responsible for her own actions.' And then: 'Black Mamba isn't real, darling. I think, perhaps ... *she* made him up. Is that right? You can tell us the truth. Did she make him up?'

'Ouch!' Cassia puts her hand to her forehead and gasps.

'Cass?' I place a hand behind her back to keep her steady.

'It's Sylvie,' she says. 'He's in there with her now. He's in the bathroom with her. Please, you have to help her. You have to *get her out of there*!'

'Alfie ...' Julia begins.

But Cassia clasps her head even tighter. 'Now!'

'Stay with your aunt,' I say to her, as I hurry back up to the bathroom.

'Alfie!'

My fingers shake as I fish the key out of my pocket.

'Alfie, don't play along with it.' Julia is at the foot of the stairs, Cassia peering from behind her legs. 'This is crazy.'

I hesitate. She's right, of course she is, but in that moment something chills me, forcing my hand: the bathroom is completely silent. I struggle for a moment to turn the key, as though it's swollen in the heat, but then all of a sudden it clicks and the door swings open with ease. My eyes turn at once to the mirror on the left-hand wall, where a vein of something red catches the light. A streak of blood – just like the night that Pippa fell. And Sylvie, like Pippa, is motionless on the floor. I crouch down and scoop her up into my arms.

'Julia,' I shout, 'call an ambulance.'

I look up, thinking she's standing in the doorway, but instead I see Cassia, looking like half a person – just as she did on that awful night. My eyes meet hers. She fixes me with a terrible stare.

She can't remember. She was too young. She only remembers the story. The story I spun for her so many times.

Mummy had an accident. She drank too much. She fell.

True, or true enough. Not a made-up story – just an abridged one.

Julia appears behind Cassia. She covers her mouth in shock. I look down at Sylvie, who's teetering on the edge of consciousness, blood coming from her forehead. A small cherry pool is forming on the porcelain floor.

'Julia,' I say again. 'Do it now!'

Four hours pass, and we're still in A & E. A young male nurse in ill-fitting teal scrubs is finishing an examination of Sylvie's forehead. He seems tired, but his hands are steady. He has a light on a stick, which he flashes in Sylvie's eyes and then waves from side to side. 'Follow its path for me, sweetie.' Her blue eyes chart, back and forth, and he seems pleased. A few more notes on his clipboard, then half a smile. 'She'll be fine.'

'Thank you,' I say.

He flicks through his papers, then adds, matter-of-factly, not making eye contact, 'The police are still here.'

'Right.'

He gestures down the corridor. 'They want to talk to her – your ... partner?'

Julia is halfway down, getting coffee.

I feel my face go pink. 'Sylvie's aunt.'

He shrugs indifferently. 'Will you tell her?'

'Of course,' I say. 'I'll get her now.'

'Daddy?' Sylvie is lying like a princess, immobile beneath the pure-white sheets of the hospital bed. She's back in frightened mode – her voice uncertain, infantile. All traces of anger and menace have vanished from her face. But I can't forget.

I kiss her hand, wary of kissing her head. 'I'll be back soon. I promise.' I turn to the nurse again. 'Thank you,' I repeat. He nods briskly as he reclips the board to the foot of the bed. Then I trudge down the corridor towards Julia. 'Sylvie's fine,' I tell her. 'No concussion. Nothing that needs to be fixed.' It's an odd thing to say, given the circumstances, and it feels strange in my mouth. I point to the officers in fluorescent jackets down the hallway, dealing with another family – another crisis. 'They want to speak to you.'

Julia nods, sipping her drink.

'I told them everything already. They probably just want to—'

'Yeah.'

We study each other awkwardly.

'Is Cass ... ?' I ask.

'In there.'

'Right.' I rub my eyes. 'I'll wait with her.'

Julia blinks. 'What about ... ?'

'I've told you,' I say. 'Sylvie's fine. I'll wait with Cass.'

She nods wearily. 'Fine.'

I touch her arm perfunctorily; she touches mine back. Then we part ways.

Cassia is sitting in an empty waiting room. As I walk in, she doesn't even flinch. She hasn't said a word to me since Sylvie's accident.

'Mind if I ... ?' I smile weakly, gesturing to the seat opposite her.

Still nothing.

I sit down, legs like lead, and close my eyes. They, too, feel achingly heavy. *We don't need to speak*, I tell myself. *To be with her is enough.* Cassia watches me in silence.

'I'm sorry,' I say eventually. 'I've been ignoring you.'

Cassia's eyes widen, but she still doesn't speak. (We both know, really, it's the other way around.)

I lean forward to stroke her hair. But she recoils out of reach. 'What is it?' I ask. 'What's wrong? You can tell me.'

She cocks her head. 'Can I?'

I nod encouragingly.

Her nostrils flare slightly, and she shrugs. 'I thought you didn't want to hear.'

'I do. I always do.'

She shakes her head, eyes narrowing. 'I thought you didn't want to hear about *him*.'

'Cass—'

'It's true. You don't want to hear about Black Mamba. Though,' she adds quietly, 'maybe you should.'

'What do you mean?'

'Oh,' she says. 'He has lots to say. So many ideas.'

'Like what?' I scoff – I can't help myself. 'Getting Sylvie to kick you in the stomach?'

'Black Mamba said to say that it was you.'

I hear her words – spoken so lightly, with no venom; almost trance-like – but I can't absorb them. They seem to bounce off my comprehension.

'Black Mamba,' she continues, 'said that I should show the doctors my tummy. That I should tell the police *you* kicked me. That I should say you gave me the bruises on my arm ...'

The sounds of the hospital drain away, and my field of vision seems to narrow.

'Why? Why would you—' I swallow hard, my throat on fire, and correct myself. 'Why would he tell you to do that? Why would he tell you to lie?'

She answers calmly, with no hesitation. 'Because that way we'd be alone together. Just the three of us.'

I shrink against the back of my seat. Her voice is cold, so cold – as chilly as the words themselves.

Her words. *His* words.

I stare into her eyes, searching for a glimmer of emotion, something I can recognise and cling to. But her eyes are ice cold too.

'Alfie?'

I jerk my head towards the door. Julia's standing there, frowning, Sylvie in tow. 'Alfie,' she says, 'what's wrong?'

I drive home; I *watch myself* drive home. My fingers shake on the wheel. Dreamy orange light streaks and streams on either side of the road. Hart House waits for us, patiently, in the dark.

Open thy marble jaws, O tomb, and hide me, earth, in thy dark womb,

Ere I the name of father stain, and deepest woe from conquest gain ...

I let Julia do everything when we get home. She undresses the girls, bathes them, and puts them to bed. I lie in the living room, lights off, prone on the sofa like a corpse. When she's finished, I don't even see her standing over me until she speaks.

'Cassia told me.' Her voice is quiet, chastened. 'What she said to you. What *he* said ...' She shakes her head, gently, as if in disbelief. 'Maybe you're right. Maybe they are hallucinating. Maybe they do think Black Mamba's real.'

'Maybe he is.'

Julia stares at me, her face frozen in the soft light of the hallway. If I could shrug, I would. But I don't have the strength in my shoulders.

'I can stay here tonight,' she says eventually. 'For a few nights, perhaps. I can stay here, with you and the girls. We can figure out what to do. Together.'

I raise my body up on my forearms, not quite believing it. 'I thought you hated this house.'

'Oh,' she says listlessly. 'I do.'

Twelve

Julia

I never thought I'd live here again. Yet here I am, in my old
room, just across the landing from the girls' room – which
was also mine, once. Mine and Pippa's. Every inch of this
house is familiar to me. I could walk around it with my
eyes closed, never losing my footing on the stairs, always
knowing the distance between doorways. The girls could
blindfold me, spin me round and push me in any direction, and still none of the rooms could wrongfoot me – the
grooves in the floorboards would betray them.

The girls are in bed now, sleeping soundly as far as I know.
They were wide-eyed and watchful when we returned from
the hospital, but the rituals of bedtime helped to calm
them. I stripped them of their dirty clothes and washed
their bodies with warm water. Sylvie's bloodstain, which
I'd forgotten about, remained encrusted on the wall-length
mirror like a crude icon. I crouched down to inspect the
mark, and it appeared, suddenly, as if on my own forehead,

or that of my twin in the mirror. Sylvie glanced at the stain when she entered the bathroom, lightly touching the stitches on her brow, as if marking herself with ashes – though her mood seemed far from pained or penitential. Cassia was more unsettled; she eyed the mark warily from the tub, as if fixated by its dark, dry ridges, only relaxing when I washed it off.

By the time the girls were clean and in bed, disappearing into the folds of the duvet, they were yawning incessantly. The day's trauma had caught up with them in a sudden, overwhelming wave. I switched off the light and felt them drop, almost instantly, into the depths of sleep – their breath settling swiftly into a shallow, mechanical rhythm.

If they're awake, they haven't left their room. I would have heard them. No one lives in Hart House anymore who can cross its boards as noiselessly as I can. That's how I know, too, that Alfie hasn't come upstairs yet. I left him lying on the sofa, his eyes glazed, as if conscious thought had left him. Maybe I'll hear him go into the kitchen soon. Maybe I'll hear the clink of bottles. There's nothing to stop him.

I took this room shortly after Dad died, when Pippa's sleep became too broken for us to carry on sharing. Alfie and Pip did nothing to it when Mum gave them the house, they just kept it as a spare room, so it's more or less unchanged since the day I left it, as though it's been waiting, all this time, for me to return.

I lie in bed, trying to relax. But the beige curtains, the

unadorned walls and the solitary wooden chair strike a depressing contrast with my homely flat.

I won't stay any longer than three days and three nights. As long as Jonah spent in the belly of the beast. As long as Christ spent in the place of shadows.

I stretch out my arm to switch off my bedside lamp and, as I do, I hear a rustling downstairs. Alfie is moving in the hallway, finally raised from the sofa. The house groans as he feels his way poorly through the dark. I wrap my hand around the lamp switch before he can see that I'm awake. The exchange we had in the living room less than an hour ago still echoes in my mind.

Maybe they do think Black Mamba's real.

Maybe he is.

I flick the switch and the bedroom plunges into darkness. But the darkness comes a second too late – for as I turned away from the lamp to lay my head on the pillow, my eyes passed momentarily over the solitary wooden chair in the corner of the room, and in that split second I saw a man sitting in it, smiling at me. Then he was gone, engulfed by blackness.

I fumble in panic for the light switch, knocking things over in the blubbery dark. When I find the switch again, the chair is empty. I look from side to side, terrified that I'll find the man right by me. I even check the ceiling, as though I might find him splayed upon it, like a spider waiting to drop. But it's a blank canvas, with only a naked bulb dangling from its centre.

I struggle to steady my breathing. Nothing like this has ever happened to me before, even though I've imagined seeing such things – feared seeing them; longed to see them – a thousand times. I know, rationally, that it's nothing unusual or worrying. That this vision is the kind of thing the brain can easily produce when stressed and sleep-deprived. Yet somehow, I still feel *altered* by it.

I rise, trembling, and open the bedroom door. The landing is as empty as my room. No one is on the spiral stairs. No noise is coming from below, or from the master bedroom, two floors above. Alfie must have moved very quickly to bed, or else still be downstairs. I have an urge to head up to his bedroom to pin his location down, but I contain it. Leaving my room would risk waking him, and he needs to rest. We all do.

I close the door and slink back beneath the covers. I stare at the empty chair, my heart still thudding. Part of me would like to put the chair out on the landing, but I know I shouldn't. I stay perfectly still, trying to trick my body into sleep.

This is how she used to find me, in the weeks after Dad died: rigid and motionless in bed. I'd moved into this room to stop her disturbing me whenever she woke, sobbing in the night. Mum never came to comfort her. Having imbibed an ocean of pills, by midnight Mum was dead to the world. Pippa's tears all fell on me.

I'd moved into the room across the landing, but I couldn't stop her waking, or coming in. I'd hear her first, pushing open the door, then I'd feel her weight as she clambered into bed with me.

'I saw him again,' she'd whisper. Her wet face would brush against mine. 'Dad's ghost ...'

'It was only a dream,' I'd say.

'It wasn't a dream. It was real.'

'Go back to sleep.'

Except there was no telling Pippa what to do when she was upset. 'I saw his face in the dark. He was standing at the foot of our bed.'

I'd shift over, reluctantly, giving her room. 'It isn't *our* bed anymore. It's yours. And *this* is mine.'

'You do believe me, don't you?' she'd say, oblivious to my frustration. 'I heard him on the landing, walking up and down the stairs. Shaking his rattle ...'

The rattle. That detail always made me shiver. When he was alive, Dad would wander Hart House by day, photographing the empty rooms, as if searching for something in the blank space; something hidden from view. And by night, when he couldn't sleep, he'd pace up and down the spiral stairs, shaking his rattle. Mum would call downstairs, despairingly, *Leave it till morning* – but he seldom would.

The rattle was an antique, its wooden handle riven with scratches, its cloth-covered head bulbous and worn. Dad never explained what he was doing – why he was shaking it; why he did it at night. He seemed to be calling for something. Something in the shadows.

Do you know why you moved to this house? he asked us: the man from social services. *Do you know about what happened here?*

'Close your eyes,' I said to Pippa, the last night she saw Dad's ghost. 'Close your eyes and imagine a door. A big red one, with a lock on it – like the box Dad kept his photos in.'

'Yes,' Pippa said. 'I can see it.'

'Good. Now imagine Dad's behind that door. Behind the lock. There. He can't get out now, can he? Whenever you think you hear or see him, remember he's trapped.'

Pippa nestled against me. 'I love you, Jewel,' she said.

'I love you too.'

Now, I close my eyes with the light on, still thinking of my sister. On my advice, she never told Mum of those visions. With my help, she began to pull away from the church – and eventually, away from Mum too. She moved out. She began to live the life that she wanted for herself.

Then she met Alfie, and never asked for my help again. Not until the week before she died.

I shudder, still struggling to believe that she perished in the cellar of this house. In the space where Dad developed his photographs; where he kept the red box; where he kept the rattle. Without daring to open my eyes, I reach for the lamp switch again. This counts as night one of three.

*

'Do you have kids?'

I'm at the clinic. This will be my last appointment for a while; I'm taking leave again. As soon as my three days in Hart House are up, I'm getting out of London – going to the coast, perhaps. I need to get away.

But before that, I'm seeing Simon one last time. He's clean cut and smartly dressed, but there are shadows beneath his eyes, and whenever he speaks of Ralf he lowers his voice, as though he's scared it might break. I'm dimly aware that he's just asked a question, but I'm struggling to take it in. From the start, this couple has puzzled me. Their love for each other is so strong that the conflict between them feels unwarranted, unsustainable. Yet the toll it's taking on them is obvious, too.

'Mm?'

Patiently, he repeats himself. 'Do you have kids?'

You'd think I'd have an iron rule when it comes to answering personal questions at the clinic. But the truth is, most clients don't ask them. To most clients, I have no interior life. I'm a mirror, their externalised self. Something to be spoken at, not to.

So I answer, 'No.'

'Did you want them?'

To my surprise, I bristle internally at his use of the past tense. 'Yes,' I bat back, truthfully. 'Always.'

'Oh,' he says abruptly. 'I'm sorry.'

'No, no. It's fine. The timing's just never been right. I've never been with the right guy.'

He nods a little vacantly, giving me a chance to reflect. It's true: I'm childless by accident – just as so many of my clients had kids before they were ready. Simon and Ralf don't have that luxury. No accident can settle their dispute, allowing one to rationalise what he wants, and the other to master his emotions, accepting what must be. This is their condition, and their curse. They must make a choice.

'It's not that I don't want to be a parent,' he says, after a moment. 'I just think it would feel like pretending. Like make-believe.'

'What would?'

'Adopting kids. Them calling me *Dad*. I suppose I'd get used to it. But could I ever fully shake the feeling that I'm ...'

Speaking automatically, I fill in the gap: 'An imposter.'

'Yes,' he says fervently. 'With their real dad in the shadows somewhere.' He shrugs. 'I'm sure we'd love them. Raise them well. I'm sure I could act the part – enjoy it, even. But then ... I'll look at Ralf, and remember that none of it's real. That I'm living someone else's life – or, at least, a life not meant for me. Does that make sense?'

He leans forward, staring intently, as if he truly expects me to answer. But I can't. If I say I understand, it'll only sound glib. Even though I do. I've felt it ever since I was a child: the fear that what I want and who I am don't align – and never will.

I wrap things up. We're almost at the hour. I remind him cordially of his new time slot, and of my colleague's name. Normally, I feel guilty when I palm off clients – a new therapist can undo weeks of progress, slow it down or stop it altogether – but in this case I don't. I *have* done all I can for this couple; all anyone can.

I usher Simon out, back towards Ralf, and whatever future awaits them – or doesn't. I leave them to make their choice.

When I get home, the girls are still at school. Alfie is sitting in the front room, gazing out of the bay window towards Peter's Park. His stubble is growing denser. I've never been able to imagine him with a beard, but soon I won't have to. Alfie's always been good-looking, but the strain of losing Pippa – and the prospect, now, of losing the twins too – has made him unkempt, dishevelled.

Less appealing. More in reach.

'I've finished work,' I say. Then think immediately, *I haven't*. 'Can we talk?'

He makes a grunt of assent.

I sit down in the armchair opposite. 'Last night you said you thought Black Mamba might be real. I wonder if you meant that.'

Silence. Then he sighs and rubs his forehead. 'I brought you here to counsel the girls,' he says. 'Now you want to counsel me.'

I open my mouth to object, but he lifts his hand.

'It's all right,' he says gently. 'Maybe you're right to want that. Maybe this is where we should have started.'

I nod, and consider how best to phrase my first question; how best to give nothing away. The vision I had last night of the man in my room had felt remote at the clinic. But now that I'm back in Hart House, it's with me again. 'Have you had any . . . hallucinations?'

Alfie gives a wry smile. 'How would I know if I had?'

'Well, have you seen him? Black Mamba, I mean.'

'Only in dreams.'

'Never in the daytime?'

'Never.'

'Not even from the corner of your eye?'

He rubs his fingers over his lips, thinking. 'I've seen Pippa,' he says quietly, after a moment. 'It started off as a fantasy. I'd close my eyes and imagine she was next to me. Or I'd open them and pretend she was in the next room. Then I began to speak to her, and make up the words she'd say back. After a while, I started hearing her laughter, rising out of nowhere – like a bubble in the air. Sometimes I think I see her, too. In windowpanes, in mirrors. I feel her presence, sometimes, in the night.'

'And why do you think that is?'

He takes a moment, rolling his tongue around his mouth. All his energy seems to have drained away.

'Because I miss her. And I can't believe we'll never speak again. Kiss again.' He hesitates, but only briefly. 'Fight again.'

I watch him closely. This may be the first time he's acknowledged that any tension existed between them. *They fought.* I feel a strange frisson as the words leave his lips – something dark stirring within me. I knew this fact already of course, because Pippa told me as much, many times. But hearing it from Alfie, in her absence, is more powerful. The urge to probe further is irresistible, and I'm aided by what I already know.

'Whose idea was it,' I ask mildly, 'to have children?'

A blank look. 'Adam and Eve's? It wasn't anyone's idea. It's just what people do.'

'Don't couples normally discuss it?'

He shrugs, still bemused. 'The timing, maybe.'

'All right then. Who wanted them first?'

Something flickers in his eyes. 'I don't remember,' he says softly. Then – a change of heart. Perhaps it occurs to him that I may well know the truth already. Or perhaps he just decides to be honest.

'She did.'

I nod contemplatively. 'Why didn't you want children?'

'I did want them,' he corrects me. 'Just not—'

'Then?'

'No.'

'Why not?'

He waves a hand vaguely. 'Is this relevant? We hadn't been together long. We were living in this tiny flat.'

I clear my throat instinctively. Their first flat was bigger than the one I live in now.

'Which was fine,' he adds, backtracking. 'We had enough room for children, I suppose, just about. But that space was ours – just mine and hers. You know?'

I nod. (He's making things worse, of course. But he's not to know that.)

'I felt prickly about sharing the space with anyone else.'

'Prickly?'

He cocks his head. 'I suppose.'

'It was your word.'

He stares down into his lap. 'I suppose I wondered whether I was still enough for her. Does that sound crazy?'

'No,' I answer truthfully. It should have been a crazy thought. But I know for a fact it wasn't.

'When we first met,' Alfie says, 'I never questioned it. Her love for me. It seemed undeniable – like a force of nature.'

'I remember,' I say. 'She really fell for you.'

Alfie smiles. 'I was flattered.'

'You were more than that,' I prompt. 'You loved her.'

'From the moment I saw her. But it was a different kind of love, I think.'

'Different from what?'

'From hers.'

I cross my legs, pat down my skirt. Try to seem impartial. 'What do you mean?'

He presses his fingertips together lightly, as if in prayer. 'My love for Pippa started small, then grew, day by day, until I couldn't see anyone else. Until I couldn't see myself *with* anyone else.'

'And Pippa's love for you?'

He smiles again, this time ruefully. 'Went the other way. A few years in, she grew restless. She wanted more. She wanted kids.' He shrugs, diffidently. 'She still loved me. It was okay. Our love met in the middle. We had enough of it to manage, between us . . .'

'Why didn't you marry?'

'She wanted that, at first. To be Mrs Marvell. I didn't. Then we had the girls.'

'And?'

He shrugs. 'Then *I* wanted to marry. And she didn't.'

I hesitate before asking my next question, but I think it's safe. 'What did you fight about?'

He turns his head, gazes again out of the window. 'You know what Pippa was like. She could be intense. Passionate.'

'You mean flirtatious,' I ask. Though it isn't really a question, and he doesn't treat it as such. 'Did you ever get jealous?'

There's a cold silence. Then, every answer possible, like he wants me to pick: 'No. Maybe. Yes. Sometimes.'

'Did you ever feel threatened?'

'What?'

'By a rival. Another man.'

'No. Well – no one specific. Sometimes she'd go out with friends. Drinking. Having a good time.' He snorts suddenly. 'Maybe that's why I hate him so much.'

'Who?'

'Black Mamba.'

'Because ... ?' I say, groping. But he doesn't help me out. 'Because he rekindles those feelings? Jealousy of another man; a phantom threat? He reminds you of the way Pippa made you feel?'

'No,' Alfie replies. 'He reminds me of my failings.'

Failings. Pippa saw them that way too. She told me so one summer afternoon, not long after Mum gave her Hart House. I had some time off from the clinic, so she came round to my flat in a cotton dress and a large sunhat and lay on my sofa, her long hair hanging over the armrest at one end, her legs dangling from the other, like she was floating in mid-air. She held a glass of white wine in her hand; she'd brought two bottles. I watched her roll the stem between her fingers as she talked about the defects of her lover.

'He doesn't understand,' she said, sipping, sipping. 'Why I can't say it back. *I'll always love you.*'

'Why can't you?' I asked, pouring myself a drink too. She might have been on the psych couch, as she sometimes called it, only half joking, but I was off duty.

'Well,' Pippa said. 'How do I know I will? How does he?' And she shook her head and closed her eyes, and my fingers clenched around the stem of my own wine glass in a fist.

'You'll make him nervous,' I suggested.

Pippa just laughed.

'Jealous, then.'

'He shouldn't be.'

'Why not?'

The question seemed to throw her.

'Do you never think,' I pressed, 'of men, besides Alfie?'

'Oh, Jewel,' she said. 'Of course I do. Just like I look, sometimes, at shoes in shop windows. It doesn't mean I'd throw out the ones I've got ... so comfortable and easy to slide on ... like sinking into a warm bath.'

She spoke that way a lot in those days: carelessly, dreamily; trailing off; mixing metaphors; her phrases full of ellipses. She used to be more precise, more considered, but I was seeing someone at the time – a guy from work who was painfully quiet; who I'd soon dump – so she spoke more freely.

'He asked me the other day who I loved more: him or the twins?' She said it with another laugh.

'And what did you say?'

Pippa wrinkled her nose. 'I wasn't going to lie. But I couldn't tell him the truth either.'

My face must have shown my confusion.

'He wouldn't understand. He's immature in some ways – like a kid, obsessed with who their parents love most.'

(That one hurt.)

'Except Alfie was an only child,' she said. 'And I don't think he ever had those kinds of worries. Which doesn't help.'

'So?' I prompted. 'What did you tell him?'

'That I love the girls, and there's no one I'd rather raise them with.' She shrugged. 'Isn't that enough? Isn't that everything?'

For a woman it might be, I thought. *Not a man.* But I didn't say that. I try to avoid clichés, especially misandrist ones. And besides – I doubt it would have been enough for *her*.

(This, of course, was how she could be so blasé – she had no need to fret. Alfie's feelings for my sister had grown, by this stage, to the point where she'd never have to doubt his love again. Or kill her own damn spiders.)

I licked my lips, trying to formulate some good advice. But then I realised that she didn't want to hear my thoughts; she only wanted to speak.

'Love's a dishonest word,' she mused, swirling the cold wine around her glass. 'We use it to describe all kinds of feelings, for all kinds of people. But no two versions are ever the same.'

I jump. Alfie has just reached across and nudged my knee.

'Are you okay?' he asks.

'Yes. Sorry. It's nothing.'

His hand had seemed to linger on my leg, just for a second. But I brush away the thought. 'All relationships struggle,' I say automatically – my training kicking in. 'It doesn't mean you're failing.'

'But it got quite bad,' he says, his eyes clear and grave, 'between me and Pippa. Just before the accident.'

'Oh,' I say. Though it isn't really a surprise. Something in the girls' behaviour – the aggression of their woozle – spoke, from the start, to problems that began before the accident. And now that I've scratched the surface, Alfie wants to share. Or feels compelled to. 'For how long?'

'A year, maybe.'

'And why was . . .' I begin, but my thoughts overtake my words and the question dies on my tongue as I remember. I blush. 'Of course. I should've thought. I'm sorry.'

'Yeah.'

I take his hand. It's the first time, I think, that he's not instinctively pulled it away. His palm feels surprisingly soft, like a baby's cheek.

'Thanks.'

We sit in silence for a moment. Then finally, I ask: 'Did you ever name him?' I can't believe I've never asked that question. But a year ago it was just too raw. 'Not all couples do,' I add quickly, 'when the pregnancy isn't carried to term. It's normal if you name the child, and normal if you don't.'

'It's okay,' Alfie says. 'We did. We named him Peter.'

I smile and squeeze. 'Beautiful,' I say. 'Just like the park.'

'Yes.' Alfie's eyes flick briefly towards the foliage, visible through the bay window – leaves shimmering in the breeze – then return to me. 'The boy who never grew up.'

A thought crosses my mind – a dark one. *The Darlings' imaginary friend.*

'I still dream about the day we scattered his ashes,' Alfie continues, smiling sadly. 'We took a handful each, me, Pip and the girls, and let the wind carry them into the sea.'

'The sea?'

He nods. 'We drove down to Collier Beach ...'

I feel his hand begin to wriggle in mine, like a trapped fish, so I loosen my grip. He runs his fingers swiftly through his hair.

'It was after we lost him that things changed. Pippa became troubled.'

'How do you mean?' I ask. Even though I kind of know.

'She closed up. Wouldn't speak to me. Her sleep became disjointed. She was having nightmares ... sleepwalking.' Alfie looks at me intently. 'She told me the same thing happened when her father died.'

He was my father too, I think. 'Yes.'

Alfie's face and body language are becoming strangely stiff. 'The day of the accident—'

'Mm?'

He swallows and tries again. 'She was sleepwalking down to the cellar, in the weeks before she died. On the day of the accident, after she got that bite on her foot – or whatever it was – I took her back to the house, and she went to lie down. She seemed all right, really.' His left leg is shaking; his foot drums steadily against the wooden floor. 'But she had the dream again. She must have. She had the dream, got up, went down to the cellar ... and died there.'

I stay silent, picking at the hem of my shirt.

'She never told me what the dream was about,' he says. 'Did she tell you?' His eyes are narrow; his face set. It's almost an accusation.

'No,' I say, and he accepts it readily – his intensity dissipating like dew beneath the rising sun.

Thirteen

Alfie

Finally, I'm starting to see things more clearly. It has something to do with feeling like a child again.

Julia's taking care of everything. Doing things herself, or asking me to do them. Breaking down each task into steps that, individually, require no thought. Her still voice steadies me, and guides me through them; reminds me what it means to be a parent.

My own parents split when I was younger than the twins are now. When I last checked, my dad was in New Zealand; my mother, charting a route across the States – Illinois, Iowa, South Dakota. Since they parted ways, neither my mother nor my father has ever stopped moving, as if they can't get far enough away from each other. Something new always awaits them, luring them on: a town or a job; an adventure or a lover. I spent the second half of my childhood bouncing between them. I saw each of them half as much as I had before, and they loved me twice as hard in return.

Then, like lightning, Pippa. Wildly in love with me, and in need of me – at least at first. So much so that I didn't think our differences mattered, or would ever matter. Not until I loved her too; until I couldn't picture life without her.

She wanted to put down roots. To have kids, and make them the centre of our lives. She was older than me, if only by a few years. She was impatient. I wanted things to stay as they were, at least for a little longer. I wanted us to keep travelling, to remain free.

Pippa kept pushing; I reconsidered. *Would it be so bad?* To be still. To belong. To have a family and raise them in one place, in this beautiful house – even if that did leave us in debt to her mother?

The truth was: it was better than I could have imagined.

And: I *was* too young to father children. And still feel too young to raise them on my own.

When our conversation has finished, Julia leaves to pick the girls up from school. I have nothing to do so I wander the house, drifting in and out of rooms and staring at their ceilings – which I notice, for the first time, are not entirely white but lightly veined, like marble.

I see things more clearly now, but that doesn't mean I *understand* them. Instead, it's like the house is revealing itself to me coyly, one piece at a time. I'm seeing things I hadn't spotted until now; things that only a child would notice. Like the eyes staring out of the wood panelling. Like the cracks that spell out letters in the tiles.

Like the loft hatch. The solid black line that marks its rim used to be matted with cobwebs, but they've been torn away, leaving only a few scraps hanging freely, rippling in the wind that whistles through the slats of the attic roof.

Someone has opened the hatch. Not me or Julia, and certainly not the girls. Which can only mean one thing: *someone has got into this house.*

I've suspected it ever since Cassia's threat at the hospital to lie about me, though when I sit and talk with Julia, my confidence crumbles and I think, *I must be mad.* Only when I'm alone again, and I spot things like those missing cobwebs, does my faith begin to re-emerge; to grow stronger. The supernatural, I know, does not exist. But Black Mamba and his intrusion into our lives – this poison, flowing through our family's blood – can't be just a product of my daughters' minds.

Someone has got into this house.

I hurry back down the spiral stairs, intending to check on the spare key, hidden in a crevice of the porch, but something slows me. It's the walls. There's something different about them. I lean against them and smell a spicy scent seeping out of the brick – sweet but smoky, like burning incense. I've never smelled anything like it.

When I reach the hallway, I open the front door and jam my hand into a crack in the outer brickwork of the house, feeling for the spare key. It's no longer there. I pull my hand out roughly, grazing the skin.

I go back inside, close the front door, and stop. A noise is coming from the cellar – a faint, dry rattling that makes me go cold all over. The keys to the cellar hang on a small iron hook. I unlock the door, feel gingerly for the light switch, then make my way down the worn stone steps. Pippa's canvases rest on one side, draped in enormous white sheets. Above my head, the lone lightbulb illuminates the wires that have hung here since Eric used it as a darkroom, casting criss-cross shadows throughout the space.

I hear the rattle again, louder this time, coming from the far side of the room, which is lined with cardboard boxes. I make my way towards them, then jump back sharply as I see one move. There's the noise again. I lean forward and pull the box away from the wall.

A rodent, scrawny and black, screeches as its body is exposed. Before I have time to react, it scurries away, vanishing into a hole in the wall.

I take a breath, then read the words on the cardboard box at my feet.

HART HOUSE.

I crouch down, rip away the brown tape. When I lift the flaps, the rattling emanates again from the heart of the box. Warily, I begin to sift through its contents. The top layer comprises a series of newspaper clippings, sallow and crumpled. I pick one out at random and unfurl the page. It's local press – a cutting from over two decades ago, covering Eric's death. I scan its contents silently. *The appearance of a suicide ... bouts of depression, ever since the tragic passing of his nephew ...* Then I cast it aside. The story is familiar to me, and, though perhaps morbid, I see nothing strange about keeping it; after all, I have a box in my bedroom marked: PIPPA.

I pick up another cutting and smooth it out. Instantly, the image on the page – murky, obscure, printed in a diseased black and white – becomes clear to me. It's a picture of Hart House from decades ago, before Pippa and Julia were born, beside the caption: 'Madman almost sets whole street ablaze.' I scan the article, gleaning what I can. The previous owner believed the building was cursed – though the clipping neglects to say why. He, too, died in this house. He died whilst trying to destroy it.

I rummage a little deeper and draw out an aged cardboard folder, dusty and korma-coloured, marked 'Susan Harris Estates'. I tip it on its side, and legal documents detailing Marian and Eric's purchase of Hart House fall out. I leaf through them and, almost instantly, years of residual guilt melt away. We didn't take advantage of Marian when she sold us the house for a snip. She, too, had paid a pittance for it.

Delving further, my hand hits something hard in the depths of the box: a large, heavy object, swaddled in more sallow paper. I pull the wrapping away to reveal an antique child's rattle. The head is bulbous and covered in cloth, and the handle is riddled with scratch marks – marks that, for a fleeting moment, remind me of the scratches on my stomach. Squinting, I look closer, and realise that the marks aren't scratches at all, but letters. Letters in an alphabet I do not know.

I drop the rattle back into the box, but my attention is caught by the paper, which I'm still holding. I thought it was more newspaper at first, but it's too thick for that; this page has been torn, barbarously, from a book. I smooth it out: the printing is old, fifty years at least. It's a reference book; the title is printed in the header. *Spirit Guide: Occult Sites in England*. And, just below it, the name of the entry that's been torn out.

HART HOUSE –

I lift up the page, fingers prickling, and blow away the dust. The musk of the paper tickles my nose.

– a Victorian terraced house in Allington Square, London, named after its first owner, Stefan Hart, a chemist who emigrated from Baden, Germany, with his sister Lina in 1851. As a founding member of the Society for Alchemical Inquiry, Stefan became a prominent figure in London's scientific circles, meeting the Prince Consort on at least three occasions.

Within a year of arriving in London, the Harts adopted two children, Frank and Mary Dawlish. Little is known of their natural parents, save for their religious fervour. In the 1863 trial of Mary and Frank, their parents were described as 'assiduous penitents ... whose sole object in life was to make amends with God ...' In that effort, the children were beaten, scolded and woken at all hours of the night, and came to the Harts 'both silent and malnourished'. The nature of the accident that claimed their parents' lives is unclear.

By all accounts, the adoption was unhappy from the start. At the trial, prosecuting counsel denounced Frank as 'malignant, savage and soulless', and Mary as 'cold and unfeeling'. Both children refused to accept Stefan as their father, resisting his authority and rejecting his love.

Soon after Frank and Mary came of age, Stefan went to Baden for a month, to visit his mother. Upon his return to London, he was shocked to discover Lina on the edge of death, having been taken gravely ill in his absence. Mary and Frank had nursed her, alone, in Hart House. Upon Lina's passing, Stefan reported his suspicions to Scotland Yard. Within a week, a coroner determined that Lina had been poisoned, and Frank and Mary were charged jointly with her murder.

The trial that followed was a sensation of the era, owing to the intervention of the sect to which the Dawlishes had formerly belonged: the Lord's Séance at Tabor, now disbanded. The Lord's Séance, and several of its sister churches, were longstanding antagonists of Stefan and his society. Upon retaining counsel to defend the Dawlish children, the churches published a series of fantastical pamphlets, claiming that Stefan had brought with him a demon from the Schwarzwald, where 'devils lurk in the earth, in the river, and in men's houses too ...' Dripping *with xenophobia, their charges continued: that Stefan had been controlled by the demon; that it had coerced him into sorcery, and the use of mind-altering drugs; that it had led him into carnal knowledge of Lina, and towards a life 'most unnatural ... brother and sister, joined as if in wedlock, succouring another's young ...'*

When Frank and Mary took the stand, the slander continued. They testified that Lina had been pregnant with Stefan's child; that in exchange for two droplets of Frank and Mary's blood, the demon had promised to destroy the baby; that as a result of this pact, both were now 'possessed by a pythonical spirit, like the damsel in Acts', and bore no guilt. When cross-examined, outrageous scenes ensued: Frank spoke in tongues, and Mary fainted repeatedly. Congregants of the Lord's Séance, seated in the public gallery, sounded musical instruments, in an attempt to force the demon to materialise; the gallery was cleared.

Guilty verdicts were returned for Frank and Mary within three days; they were soon hanged.

I turn the paper over, but there's nothing else; only the subsequent 'H' entry, HATFIELD PEVEREL, so I scrunch it up tightly and hurl it back into the box. The details of the story are difficult to take in, that this happened in my *home*. I feel deceived, as though something familiar to me has suddenly become strange. Just like my daughters.

A cold draught ripples through the cellar. I sit on the stone floor, hugging my knees. The prospect that I'm wrong – that no one has got into the house; that instead, a darkness was present all along, inside the girls and buried in the walls around us – feels almost unbearable.

I hear a hissing noise, and turn to see one of the white sheets that cover Pippa's paintings slipping to the floor, slowly at first, then all at once in a big billowing sweep. The unfinished painting: Pippa's final opus, begun in the last weeks of her life, between those fractured nights harried by bad dreams. I stare at the two silhouettes, the man and the woman – he, tall and proud in the centre of the canvas; she, reaching towards him – and I wonder at the ring of red smoke snaking above their heads. The shape of that ruby halo has always been vaguely familiar, but until now, sitting on the cellar floor where Pippa died, I've not been able to place it.

But now I look up at the ring-shaped groove in the ceiling where the lighting rig used to hang, and I see things more clearly than ever. The painting isn't an allegory; it doesn't have a classical theme. Its setting is right here, in the cellar; the red, the safelight of the darkroom that it used to be.

When Julia arrives home with the girls, she gives them a minute to change out of their uniforms and then sits them down on the living-room floor with paper and pens. Even if the girls have pegged these drawing sessions, rightly, as a form of interrogation, they haven't rebelled as yet.

'Join us,' Julia says to me. It's an offer, not a command, but I do it anyway.

The girls look expectantly at their aunt.

'Let's all draw ourselves,' she says, 'in ten years' time.'

The twins frown. 'Ten years?'

'Yes. You'll be eighteen, practically. You'll be adults. I want you to picture yourselves. Where you'll be, what you'll look like, who you'll be with. Can you do that for me?'

The girls cock their heads, chewing their hair uncertainly, and Cassia puts her thumb in her mouth.

'We'll be with Black Mamba,' Sylvie murmurs, glancing at her sister.

Julia ponders for a moment, then says, 'Imagine, for me, that you'd never met Black Mamba. Where would you be in ten years' time? Without him.'

Cassia removes her thumb and shakes her head. 'I don't think I can.'

Undeterred, Julia smiles encouragingly. 'Give it a try.'

They draw diligently – all three of them – for twenty minutes, while I stare at a blank page, unable to see past the next ten days, never mind years.

Where would I be in a decade's time? Without Black Mamba.

I close my eyes and try to let my fingers guide me, surrendering to automaticity. But nothing coherent emerges on the page. It's as if my future simply doesn't exist.

The girls have finished. Julia leans forward to inspect their work. Cassia first. She's drawn herself and Sylvie – tall, in long flowing dresses, with hair that comes down to their feet. I'm not part of the picture.

'Beautiful,' Julia enthuses, running a finger down the girls' hair, admiring the fine gold flecks. 'And yours?'

A little reluctantly, Sylvie rotates her drawing. We all lean in. She has sketched herself, tall and slender in a painter's smock, standing beside a man who's crudely drawn – at least by the girls' standards.

'Who's that?' Julia asks.

Sylvie shrugs. 'A man.'

'Your dad?'

'No.'

Julia frowns. 'And it isn't Black Mamba?'

Sylvie shakes her head, shyly, and shrugs again. 'He's just a man,' she mumbles. 'Any man.'

Cassia says nothing. There's total silence, in fact – a pinched, painful pause.

'All right,' Julia says gently, collecting up my half-hearted scribbles with her own. 'I think that's enough for today.' When she reaches across to retrieve the twins' drawings too, Sylvie snatches hers away, hot and flustered, and screws it up tightly in her fist.

Julia

Night falls slowly around Hart House at this time of year. Peter's Park is bronzed for hours in the twilight, with darkness coming only very gradually, the sky cooling from a warm rose to an icy blue, to a dull purple and then, last of all, to a cold, hard black. At the same time, inside the house, the walls and ceilings also change colour in the fading light, while shadows stretch silently from the skirting boards and doorframes until all of the carpets are covered. This is night two of three.

I'm already half asleep when the noises start: the creak of a door across the landing – the door to my nieces' room – and then, footsteps. I rise from bed without switching on the side light, and tiptoe across my room towards the doorway. The girls are walking on the landing in single file, out of their bedroom and towards the spiral stairs. In this light, I can't make out who's leading, but I can tell that both girls have an index finger raised, as if to learn the path of the wind – though the air on the landing is, of course, quite still.

I whisper to them to get back into bed, but they ignore me. It's only as I follow them down the stairs that I realise they're asleep. You must never wake a sleepwalker – I remember that from my experience with Pippa – but I'm curious to see where this will end.

When they reach the bottom, they turn immediately towards the cellar. The girl in front wraps her hand around the doorknob and twists. The girl behind mirrors the gesture exactly, grasping at the empty air.

They won't get in, I think. Alfie keeps the cellar locked up at all times – sealed off, just like the attic.

It opens with ease. Moving almost like machines, the girls shuffle down the stone cellar steps. I follow them, grasping for the light switch so that I – and they – don't trip. The single bulb that hangs from the ceiling is large and bare. It should make the cellar bright, but the room is deep, as though sinking into the very earth, and the light itself gutters, like a candle: the result of a faulty connection.

The girls reach the bottom of the stairs and process into the centre of the room. Beneath the dull, flickering bulb, they turn to face each other, and both lift a hand. Gently, their fingertips touch. I pace around them, staring at their impassive faces. Their blue eyes are open, but blank. Their lips are pursing into shapes – but no sound comes out. I've never known the twins to sleepwalk, and Alfie's never mentioned it, though I suppose it would explain a number of things: the light coming on in his en suite, and the girls not remembering using it; the noises he's heard in the night.

I watch them for a few minutes, standing – sleeping – on the spot where their mother died. But when I realise the words they're mouthing will never be spoken aloud, I stand between them and take their hands, the hands that aren't raised, and whisper, 'Let's get you back to bed.'

They seem to hear me, though they don't wake.

'Come on. That's it. This way.'

The three of us head back towards the cellar steps, but before we reach them I turn my head, look past Sylvie's shoulder – and gasp. The far cellar wall is lined with cardboard boxes, containing what I thought were just Pippa's old things. But on top of one of those boxes lies Dad's rattle. The sight of it stuns me. I haven't seen it in over twenty years; I had no idea it was still in Hart House. If my hands were free, I'd reach over and lift it, to be sure I'm not mistaken, though such a test is unnecessary. The rattle's swollen, cloth-bound head and wooden arm, all worn and scratched, are instantly recognisable; the sound it makes when lifted is ingrained upon my memory.

'Let's go. Come on. To bed.'

I release the twins' hands only when we reach the top of the cellar steps. I move to switch off the light, to shut the door. The last thing I see is the painting Alfie showed me, months ago – the only one uncovered.

The subject, to me, unmistakeable.

Pippa told me about her nightmare three days before she died. She came round to my flat in another floaty summer dress, with another bottle of wine. Bangles on her wrists and bags beneath her eyes. She hugged me tightly when I opened the door. It was the last time I ever saw my sister.

'I'm sleepwalking again,' she announced. She was trying to look casual, lounging on the sofa in her usual way, wine glass in hand. But I could tell she was troubled.

'How many—' I began. But she interrupted with a question of her own.

'Have you ever dreamt of Dad?'

I was about to pour myself a glass too, but my wrist froze at her words – the bottle suspended, horizontal in mid-air. 'No,' I said, crossing my fingers.

'Never?'

'Honestly, these days, without photographs, I can barely remember what he looked like ...' That part, at least, was true.

Pippa sipped her sauvignon, looking absently around the room. 'Nor can I,' she said. 'But I remember his voice, or at least I think I do. I hear it every night. I've been having the same dream, over and over. I wake, at home, in bed, and everything's dark. But Dad's calling me so I follow his voice, down the stairs, towards—' She broke off, tapping her knee. 'When did Dad turn the cellar into a darkroom? When we were six? Seven?'

'Around then.'

Darkrooms weren't uncommon back when Dad built his. Even so, we'd known for a long time that our family – our church – saw photographs differently from other people. They held, we believed, a special power: to reveal; to *summon*. It's why I haven't seen a photograph of Dad in years; it's why no photographs have ever been displayed at Crescent Place. Until Mum gave Hart House away, none were displayed there either. All our pictures were kept in a locked box in the cellar – scarlet with a white cross drawn on the lid. Just like the box in which Sue keeps all her photos of Michael. Sealed. Protected.

'What happens next? In the dream.'

'I walk down the cellar steps, into the shadows. But it's not the cellar as we know it now. It's a darkroom again. The safelight is back, with its red bulb, and the whole room is glowing ... like it's on fire.'

'And?'

'Dad's waiting for me, in the middle of the room. Standing with his back to me. I reach out to touch him, but when I do ...'

'Yes?' I prompted.

She paused, then drained her glass. 'He turns, and I wake, knowing ... that it wasn't him. That it was someone else. An imposter, in his place.'

I sat silently for a moment, soaking it in. 'When did they start? These dreams ... these nightmares ... ?'

'When—' She stopped, then tried again. 'When ...' And she closed her eyes and touched her midriff lightly, as though she was scared the skin might break.

I came off my chair and knelt next to her as she lay on the sofa. I took her hand in mine, pressing lightly on her palm.

'Alfie's found me a couple of times in the cellar. Alone. Terrified. He's guided me back to bed. I haven't told him, though. About the dreams. You know how he gets with that kind of thing ...'

'Yeah?'

'Yeah. He isn't keen on ...'

'Flights of fancy?'

It was just a suggestion, but Pippa looked at me darkly. 'That's what he calls them too.'

The twins have no memory of last night. Or at least they say they don't, and I believe them. We're in the living room: they're on the sofa; I'm on the floor. It's a trick I sometimes use with kids at the clinic. Make yourself smaller, lower. Less intimidating.

I describe their movements last night and they react with surprise, which again feels authentic.

'What did you dream of?' I ask casually. Alfie isn't with us; he's yet to emerge from his bedroom, even though the girls and I have eaten and dressed.

'We didn't,' they say in unison.

'Everyone dreams,' I tell them. 'Every night. It's just sometimes hard to remember.'

It's a Saturday, so I have the whole day to talk to them; to get somewhere.

'Is he here?' I ask, and they smile. Though I don't believe in him, they've forced me back into pretending. Which for them is victory enough.

'Yes,' says Sylvie.

'As what?'

'A moth.' Cassia looks up, points into empty space with a dainty finger. 'There he goes.'

I watch their eyes wander from one corner of the room to another, tracking Black Mamba's movements in perfect harmony.

Then Cassia's finger drifts towards the open door. 'He's gone,' she says, indifferently. 'Upstairs ...'

I lean closer to the girls, placing my hands on their knees. 'Where upstairs?'

I see, instantly, that my question has struck a chord. They share a glance, still smiling, as if they're debating whether to share a secret with me. I decide to wait for their answer – but then suddenly, before I even know what I'm saying, I find that I'm speaking again. 'People ...'

They stare at me intently.

'People, moving about upstairs.' The words come to me, automatically, and it takes me a moment to remember where I've heard them. 'That's what your dad said you could hear ... on the night of the storm.'

'Yes,' says Sylvie. '*Yes.*'

I take out my phone and scroll to the snap of Sylvie's workbook.

'*Black Mamba lives with us,*' I read, '*but Hart House isn't his home. His home is somewhere else. We want him to take us there, but he says it isn't time. When the time comes he'll take us, but we won't be able to come back to Hart House—*' I break off. 'Where is Black Mamba's home? Where did he come from? How do you get there?'

'He comes from behind the door,' Cassia says, perfectly calmly.

'Which door?'

'The red one. The red one, with the white cross. The door that only *we* can see.'

I place a hand over my mouth. Of course. *How didn't I realise this before?* It's been staring me in the face, from the very first question I asked them, on the night they first spoke his name.

How did he get into the house?

Why, through the door, of course.

Deep down, I've suspected it all along, but now I know it to be true.

This is all my fault.

Fourteen

Alfie

And we're at the beach again – Collier Beach, with its cold winds and pebbled shoreline – and the girls are whirling into the sky, like angels; their white fists clinging tightly to the cords of their red balloons; their shoes kicking above my head. Straight in front of me, I see Pippa. She's running down the shingle, towards the sea. Running into the black water and whatever awaits her beneath, ready to drag her down to the seabed, out of sight, out of sound. I know how the dream will end, because it always ends the same way – with Pippa restored and striding through the sea, grinning maniacally with seaweed in her hair, crying, *I got you, I got you!* So I close my eyes and wait for her to be taken, and when the screaming starts, I cover my ears to block that out too.

Just a few more seconds, I think, and then—

I lift my palms, cautiously, from my ears and listen intently to the wind, and every sound threaded through it: the shrieks of gulls; the breaking of waves against the shore. Pippa's screams have ceased. I open my eyes.

Panic seizes me. Somehow I've moved down the beach, close to the water's edge – so close I can feel the cold sea soaking into the fabric of my shoes. I look up into the air and see the girls, floating high above the water, still holding their red balloons. They stare down at me with blank expressions.

'Pippa?'

I look down the shoreline and out to sea. But she's nowhere to be seen. Ahead of me, the sea is vast and glittering; empty but for a single figure – a tall, black crane standing a few feet in front of me, its spindly legs half submerged in the water. Its face is turned away from mine, foreshortening its sword-like beak, and its wings are tucked neatly behind its back. I watch its body rise and fall as it breathes, just as I breathe, and I stare at the back of its feathered head, pregnant with thoughts, written in a code unknown to me. It begins to breathe harder and faster, mimicking my own quickening breath, and then suddenly it turns to face me. Its dark eyes stare into mine, shining like black beads in their sockets, and its whole body starts to shake, as if it's readying itself to spread its wings.

Alfie!

My heart almost bursts with relief at the sound of Pippa's voice directly behind me. I turn to face her, as suddenly as the crane turned to face me. She stands with a conch in her hand, full of black ash. Without a word, she thrusts her arm forward, tipping the ash into my face, and I scream as it burns through my eyes.

I wake up sweating, brushing frantically at my face, the smell of ash and salt-water still in my nostrils. It takes me a moment to calm myself. It felt even more real than usual. I run a finger across the surface of my memory, struggling to find the seam between the present moment and my dream.

Still shaken, I stumble out of bed and into the shower. I lift the lever and warm water stutters from the showerhead, as if I've surprised it, then settles into a steady stream. I rub my hands over my body, washing off the nightmare and, not for the first time this year, I notice I'm putting on weight, as though I'm slowly melting out of shape. It's a mild morning but, even so, the shower door steams up, until it's almost entirely covered in an incongruous frost. I cut the water, turn to get out, and freeze at what I see, imperfectly, through the mist.

The black crane is just the other side of the shower door. I see its unmistakeable silhouette – the long, stalk-like legs and slender neck; its scimitar beak. I smell its dank, salty feathers, and I can hear the rattle of its slow, steady breaths. My spine touches the cold cubicle wall as I try to back away, feeling like a child again, weak and terrified. I screw up my eyes – not quite brave enough to close them fully – reducing it to a shape against the glass.

Get a grip, I say to myself.

But it's only Julia's voice, calling me from elsewhere in the house, that brings me to my senses. I wrench open the shower door and stare out, stupidly, into the bathroom, which is bright and empty save for a tiny, plush black moth, fluttering above the towel rail, beating a path towards the open window with its veiny wings.

'I have a theory,' she whispers through the crack in the bedroom door, 'about what's going on with the girls. And what we can do about it.' Julia is standing on the landing outside the master bedroom, directly beneath the attic. Her face is turned away, discreetly, while I dry myself and change.

'A few months ago, I started to wonder if the girls created their woozle together, or if one of them was taking the lead. Remember what I said about it being a product of the twinship? How the girls were retreating into themselves ... using the woozle to strengthen their bond with each other? Well, I began to think – what if one of them is *using* Black Mamba to bind the other to her more tightly?'

Shadows play on the carpet as Julia fidgets. 'At first, I thought it must be Sylvie. She's always been the more volatile personality. Needier. Less independent than Cassia. And Cassia's injuries seemed to fit the pattern. I also thought of something their teacher told me. Miss Addison said that Cassia was falling behind in maths – a subject Sylvie's *always struggled in*. I wondered if Cassia was holding herself back deliberately. For fear of Sylvie's reaction.'

There's a moment's silence, as if she's waiting for me to say something. When I don't, she continues, as if in a confessional: 'I blamed you. I thought you were overlooking Sylvie's anger. Ignoring her mistreatment of Cassia. Out of—'

'What?' I ask wearily. 'Favouritism?'

'Yes. Like my father favoured Pippa.'

'Maybe I was.'

I catch Julia turning her head slightly, glancing through the crack in the door. Hurriedly, she looks away. 'But then, after I found out what Cassia said to you in the hospital, I thought: what if I'm wrong? What if it was Cassia who invented Black Mamba? We've always thought that she's the strong one. That Sylvie's the sensitive one, who really needs her sister. Now, I think it might be the other way round. Cassia was always closer to Pippa, Sylvie closer to you. The accident must have left Cassia feeling especially vulnerable. Fearful of being shut out – think of the girls' drawings! Fearful of rejection ...'

'By me?'

Julia's voice is small, but still she answers. 'By you.'

I pull my jumper over my head, my face prickling. I don't want to believe it, but her theory is compelling.

'So she's rejecting you pre-emptively. Pushing you away, and pulling Sylvie towards her. Holding herself back in school – doing everything she can to protect their bond and to strengthen it. Even if that means accepting – or actually encouraging – abuse.' Julia halts; clears her throat. 'We have two problems: Sylvie's anger, and Cassia's dependence on her sister. But together we can fix them. I can help Sylvie master her emotions. And you can work on your bond with Cassia.'

I sit down on the edge of the bed, fully dressed now, and listen attentively. This, I want to believe.

'Let's separate them. I'll take Sylvie out for the day, just the two of us, and I'll talk to her. About everything. I'll try to find out where her anger's coming from. And you ... you should stay here, in the house with Cassia. Just you and her – no pressure to talk about anything. Not if you don't want to. Just play together, cook together, relax together. And hopefully, the two of you can start reconnecting. She'll be reminded of how much you love her.' Julia hesitates. 'Then,' she concludes, voice wavering, 'we'll come together again. The four of us. As a family.'

There's silence for a moment. I hear her breathing softly through the crack. 'All right?' she asks.

'All right,' I say.

Julia

Sylvie follows me uncertainly outside. Her reticence may be down to mistrust, or simply the heat. In any case, I smile; try to reassure her.

'Come on,' I beckon. 'We won't go far.'

Today is the hottest day of summer. The sun is keeping

everyone inside, in the warren of cool, dark houses that surround the square. Peter's Park is glowing in the heat. I walk with Sylvie down the stone paths that curve around the flower beds. It's too sticky a day to hold hands, so we shield our eyes from the sun instead, and fan our faces. We wander west, into the depths of the gardens, to admire the roses and peonies, but the back of my T-shirt is slick with sweat and Sylvie begins to sag, so we leave the path and head into the long grass, under the shade of the trees. When we reach the pink chestnuts we give in and lie down on the grass, close our eyes, almost sleep. There's no breeze among the leaves; the only sound is birdsong – and Sylvie when she sits up, abruptly.

'Auntie Julia?'

She doesn't look at me, instead she picks at the tall grass. She's been subdued ever since coming back from the hospital, as though her actions that day shocked even herself. I lean forward and brush away a strand of her golden hair. The stitches in her forehead have long since dissolved, but a thin scar remains just visible, marking her out like Cain. It doesn't look as jarring as usual to see the twins apart.

'Am I going to die?'

Her question stuns me with its frankness and I'm unsure how to respond. Hart House is out of sight from here, obscured by leaves and branches. Somehow, that makes this easier.

'We all will, one day ... yes. But you won't die for a long, long time. So you mustn't worry.'

'And ...' She frowns, vacillating. Holding a perfect blade of grass between her fingers, she splits it at the sheath, then pulls it carefully apart. 'What do you think *happens* when you die ... ?'

Dad's rhythmic voice – thrumming in my ears. I feel the curve of his arm; the weight of his body.

'Some people think you go to Heaven. You've heard of Heaven, haven't you?'

Sylvie looks up, eyes narrowing. 'Of course.'

'Well, then.' I swallow hard. 'You'll probably know, too, that not everyone believes in it when they grow up. Including me.'

There's silence, as Sylvie's query remains suspended in the air. I remember, suddenly, what Alfie told me about the death of their pet rabbit – how the girls hadn't cried, but remained still and impassive, and full of questions. *Where's he gone? Can he come back? Will we ever see him again?* Questions that Pip couldn't answer, lying numb on the sofa, still shaken by the death that had taken place inside her; questions that Alfie evaded.

'When you die,' I begin – cautiously, but with resolve – 'I don't think you go to any physical place. I think you're just ... at peace.' I place my hand on Sylvie's back and rub lightly, my thumb pressing in concentric circles. 'Does that make sense?'

She shrugs and continues shredding the grass.

Something occurs to me, and I remove my hand.

'Sylvie ... have you asked anyone else that question?'

She pauses, another blade pressed between her fingers. 'Grandma, for instance?'

She nods.

I grit my teeth and draw a deep breath. *I knew it.*

'Did she tell you about Sheol?'

Sylvie nods again, then whispers into the ground: 'The place of shadows ...'

'Your grandma,' I say firmly, 'has a lot of strange ideas. And that's all Sheol is. An idea.'

Sylvie's eyes bore into mine. 'And what is it? The idea?'

'Your grandma believes,' I explain, with all the neutrality I can muster, 'that the dead aren't in Heaven, not yet, but are still here, on Earth, trapped in the shadows. Waiting for seven trumpets to sound, and Christ to return. Waiting for the New Jerusalem to be created – Heaven on Earth – and Gehenna, too, for the wicked. Waiting for the judgment—' I break off. 'But it isn't true, Sylvie. None of it is. The dead are either in Heaven, or they're nowhere at all. But they're not still here, on Earth. They aren't trapped. They aren't waiting. We can't see them or speak to them. We can't be with them again, and they can't be reached. You understand that, don't you?'

Sylvie says nothing. Her expression is inscrutable, but she seems calm, at least. Stable and engaged enough, I think, for me to ask some questions of my own.

'We need to talk,' I say. 'About what's true and what isn't.' I study her face carefully. 'We need to talk about what happened here.'

'Here?' she repeats.

'Yes. Right here, on the grass we're sitting on now, under these trees. We need to talk about what happened to Mummy.'

'Why?'

'Because it's important to share how we feel. It isn't good to keep our feelings locked inside.'

Sylvie is silent for a moment. Then she says, 'Okay.'

Relieved, I rub her back again. 'Tell me what happened,' I say gently. 'The day she died. Tell me in your own words.'

'It was warm.'

'Like today?'

'Yes. But the grass was short. We were hunting in it, for bugs. Me, Cassia and Mummy.'

'Bugs?'

'Yes.'

'What kind?'

'They weren't real. At least, I thought they weren't. I thought it was just a game.'

'A game?'

Sylvie glances up at the sun, then jerks her head away, blinking. 'It was my fault,' she whispers.

'Your fault?'

'Yes. It was my idea. To pretend we were hunting for bugs, and putting them in jars. It was all pretend. The bugs were invisible. We imagined them. But then ... something bit Mummy. Something in the grass. And somehow it all became real.'

'It wasn't your fault,' I say. I try to put an arm around her, but she pushes me away.

'It was,' she insists. 'Mummy was Cassia's, and I took her away.'

'What?'

She's crying now. 'I did. I took her away ...'

'If there's one thing I know is true,' I say, 'it's that none of this was your fault. It was an accident. Your mummy was bitten, or stung. Your daddy thought she'd be okay, after a lie-down. So did she. It had nothing to do with the game you were playing, I promise. You didn't do anything wrong.'

This time she comes to me, leaning into my body, sobbing into the folds of my T-shirt. I put my arms around her and whisper those last few words again and again, knowing all too well how hard she'll find it to believe them. Once a story has been constructed, it can't be easily rebuilt.

When she finally calms, I speak again.

'Who saw Black Mamba first: you or Cassia?'

'Cassia.' The answer is immediate and, without prompting, she continues: 'Cassia woke me. She said there was a man in our room.'

'And you couldn't see him?'

'Not at first. I thought she was pretending. But then, like the game we played with Mummy, it all became real. I started to see him too, as a bird, a fish, a bear, a—' Sylvie leans forward, dipping her hand into the long grass. Her bare arm looks silver in the light. 'He's here now,' she says, sounding surprised.

'Black Mamba? He's here? Right now?'

'Yes.' Her blue eyes are pellucid and grave. 'As a snake ...'

'A snake? Ah. All right then.' *His very first form.* 'You can see him?'

'Yes. He's wrapping himself around my arm. Squeezing tight.' She shifts on the ground, as if the snake is moving; both her elbows bend until crooked, as though managing his weight.

My eyes narrow reflexively. 'You're not pretending?'

Sylvie tosses her head, her eyes still red but her cheeks already dry. 'He's speaking to me,' she says, wincing slightly. 'His tongue keeps flicking my ear.'

For the first time, I believe her. All sense of artifice, of cold design, has been stripped away in the absence of her sister. She's telling the truth. Or at least, she thinks she is.

'What's he saying?'

Sylvie straightens up, closes her eyes. Lets him whisper.

'He says we should go back to the house.'

'Yes?'

She nods solemnly, then adds, 'They're fighting. Cassia and Alfie ...'

My skin crawls. 'Who?'

'Cassia ... and Alfie.'

'Daddy, you mean?' I say, but she shakes her head, her eyes now wide with fear.

'No,' she says slowly. 'That's Black Mamba. He says we

have to call *him* Daddy from now on. And Alfie ... Alfie isn't happy ...'

I stare at her, trying to make sense of the words, but as she intones them, Sylvie's face seems to shift somehow, almost imperceptibly, until I think I'm looking at Cassia. I feel woozy in the heat, and then my phone is ringing and it's Alfie's voice at the end of the line – unable to choke out more than two words at a time.

'*She won't ... call me ...*'

'I'm coming,' I say, standing up. I motion for Sylvie to follow and, when she doesn't, I grab her hand and pull her up. We hurry back through the park, my plan for the day drawn to a sudden, stillborn end.

Fifteen

Alfie

It's late. Darkness has fallen, throwing a filmy veil over hours of shouting and tears. The house is still. Julia has prepared dinner – lamb stew – and we're eating in the dining room, with its windowless walls and harsh, unnatural light. Steam is rising from our bowls like ghosts. My daughters are silent as they chew; *they are still my daughters*.

They are still my daughters, but Black Mamba is seated at the head of the table, leaving the four of us to crowd around it lengthways, heads down. We don't say grace before eating; we never have. There's never been a God in this house – and now, no one is above Black Mamba.

The table is draped, as always, in a red velvet runner, ancient and plush, which I study as I eat. We inherited the table and linen from Marian; she had no space for them when she went to live with Susan, so they stayed in Hart House. It's the kind of dark, fusty velvet on which Tarot cards should be placed. My irreligious mother had a set, which she let me play with when I was a boy. I look at the faces around me and lay down the major arcana: the Sun for Sylvie; then for Cassia the Moon; the Priestess for Julia; and then for *him* – I don't look up, even though there's nothing there to see – the Devil. Before myself, I deal the Fool.

Julia coughs. 'Could you pour some water for your dad?' she asks Sylvie, nudging her elbow.

But before Sylvie can answer, her sister smiles glassily and intervenes. 'He'd rather have milk. He's turned into a big black cat. Alfie – could you fetch a saucer for him, please?'

Julia frowns. 'Unacceptable,' she says.

I don't react, unmoved by it. There are cards left for the empty spaces, I think. Judgment for your mother; the Magician for your father, to be replaced swiftly by the Hanged Man.

'Dad, Dad, the fat black cat,' my daughters start chanting. *They are still my daughters.*

'He's climbing on the table!' Sylvie reaches towards me, but her hand stops, prematurely, and she strokes the air.

The Lovers falls in the place where Pippa used to sit; where Julia sits now. When I glance down, my own card has been swapped for Death.

'Look at those beautiful whiskers!'

'Look at his beautiful tail!'

I seize the velvet runner and pull. It comes away with astonishing ease. Cutlery falls with a crash. Bowls of stew are upended – two thirds full, still, and hot; one hits the floor and smashes into pieces. Shocked, appalled, frightened faces, spattered with lamb, stare at me dumbly as the pepper pot rolls across the floorboards and something dark and elegant leaps from the table with rage-stiffened limbs, then melts into the shadows.

Cassia stares at me. She doesn't speak.

I can't look at her face. I know how it will appear to me: just as it did the night Pippa fell. She woke to the sound of my shouts. She left her sister sleeping and followed us into the bathroom. She was only three years old, but she remembers – I'm sure of it.

Pippa and I had been trying for a third – a boy, she hoped – trying and trying, with no luck. That night, she'd been out drinking with friends.

Is Mummy okay?

Shh – she'll be fine. Don't wake Sylvie.

I glance up. Julia is standing aghast in the corner, surveying the wreckage. Sylvie's holding on to her auntie's leg, trembling at the destruction I've caused.

Cassia's the only one still seated. *I can't look at her face.*

Shame, and an overwhelming urge to run, possess my limbs. I lurch towards the hallway.

'It's not your fault, Alfie,' Julia calls after me, her voice catching. 'None of it is.' And then, as if these words might block my path: 'It's mine . . .'

But I'm already gone – out of the front door, over the step; racing towards Peter's Park until I'm hidden among the trees; sprinting into the dark, balmy night.

Julia

This is how it started:

It's three years ago. My sister is still alive, and she and Alfie are in the bloom of love. Mum hasn't yet given them the house; instead, I'm still living here with her. This weekend we're looking after the twins. Alfie and Pippa are going away; Sunday is the anniversary of the day they met, a day they mark each year with a trip to the coast. They walk down Collier Beach together and stay in the same hotel every year: a Victorian guesthouse near the seafront – boarded, elegant, the colour of cream. When they arrive on the first night, a cold bottle of champagne will be sitting in a dripping silver bucket, and the bed will be covered in a drift of petals. She has shown me pictures.

They drop the girls off early on Saturday morning. The twins flit about the house like linnets, chirring with excitement. They flurry up and down the spiral stairs and bounce on the beds; their shouts ricochet off the walls. They've always loved Hart House.

Pippa stands unsteadily in the kitchen, handing me their things – unpacking the girls' bags and placing each item into the palm of my hand, individually. With each one comes an explanation.

Alfie and I share a knowing glance.

'Enough,' I say firmly. 'Get out of here. Have fun.'

Pippa hugs me tightly.

'We will,' she whispers, giggling slightly in my ear, and I clench my teeth. I know they're trying for another child. When Alfie says goodbye, I don't look up; I busy myself with the girls' belongings. I hear him talking briefly in the hallway with my mother – the low timbre of his voice, deep and smooth, echoing gently in the recesses – and then he's gone. The only sound left in the house is the laughter of his daughters, who have my blood in their veins as well as his.

The girls play with their grandma. She sings to them, reads to them, dresses them in matching clothes and combs their hair. I'm supposed to watch them at all times, and intervene the second our mother's songs drift in the direction of a hymn, or she starts to tell them a story from scripture. But this morning began with period pain – light spotting, but terrible cramps – so I leave them playing. I go upstairs, take some tablets and lie down, holding my tender stomach and trying not to think about the cry of gulls, the smell of the sea.

When the painkillers kick in, I come back downstairs. The girls are painting together, working on a single picture. I recognise the subject instantly: Jonah and the fish. Cassia is dabbing at its great blue, purple scales, and Sylvie is perfecting the holy man trapped in its belly. Mum is sitting between them, cooing, whispering, guiding their hands. When I enter the living room, she looks away guiltily.

I'm about to say something, but a deep twinge in my stomach leaves me too winded to argue. *They're only stories.*

Myths, allegories, just like the pictures that Pippa paints; just like the games of make-believe the girls play – they can't tell the difference. And then I think of Alfie, walking along the beach with my sister, his body next to hers, and I close the living-room door and leave Mum to it.

They've been trying for a while now. Pippa badly wants a boy, but Alfie hasn't delivered (her words). Still, she's staying optimistic. I've seen her expectations build as this weekend has approached. *The sea air might do my body some good ...*

I return upstairs and lie down again – though not in my room this time, but in the girls' room, on the bed I used to share with Pippa. I breathe in my nieces' sweet scent, and clutch my stomach.

(This will be their last romantic weekend away together – though none of us knows it. The next time Alfie and Pippa go to Collier Beach, it will be for another purpose. There will be no dripping silver bucket, no drift of petals; they will scatter ashes instead. The winds will be high, and the sea wild, and my sister will die herself within the year.)

When I next go into the living room, to my alarm I find Mum towering over the girls, who are lying on the floor. The art materials have been cleared away, and the twins are in identical positions. Mum is adjusting the placement of their arms and legs, making each of their bodies the perfect mirror image of the other.

'What on earth ... ?'

The twins sit up, instantly spoiling her careful arrange-
ment. They look relieved to see me.

I shoot Mum a dark look, and am chilled to see a photograph, flapping in her hand.

'What's that?'

She presses it swiftly to her chest. 'Just a picture.'

'Of who?'

She hesitates, but then answers, her face set in defiance.
'Their grandad.'

'Dad ... ?' I turn, dizzily, and then in astonishment
I spot the red box painted with a white cross – the box
where Mum keeps all our photographs – sitting baldly on
top of the bureau. It's been in the cellar for years; this is
the first time I've seen it out, and unlocked, in more than
a decade.

I order the girls to go upstairs and play.

'What did you tell them?' I ask, as soon as they're gone.

'Everything,' she says.

I close my eyes despairingly.

'Oh!' she cries. 'I don't expect *you* to understand. I just
want to see him again. That's all. Hear his voice a final
time. Be with him for one more moment.'

'I do understand,' I say, relenting and putting my arms
around her. 'But you can't. He's gone.'

She laughs and wrenches an arm free to wipe her eyes;
then she shakes her head. 'That's not true, though, is it?
The dead are never gone. You should know that better than
anyone.'

*

When I put the girls to bed that night, they're frightened, holding the covers tightly like a shield.

'What if we see him?' they ask.

'Who?'

'Grandad.'

'You won't,' I insist.

I climb into bed beside them. They're small and precious, only five years old, and their faces are still toddler-chubby. Sometimes they stumble over their words; Sylvie, in particular, still lisps a little. They are both enigmas. Their minds are like Chinese boxes, closed to everyone except each other.

'We might. Grandma thinks we will. Grandma thinks he's still here ...'

I'll tell them tomorrow, I think. *As soon as they're back from the beach.* I'll tell them what Mum has done and said. The twins will be kept away from her – perhaps from me, too. It's for the best.

'If you see him,' I say – remembering, suddenly, what I told Pippa after Dad died, when she couldn't stop dreaming of him – 'just imagine a door. A big red one, with a lock on it, like the box Grandma keeps her photos in. Then, imagine Grandad is behind that door. Locked away, so you can't see him. Gone.'

It isn't make-believe, I tell myself forcefully, *if it's true.*

The girls fall asleep in my arms. For hours, I watch the shadows as they peacefully dream.

*

I'm going to tell them.

I'm going to tell them, until the moment they walk in through the door the next morning and I see my sister's smile, as bright as the sun on a clear winter's day – and the words leave me, suddenly, vanishing on my tongue like ice. She greets the twins then hugs me, pressing me so close that I can smell Alfie on her clothes, on her skin, in her hair, and she says, 'Maybe this time.'

Her voice is so hopeful; her mood so light. Alfie nuzzles just beneath her ear and she shivers and laughs, pushing him playfully away. He grabs her hips and pulls her to him, and they kiss.

I look away; say nothing. They break apart just long enough for Pippa to thank me as I pack up her daughters' things.

Three months later, she'll tell me they're expecting a boy.

The sound of the front door closing makes me straighten up, abandoning the final shards of crockery scattered over the dining-room floor. I push my hair out of my eyes, and smooth out the surface of a clean runner, silk-blue. Alfie's back. He's been gone for an hour, perhaps longer. While he was out God only knows where, I put the girls to bed and tidied up. I binned the remnants of dinner.

He shuffles sheepishly into the dining room, then sits down, head in hands.

'I'm sorry,' he says, without looking up.

I make a noncommittal noise and stay on my feet. 'Where did you go?'

'For some air.'

There's silence for a moment. Then I ask: 'Are you still upset?' The question sounds odd to my own ears, my voice stilted.

'Of course I am,' he answers, dully. 'Pippa's dead. Yet I'm the one they want to replace.'

I say nothing, do nothing, until finally he looks at me. His eyes glitter. 'When I walked out, you said that this wasn't my fault.'

'It isn't—' I start, but he cuts me off.

'Julia, listen to me. I've got to tell you something.' He takes a deep breath. 'Do you remember when Pippa fell in the bathroom and hit her head?'

I nod, slowly. 'She came home drunk. It was ... an accident.'

'Yes and no,' Alfie says quietly. 'We'd been having problems. She wanted another kid – she'd always wanted one of each – but I was struggling to cope with the ones we had. I was exhausted. Frustrated. She went out drinking with friends. To cheer herself up, I guess. When she came back, she was drunk, and we fought. She said it was my fault we couldn't get pregnant. As if my reluctance was ... cursing us somehow. You know Pip. She could be daft like that. Superstitious.' He shifts in his seat. 'We must have woken Cassia. She followed us into the bathroom, where our fight ... became physical.'

There's a taut silence.

'She started it,' he says, and his lips curve upwards into a weak, incongruous smile, perhaps at how childish that sounds. 'Pip was hitting me, and hitting me – and I pushed her, just to get her away from me. I didn't mean to hurt her. In that sense, it *was* an accident. You have to believe me.'

The room rings with silence. He hangs his head, then gruffly continues. 'Cassia saw what happened. She was only three years old. I didn't think she remembered. I hoped she didn't. Do you think …' He swallows uncertainly. 'Could that be why she's doing this? Rejecting me. Inventing this other man – this monster?'

At last, with care, I speak. 'I'm sure that won't be the only reason. Behavioural disorders rarely have a single cause.'

It's as if he doesn't hear me. 'I didn't mistreat her,' he says. 'Pippa, I mean. I loved her. We loved each other. Maybe we weren't right for each other. Maybe we were too different, or wanted different things. But we *were* in love.'

'I believe you.'

He looks up, startled for a moment, then eyes me cynically. 'I'm not sure how you can – not after the last few months. Pippa's gone. You can never ask her. And you know how bad things got between us. You can't trust me, not completely. I don't see how.'

I shrug indifferently and turn away.

How could I begin to express the feeling I had the day they returned from Collier Beach and saw them kiss and smile in each other's arms? Or the memories that sight had evoked for me; the myriad smiles I'd seen them share, in furtive glances that had caused me so much joy, and so much pain.

'I just do,' I say lightly, crouching back down to clear away the rest of the shattered plates.

After clearing up, we stand limply in the hallway, as though we're both forestalling our separate paths to bed. Our tiredness hangs around us, almost palpable in the warm, heavy air, but still we linger at the bottom of the stairs.

'Why *did* you say it was your fault?' he asks abruptly. 'When I ran.'

I try to explain. He knows some of the details already – more than I expected. He is calm as I describe how Pippa and I were brought up to believe in a spirit world. Dad's obsession with mediumship likewise comes as no surprise. When I confess that Mum has been sharing her faith with the girls – secretly, and not for months but for years – he stiffens slightly, but then he relaxes and throws up his hands.

'She means no harm,' he says.

'No,' I sigh. 'Nor did I.'

I tell him what I think is going on – how the girls are convinced that the dead can still be found, somewhere in this house; their grandad, and their mother too.

Alfie nods receptively. 'People, moving about upstairs . . .'

'It's because of me. I told them something, a few years ago. Something stupid about a door. It was a symbol for the permanence of death. The completeness of the separation. But it only confused them.' I look down. 'I'm sorry. I should have told you. I should have—'

'Stop,' he says, with surprising gentleness. He touches my chin, lifting my gaze to meet his. 'Nothing Marian believes, nothing you've told them, could have led them to Black Mamba. They want a new father. I'm the reason he exists, not you. I drove them into his arms ...'

I shift uncomfortably on the spot. I'm still not being entirely honest. In everything I told him, I avoided mentioning the strangest aspect of my family's beliefs: those fallen creatures that move between our world and Sheol, that provide the link between the faithful and the dead. The word *demon* hasn't passed my lips.

'C'mon. We should check on them,' he says, and we make our way awkwardly upstairs.

'It's okay,' I say. 'Let me.'

I wait outside the girls' door for a few minutes, listening carefully as Alfie pads up the remaining stairs, yawning; his feet as soft as paws on the carpet. I look up from where I stand, and watch as a trapezoid of light swings over the ceiling and the loft hatch, then vanishes as he shuts his bedroom door. The staircase and landings are plunged into darkness, and me along with them. I turn the handle and enter their room.

Cassia is awake. She's sitting up in bed, her eyes wide like a doll's. The curtain has been left slightly open, and her pale face has a kind of ghostly luminescence. I skirt around the edge of the bed towards the window. There is a full moon outside, and I draw the curtain across the rail as quietly as I can. Even in the dark, Cassia's face unnerves me. It has the uncanny quality that all children's faces possess, from certain perspectives – as if they're not quite the faces of real people but, rather, approximations of people; puppets that adults craft and play with.

'Is he back?' she asks, before I've even settled on the edge of the bed.

'Who? Alfie?' My tone is biting, and seems to make her flinch.

She blinks; almost looks tearful. 'Mm.'

'Yes,' I say. 'He's back.'

She glances down at her sister who is fast asleep, her drool forming a small, dark puddle on the pillow. 'Is he ... okay?'

I gaze into Cassia's eyes and wonder: is it remorse I hear behind her words, causing her voice to waver – or merely fear? Is she, like Sylvie, a true believer in the man they've invented, consciously or not, between them?

There's only one way to be certain: through the cold, hard cast of a confession.

'Of course he's not,' I say. 'How could he be?'

Cassia takes my hand and squeezes it tight. 'It was the only way. We had to call him "Daddy" before it got dark on the third night ... He said that if we did, he'd give us what we wanted. He'd—'

'Stop it,' I say. Her nails are digging into my skin. 'Just stop it.'

I pull away, and the fantasies come to a sudden halt. Chastened, she stares at me coldly and wipes her eyes.

'Tell me,' I say, after a moment. 'Who saw Black Mamba first? You or Sylvie?'

She stares at me uncertainly. 'We saw him together. He came into our room.'

'Really?' I say. 'Because that's not what Sylvie told me, in the park this afternoon. She said *you* saw him first. That she couldn't see him at all, to begin with ...'

Caught in a lie, at last Cassia seems to falter.

I press on.

'My dad died when I was your age, more or less. Before he died ... on the day he died ... I told him a lie.' As soon as I've said it, I begin to feel dizzy. *I've never confessed this to anyone.*

Her eyes seem to sharpen in the gloom. 'What lie?'

'It doesn't matter now,' I say, with false conviction. 'We were playing a game, that's all. A daft game. Dad believed in the power of the mind. And that being a twin ... being *with* your twin ... could make that power greater.'

That's why he went for Mum, I think cynically – as I've thought many times before. *Twins ran in her family.*

'Oh, it was stupid. So stupid. But still ... I lied to him. And, because he died that day, I can never admit it. I can never tell him I'm sorry.' I pause a moment, letting the words sink in. 'You think your dad loves Sylvie, not you. But that isn't true. He loves you, Cass. He does. And I know you love him too. You need to call him Daddy again. Not for me. Not because I've asked you to.' I lean forward, pressing a hand against her heart. 'For you. And ... you need to tell him the truth.'

Slowly, but seemingly without ambivalence, she nods.

So I take the plunge.

'Is he real?' I ask, hammering my fluttering voice into words as hard and unyielding as I can make them. 'Black Mamba. Tell me the truth. Is he?'

A silence that seems to stretch out forever. And then:

'No,' Cassia whispers, exhaling audibly, as though flooded by relief. 'He isn't. I've never seen him ... When Sylvie said she could see him too, that scared me. But he isn't real.' She shakes her head firmly. 'He isn't.'

At first, I'm too stunned to speak. So I study her face. For a heartbeat, I'm convinced I see something pass across it: a glimmer of satisfaction, like a chess player sitting back, pleased with her move; a look that reminds me of Mum. My muscles tauten. Until now, I've never seen a resemblance between the girls and their grandma. But the likeness fades before it's truly sunk in. Before I can question it, I see only a child again.

'Okay,' I say, trying to remain calm as a tear of relief falls down my cheek and onto my lips. It's all I can do not to laugh. 'Okay. You made him up. Everything will be all right.'

'But I didn't make him up,' Cassia says – and my stomach drops. '*You* did.'

I pause again, the tips of my fingers trembling against

the fuzzy surface of the bedcovers, then I close my eyes and nod. What else can I do?

I didn't think she remembered. I *hoped* she didn't.

The moment I close my eyes, I'm back in this very room, that night three years ago. Alfie and Pippa are making love, miles away, in a painted guesthouse by the sounding sea, while the girls lie asleep in my arms. For hours I watch the shadows, until she – Cassia – shifts beneath the covers, her sleep purling unexpectedly at the hand of some unknown force, which eventually throws her awake.

'I saw the door,' she cries, clutching at my body like driftwood, 'and it was opening!'

'It's all right,' I murmur; shushing her. 'Whatever comes out, I'll protect you.'

'And what if you can't?'

I rub my eyes. I haven't slept; I can't sleep. I can't stop thinking about them. About *him*. Not Alfie, but his image; the version of him that stalks my mind.

'Then imagine there's a guard on the door,' I say, exhausted. 'A man. Big and tall. Strong as a beast. He'll keep you safe. He'll protect you.'

Cassia perks up a little, pressing tightly on my arm. 'Just like Daddy?' she asks, her eyes wide with hope, the mother of belief.

'Yes,' I whisper, more grateful than ever for the dark. 'Just like Daddy.'

*

I moved out of Hart House one week later. And – I remind myself as I leave the girls' room, treading softly across the landing – I will move out for the second time tomorrow. This is night three of three.

It'll be easier to leave now, with Sylvie beginning to heal; beginning to realise that Pip's death wasn't her fault. This is the first step towards assuaging her anger, rebuilding her self-esteem. And Cassia, likewise, has taken the first step towards bonding with Alfie: she's accepted he can't be replaced. Her connection with her father will heal in time, as they move on, the three of them, without me.

I close the door to my room and clamber into bed without even bothering to switch on the light. I know every inch of this room, every inch of this house. Even in darkness. Even with my eyes closed.

I wake up the moment the door opens, the hinges creaking in their sockets. I see the moonlit landing and a silhouette pressed hard on it like an ink stain.

'Cassia?'

The shadow moves and I realise it's too big to be a child. It's Alfie. He stands in the doorway, his back straight and tall, his arms by his sides – his whole body colourless in the dark.

'Couldn't you sleep either?' I ask, reaching for the cord of my bedside lamp, feeling for the switch. But he steps forward, raising one of his palms, as if to warn me off. I sit up, squinting. He's naked. I can make out the sheen of his bare skin, the hair furring his chest, his cock thick between his legs. Silently, he steps towards the bed. I saw glimpses of his body this morning, through the crack of his bedroom door, as he dried and changed, but I've never been confronted with anything as stark, as unavoidable as this.

He edges another inch closer, into the path of the window, and suddenly his face is awash with moonlight.

It isn't Alfie.

My shock is sheer, limitless, terrifying – the sight is like a mountain cliff falling away and disappearing noiselessly into the sea; the feeling is almost indescribable.

It's him: the man I saw, fleetingly, on my first night back in Hart House. The man who sat in the wicker chair, grinning, and disappeared when I switched on the light. He looks like Alfie, at surface level. He has the same face, the same teeth. He's leaner, perhaps, and has more hair on his body, though his height and breadth are the same. But his eyes – his eyes are all wrong. They have no expression, no feeling, no visible whites. They are the eyes of the *love cervere*, the great panther – two huge black pupils swimming in pools of molten gold, flecked with earthy streaks, veins of ochre, green needles.

I sit, stock still, every cell in my body frozen. I don't know what to do; there's only one thing I can say.

'Black Mamba ... ?'

I whisper it faintly, but he hears me. He recognises his name, cocks his head, half smiles. Edges closer.

Overwhelmed by panic, I grab the cord, switch on the light. But this time, he doesn't vanish. Instead he leaps away from the brightness of the lamp, snarling and cringing; his great black pupils constrict into slits beneath its glare and he slinks into the shadow of the doorway. I jump out of bed and follow, catching a glimpse of something on the landing. His eyes, perhaps, flaring in the darkness. Or a trick of the light. I step towards them. It's not a choice; it's a compulsion. It isn't enough that he's no longer here in my room. I need to believe that he never was; that I dreamed his presence.

Something begins moving up the stairs towards the floor above, dipping in and out of the shadows – but I can't quite make it out. The rounded windows that line the spiral staircase let in masts of ethereal light, which I watch closely, waiting for him to pass.

I blink in amazement. There he is, walking *backwards* up the stairs. Low and crouched, his legs stretching out behind him, he's feeling his way carefully to each new, rising step, moving slowly but with total ease, like he was born to do it. His eyes remain trained on me.

I trail him upstairs. Up and up, until I reach the top floor. Until I'm outside Alfie's bedroom.

And then he's gone – as suddenly as if he was swallowed whole by the house. I stare around, stupidly, but the landing is empty. I look up. For one hideous moment I'm certain he's climbed into the attic, and that I'll have to follow him there. But then the door to Alfie's bedroom begins to open, and those gaping, animal eyes flash in the darkness, like beacons guiding me to the shore.

Alfie

I wake to the sight of the bedroom door opening noiselessly – and Pippa, standing on the threshold. I gasp her name, almost choked with wonder as she glides towards me. Her movements are slow, almost mechanical. Her nightdress clings to her in the airless heat.

'You've come back,' I whisper in amazement, my voice catching. 'I knew you would.'

She says nothing. She's sleepwalking; I see it, as she draws near. Her eyes are open, but when she looks at me, it's as if she can't see me.

She crosses over to the bed and pulls back the sheets. I'm naked, as I always am on a summer's night, and for a moment I feel self-conscious. My body isn't what it was, but she doesn't seem to care or notice. Instead she gets onto the bed, pulls her nightdress up to her waist and tries to straddle me. I sit up, putting a hand to her face.

'Hey, Pip,' I say. 'Wake up.' But she forces my shoulders back down and lifts her leg over my hips, her body pushing against me as she brings her face parallel to mine.

'I'm awake, Alfie,' she whispers. 'I'm awake.'

She reaches down between my legs and I gasp as she slips me inside her. I can smell the sea-salt in her hair and when I close my eyes I see her, wading through the waves, laughing – kelp and green fingers in her sodden hair – crying, *I got you, I got you!*

After we come, we lie in the silence of the house. My face is wet with tears, but Julia didn't seem to notice. She's sleeping now, as I stare through the skylight at the heavens – purple-blue, dark as a bruise; disfigured by a glitter of stars.

Sixteen

Alfie

I dream, and time passes, though I'm not sure how much. When I wake, so does Julia, and she lifts her head off the pillow, blinking rapidly and staring in confusion – first at me, then at the bed.

'It's all right,' I say.

But she moans – a dry, throaty groan of disagreement – and sits upright, clutching the sheets around her.

'What have we done?'

'Nothing we should be ashamed of,' I answer firmly.

I almost believe it, and if she lies back down next to me, I'll believe it implicitly. So I smile sheepishly and beckon her closer. But she stays upright, shaking her head.

I want her beside me. I want to kiss her slender neck, so like her sister's; put my mouth on her breasts. I want to fall back to sleep with her warm weight next to me; come to at the tug of the covers as she shifts in sleep; listen to the gentle rhythm of her breath, rising and falling like piano scales.

'Come on,' I whisper. 'We don't have to do anything. Just stay with me, please.'

And she cups her hand to her mouth as if she might be sick.

I rise instinctively, reaching out to reassure her, and my half of the bedsheet slips away, revealing my body. Julia lifts a hand to cover her eyes. They are stone-blue – eyes of great control and intelligence, but warmer than Pippa's, which used to shine coldly, like the sea.

I lean across the bed and take her hand. She's no less beautiful than her sister, but she's not her sister.

We sit in silence in the dark and she allows me to hold her smooth palm, as if indulging a child. Then she turns, pulls away, as though she can't stomach my touch for a second longer.

'Don't look,' she says.

Her nightdress is bunched up in the bed. I hand it to her, averting my eyes. I feel her weight leave the mattress.

'Where are you going?' I ask. By the time I turn, she's already out of sight.

Her answer echoes faintly in the stairwell: 'For some air.'

Though her words are the mirror of mine from when I stormed out at dinner, there's no archness in them – at least, none that I detect. I check the time. It's the middle of the night. She can't go out alone at this hour.

As I jump out of bed, a sudden dizziness overtakes me, and I'm forced to slow down. My legs feel leaden as I slide on my underwear, as though the mere thought of following

Julia out of the house is causing my body to resist. I open a bedside drawer and retrieve a dark, loose-fitting top. As I pull it over my head, the skin on my neck feels painful and raw, and I step into the en suite to check it in the mirror. Long, chalky scratch marks, as deep as the ones that appeared on my chest, cover my throat, passing over my Adam's apple then disappearing beneath my collar. I lean forwards, and peer even more closely at my reflection. *What big eyes you have*. They seem wider than usual. I stare at the image in their pupils – the tiny, doll-like replica of myself that peers back at me, as though trapped inside.

It's the heat, I think. *That's all*. Then the front door slams.

I leave the bedroom and hurry down the spiral stairs. When I reach the girls' room, I take care to move without making a noise. But despite my best efforts, the door to their bedroom creaks open when I draw near, and Cassia's standing there, her eyes shining like moons.

'Who's there?' she whispers.

I hesitate, uncertain of what to say; what name to award myself. 'It's me,' I say eventually. 'What are you doing out of bed?'

'I can't sleep,' she says. 'I need the loo.'

I think of Julia, overwhelmed – wandering around Peter's Park in her nightdress at 2 a.m. – but make my decision. 'Of course,' I say. 'I'll take you.'

I stretch out my hand, feeling self-conscious as it hangs in mid-air. Cassia stares, as if weighing it up, then meshes her tiny fingers with mine. It feels like ages since we've been so intimate – though perhaps it's mere days – and, for a moment, the proximity embarrasses me. But then she squeezes my fingers, and I settle into it. I turn on the spot and we walk, hand in hand, back up the stairs.

When we reach the bathroom, I flick the switch, and instantly the tiles are spangled with electric light. The room is tiny, but full, like a cup of memories. Until now, I've only been able to see the bad in it – my fight with Pippa; her bloodstain on the mirror, and Sylvie's too – but now I smile as my mind is flooded with a whoosh of half-forgotten sounds and sensations: echoes of all the times Pippa and I bathed the girls in this tub, and they splashed, and their laughter ricocheted off the tiled walls. I remember how Pippa would squirt in some bath oil, which shot out of the bottle with a raspberry, and caused the tub to froth with bubbles. How she'd lather their chins with foam and muse, *You should be women ... yet your beards forbid me to interpret that you are so*, in that faraway voice she had.

These happy memories, which outweigh the bad a hundred times over – a million times – were lost to me. Yet now they rush, unbidden, into a kind of palpable reality, as though the mere illusion of having spent just one more night with Pippa has summoned them to me. Without a word, Cassia heads inside and closes the door. When she emerges, the bathroom is still bright and glowing. My eyes smart beneath its glare, and I'm embarrassed, again, to find them full of tears.

'You know,' I say, 'I loved Mummy very much.'

Cassia nods, then takes my hand again, this time of her own volition. 'I know,' she says, and then adds in one big, breathless gulp: 'I'm sorry.'

I crouch down. Her eyes are full of tears too.

'For what?' I ask – too doubtful of myself, too guilt-ridden, to take anything for granted.

But she won't explain, and now her tears begin to fall. I stand limply for a moment, utterly thrown. The contrast between this Cassia and the one who spoke to me so coldly earlier today is unnerving.

'Shh,' I whisper, unsure what else I can say. 'It's all right. Everything will be all right. I love you. I love you.'

When we return to their bedroom, Sylvie is awake as well, and sitting up, bleary-eyed, in bed.

'I thought I heard you leave,' she whispers to me, as I guide her sister through the dark.

'I'll never leave you.'

I pull the covers over the girls' bodies, right up to their chins until all I can see are their faces. Every day, they look more like their mother.

'I heard it opening,' Sylvie continues. Her eyes are wider now. With each moment, she seems to grow more anxious, more awake. 'The door.'

'That was only Aunt Julia,' I say.

'Leaving?'

'Leaving.'

'Is she coming back?'

Cassia, now. I turn to stroke her hair.

'Yes,' I answer.

'And ... will she stay?'

I study her face, but it remains inscrutable. As it's always been.

'Would you like her to?'

'Yes,' she replies softly, after a moment.

'Yes please,' Sylvie adds. I reach forward to stroke her too. She's now as alert as her sister.

'You need to sleep,' I sigh.

'Can't you *both* tuck us in?' Cassia says.

I check the time again. God knows where Julia is now, and what she's thinking. 'All right,' I say. 'I'll see what I can do. But stay here, in bed.'

They glance at each other, conferring. Then they answer in a single, still voice.

'Yes, Daddy.'

I'm stunned, but try not to show it. *They called me Daddy.* What is it? An act of rebellion; a profession of love? A flash of guilt?

I'll never know for sure. *We'll* never know, whatever Julia might think. The girls' minds are closed to us; we're separated from them by the gulf that exists between every adult and child – a gulf made greater somehow, in the twins' case, by the bridge that exists between them. I stroke their cheeks and cup their chins, then back slowly out of the room, unwilling to break eye contact with them until the very last moment.

Feeling lighter than I have in months, I descend the remaining stairs, only starting to tense again when I reach the hallway, when I near the door. Julia is just outside – but inside, it feels like a spell is being broken, and I'm scared to endanger that by leaving the girls alone.

By leaving them alone *with him*.

So I go into the living room instead, feeling my way through the darkness, guided only by a green pinprick on top of the bureau – Julia's phone charging – and the light from the bay window. When I draw back the curtain, Allington Square is empty. I scan the perimeter, hopefully, but there are few shadows in which someone could hide. The streetlamps cast a soupy orange light, and only a couple of cars are sitting at the kerb.

I shake my head, cross with myself. What had I expected: to see her sitting, weeping on the doorstep, ready for me to scoop her up and carry her back to bed? She must have gone into Peter's Park.

I begin to step back from the window, but as I do, I notice that the top drawer of the bureau is ajar. I slide it open all the way. Inside are several leaves of paper; I pull them out, and realise what they are. They're the sketches from yesterday – Cassia's first, then my mess, and then ... Julia's.

'Let's all draw ourselves,' she'd said, 'in ten years' time.'

I lift up her sketch to view it in the light of the streetlamps. She doesn't have her sister's talent: the stick figures resemble a rabble of insects, trapped in amber. Only after squinting do I start to make them out. It's a family. Julia drew herself and a child. And a man. I squint, with even more purpose this time. But I don't think it's meant to be me; it could be anyone.

It *could* be me.

There's a house in the picture too, but it isn't this house; it's a cottage, broad and many-chimneyed, with a wild garden, somewhere far from here – somewhere beside a pencilled sea. As I look at it, my body feels hot again, and I steady myself against the bureau. *I want this too*, it dawns on me. The cottage. The family. *Julia*. Not as a proxy for Pippa, but for her wry, smart, beautiful self.

The girls will be fine on their own for a few minutes.

I rush out into the hallway, towards the door – but then I freeze. The picture slips from my grasp at what I see: the hall has been transformed. Light is coming from underneath the cellar door – red light, bright and potent, soaking the entire hallway in its bloody shade. I feel my pulse beating in my throat. This can't be real, it can't be. I can still choose. Pull away, gather up the drawing from wherever it's fallen – and find Julia. We can sell this house, or destroy it; we can start again, the four of us.

I just need to walk away.

Open thy marble jaws, O tomb, and hide me, earth, in thy dark womb.

The cellar door opens, smoothly and silently, and light pours out. Pippa's down there – I can feel it. This isn't make-believe, or a waking dream. She's waiting for me.

I make my way down the steps, afraid that if I move too fast her presence – or at least, my conviction – will dissipate. But it doesn't. The sensation only grows stronger as I advance. I'm afraid to breathe. Afraid to blink. *Where is she?* I can't yet see her, but I know what she'll look like: solid and corporeal, her dark hair and pale face both shades of red; her eyes, drained of their colour – the irises scarlet, tipped with inky dots – but uniquely hers. And her face, her smile. Unmistakeable.

There's a droning sound, like the hum of old electric lights. A chorus of inchoate voices. I strain to hear hers within it, to pick out the call of my name.

'Please,' I whisper. 'I know you're here. Come out. I wasn't going to ... I'd never ... Forgive me.'

But there's no reply. The droning grows louder. It's coming from the ceiling, from right above my head. I look up. There's no safelight, no infrared bulb – only a writhing circle of bright red smoke, like the swirling fog from one of Pippa's paintings. To see it is to feel it blaze. My skin stings, wriggles – moves as if it has a mind of its own.

I look around the cellar dazedly, watching the smoke spread – then close my eyes and sway on the spot, swooning in the unforgiving heat. Shakily, I lift my hand.

Here she is. The tips of her fingers, pressing softly against mine. At first, I think it's merely a draught, but then I sense the weight of her palm too, and when I step forward, I feel her warm breath on my cheeks.

Noiselessly, we kiss. In my mind's eye, I recall the shape of her mouth; I picture her lips, bright red in this fearsome light. Rose, delicious.

Then we come apart. Smiling, I open my eyes.

My hand is pressed against the hand of another man.

He's my mirror image – identical, it seems, in every respect. His movements lag a few seconds behind mine, so I watch, dizzily, as his lips close. As he smiles. As he opens his eyes.

Piercing yellow; blackly slit.

His eyes glow like imprints of the sun – an afterimage – but only for an instant. As soon as I tear my hand away, he vanishes. I jump back, but when my feet touch the cellar floor, it ripples in a way that stone can't, or shouldn't. Then it bursts.

There's a split second in which I see it coming – the transformation from stone to black water – but before I can scream, something powerful snatches me under the surface.

Solidity is swallowed by delirium. I'm being dragged through the cold depths with such ferocity it's as though my skin is being torn clean away. A half-second of pain, and then: the water is a balm. My body feels smooth, cool, like a patina has been removed.

I try to scream again, but the sound that emerges is a warble of bubbles. I try to kick off whatever has me in its grip, whatever force is dragging me down through the water, but there's nothing there: only the gravity that pulls anyone down when they choose to jump. Even though I didn't. *I didn't.*

Below me I see nothing but blackness, stretching on forever. I try to swim upwards, towards the surface, back into the cellar. But the pull is too strong. Already the red light, shimmering above my head, is scarcely visible through the water. I fall, and keep falling, until it's grown so pale and small that it's little more than a pinprick; a haunting, pinkish glimmer high above my head – as faint, and as alluring, as my memories of the woman I loved.

Seventeen

Julia

From where I stand, alone among the trees, I can still see the house in the middle distance, though my view is obscured. The front steps are shrouded by the shrubbery that stretches before me and the façade is bisected by the park's iron railings. Looking at the house through this curious frame, I lean against the ridged bark of a magnolia tree and watch as the lights come on, one by one: first in Alfie's bedroom; then his en suite; the main bathroom; and the twins' room last of all. The way they light up makes me think of a doll's house – the kind of toy that Pippa would play with for hours on end, and I'd ignore – but this isn't a game; it isn't make-believe any longer.

I fucked him. Her Alfie. Their dad.

I can't go back inside. I can't even stay this last night. In the darkness, I could pretend it wasn't him I was touching – but I can't face him tomorrow, in the light.

Time passes, and my mind is so disordered that when the front door closes, I barely hear it. But the sound reverberates mesmerically through the empty square, and then I see him cross the road, unlatch the rusty gate, and head towards me. He is a silhouette, at first – the shadow of a man against the bushes. Only when he draws near does he resolve into himself: his awkward, lumbering frame; his head of dirty blond hair; his thickening beard. *Pretty, in a manly sort of way.* That's what I thought of him when we first met. Now he's more careworn, but still, he looks good as he approaches. Bathed in moonlight, his skin shining as if brand new.

He stops several yards off, as though suddenly wary of me.

'Are you all right?' I call over.

The question hangs in the air, strangely, for he has come to check on me, not the other way round. But then he lifts a hand to his throat, massages it gently, and speaks.

'I fell.' His voice is soft, expressionless. 'And then … I was trapped. But now …' He holds up his large hands, turning them over as he speaks, staring at them dreamily.

'You fell? What do you mean?'

My voice trails off as I notice that in his right hand he's holding a piece of paper: a drawing of some kind. He seems to see it only as I do. He unfolds it, smiles fondly, then scrunches it up again and puts it in his pocket.

'Ignore me,' he says. 'I was imagining things. I must have been. I know, now, what's real, and what isn't.'

'Oh. Good.' I take a deep breath, trying to gather my thoughts. 'While I've been out here, I've been thinking. Tonight ... what happened between us ... It was a mistake. I'm sorry, but I can't be a part of your life. It's for the best. I've got to move on – we both do.'

Alfie muses for a moment. Then he says hesitantly, as though feeling the words form unexpectedly, 'I don't think I want that.'

'No?' I whisper.

'No. And I'm not sure you do either.'

He takes a step closer until he's standing, I realise, right where it happened – where Pippa played, barefoot, with her daughters; creeping through the soft grass till a fang or stinger pierced her sole; injected the venom that would stop her heart. Yet he doesn't seem to notice.

'I want you to come back,' he says. 'And not just for tonight. For good. I want you to live with us, in Hart House. I want us to be together.'

He pauses frequently between his words. Yet, somehow, I don't have the time to interject.

'I know you love the twins. And they love you. They're growing up so fast. Maturing. And I'm not sure I'm enough for them. I'm not sure I can do this on my own.' His voice is low, butter soft. 'They need you.'

I can't work out what to say; whether he's trying to guilt trip me, or state a simple truth. But he isn't finished.

'And so do I.' He smiles, his teeth shining in the moonlight. 'We're yours if you want us, Julia. You can have me.

All of me. I swear: I *want* to be yours. Please, come inside, just to think about it ...'

I hang back, not knowing what to say or do. This can't happen. It's all too much. And yet – I want to touch him, kiss him, tell him that I want him too. I keep still – stuck in stasis, not trusting myself to move or speak.

And then I glimpse the doll's house over his shoulder, and gasp.

'Alfie,' I say. 'Look!'

In an instant, all the lights – in his bedroom, and the girls' bedroom, and the hallway – turn off, as if the house has been blown into the night sky, or fallen into a crater in the earth.

'Girls?'

The darkness seems to thicken around me as I move, like a brake of thorns. Hart House: its insides as black as the womb. The space that I shared with my twin from conception. Alfie moves through it ponderously, into the hallway, and the living room, and the kitchen, flicking switches on and off as he goes, to no avail. The darkness in the house is absolute – except above.

'Girls?' I say again, groping my way towards the bannister, gripping the newel as I look up. I can just make out the lights, winking, flickering, high above us, maybe on the third floor. The lights are frightening, otherworldly. They look as if they're floating freely in mid-air, unchained to any observable source.

'Alfie?'

I hear him open another door, and then I feel a sweep of cold air. It must have been the cellar. 'Alfie?' I say again.

'I'm here,' he says, surprisingly close.

'Look.' I point to the lights that twinkle above our heads. We take the stairs, and as we get closer, I realise they're flames. *Candles*. And with that realisation, I smell them – their sweet, spicy, charring scent; the odour that filled the house the day Dad died, and lingered afterwards.

I halt on the first-floor landing, covering my nose.

'Julia?' he whispers.

I take a deep breath. I've stopped just outside the twins' bedroom, so I open the door.

'Girls?' I say, for the third time. But the room is empty.

We continue up the stairs, stepping into the aromatic air. Our path grows brighter as we pass the second floor. At last, we reach the candles, which have been placed in the tiny alcoves that line the staircase; they gutter as we file past. The candles are a mismatch: new-looking ones, smooth and tall, mixed in among the half used – stubby and misshapen where the wax has melted and hardened again. Some are pale yellow, marbled with swirls of red. Others are shell-pink, studded with sparkles, which glint in the nimbus cast by their flames. The scent they give off is overwhelming.

We reach the top of the stairs, but our path to Alfie's bedroom – which I realise, faintly and with dazed embarrassment, was where we were headed – is blocked by a metal ladder. I look up. The loft hatch is hanging open like a mouth, wide and toothless.

'Did you ... ?' I half ask Alfie. But I know he didn't.

We both jump at the sound of the boards creaking above our heads, and then at the flash of dark, heavy fabric, like a wedding dress soaked in tar, that appears in the attic's mouth. It's a figure, moving slowly into view; anonymous at first, and then, as I hear her wheezing breath, oh so familiar.

'Mum!'

Surprise and relief course through me. I hold the ladder steady as she clambers down, gripping the slide rail perilously with only her right hand. A bundle of candles is tucked beneath her left elbow. The ladder groans under her weight – its serrated rungs threatening, as she staggers down, to snag her hefty black dress at any moment. Still in mourning, after more than a year.

'Thank you, darling,' she pants, when her feet are on solid ground. She kicks the tail-end of the ladder, and it folds up with astonishing obedience, travelling neatly into the attic and pulling the door shut after it with a snap.

'What are you doing here?'

Mum frowns. 'Isn't the question, really ... where were you?' She strikes a match, brightening her face – and ours, presumably – with a sudden halo of light. I step away from Alfie, instinctively. Back into the shadows. 'The girls called me.'

I start. 'They called you?'

'Yes. On your mobile, Julia.'

I go, instinctively, to thrust my hands into my pockets – forgetting, momentarily, that I'm in my nightclothes. It wouldn't matter anyway; I left my phone downstairs, charging on top of the bureau. And the girls know the code.

'Where are they?' I say.

'They were terrified,' Mum continues. 'Alfie had left them alone. Left them, apparently, to follow you ...'

My face goes red. 'He was only gone for a minute.'

'A minute? Julia, I've been here for half an hour. And you know how long it takes me to get over. What were you doing outside?'

Half an hour? It doesn't make sense. But then nothing makes sense tonight. 'Mum,' I say. 'Just tell me: where are the girls?'

She touches my shoulder. 'They're fine. I checked on them as soon as I got here.'

'But where are they?'

She shushes me as she places another candle in an empty alcove, and lowers the lit match delicately to the wick. It sputters and then reluctantly yields a small flame. Smoke drifts soundlessly through the dark air. 'They're fine,' she tells me again.

Alfie's nose twitches at the strength of the candle's aroma. 'That smell ...' he murmurs, closing his eyes as though it's awoken a half-forgotten memory in his mind, too.

Mum nods, smiling. 'Gorgeous, isn't it? Makes you feel ... oh, I don't know. More alive, somehow.'

'What are they?'

She turns to me, wide-eyed. 'What do you mean? They're just candles. We had them when you were kids. I knew there'd be some left in the attic.'

'Oh.'

'They belonged to the church, I think,' she adds, waving her free hand vaguely. 'We used them on Sundays ... in rituals ...'

I blink uncomprehendingly. 'But why have you lit them?'

Mum looks at me as if I'm crazy. 'The power's out.' She flicks the nearest light switch on and off, to prove its impotence. 'Old house,' she says, shaking her head. 'Dodgy circuits. The one thing Eric never fixed.' She looks at Alfie expectantly. 'Is there someone you can call? Or do you want to take a look yourself, down in the cellar?'

Alfie looks past her, as though he's not really listening. 'This house,' he murmurs slowly, as if entranced, 'was in a bad way when you bought it.'

'That's right,' Mum answers softly. 'And it had a bad reputation.'

I close my eyes, feeling nauseous in the fragrant air and the heat.

Do you know why you moved to this house? asked the social worker with the bald head and glasses, in his thin, reedy voice. *Do you know about what happened here?*

Yes, sir, we could have said. Should have, perhaps. Who didn't? Everyone knew about the Hart siblings, including

282

all the kids at school. *Your house is cursed*, they told us. *Haunted.* Yet it didn't feel possessed when we moved in – at least not to me. Quite the opposite: it felt abandoned, hollow. The previous owner had gone mad within its walls, and set the place alight in a vain attempt to rid the world of it. When Dad bought it for a pittance, more than a decade later, its insides were still gutted. Whole walls were covered in soot and char, like bark swathed in lichen. I remember him painting them pure white, moving his brushes slowly, reverently, as if he was blessing them with holy oil. I wasn't afraid, but nor did I share his excitement. Even at that tender age, I felt as empty as that burnt-out, derelict house. This was the first test of my faith – the faith I never had, could never muster, even when I believed in God.

'Alfie,' I whisper. 'Something's not right.'

Mum's moving ahead of us, out of earshot.

He lowers his voice too. 'What do you mean?'

'I've been able to smell these candles for weeks now. Haven't you?'

He shrugs, his face in shadow.

'And didn't you say,' I continue, remembering suddenly, 'that you thought someone had been in the attic? What if Mum's been coming round, secretly, all this time?'

'You think she'd do that?'

'Oh, it's exactly the sort of thing she'd do. Filling the girls' heads with God knows what. Behind your back. Behind mine.'

'The spare key *was* missing ...'

I hurry down the stairs after my mother. 'Thank you,' I say, 'for coming over to check on the girls. But you should go now. You really should. It's so late.'

She waves her hand again, this time dismissively, and moves to light another candle. 'It's okay. The girls didn't wake me. I don't sleep well these days – it's the pain. You needn't fret.'

We follow her jerky movements down the staircase. *It's the pain. You needn't fret.* The strangeness of her sentences, strung discordantly together, seems to ring in the hazy air.

We've reached the twins' room. Mum opens the door briskly. 'Girls?' she says. But then she falters. 'That's strange. I swear, a few minutes ago ...'

I push past her. We both do. Into the twins' bedroom, which is still empty, just as it was on our way up. The blue duvet is lying crumpled on the floor.

'Sylvie? Cassia?'

A sound floats across the landing, through the scented air. The sound of bodies moving in the spare room. My bedroom.

I burst in, and the twins emerge, casually, from under my bed. They smile at the sight of me. 'Thank God,' I say, without thinking. I pull them towards me in a hug, so tight it's like I'm stitching them into my nightdress, sewing their bodies into mine with the strength of my embrace. 'You're all right,' I say, and relief courses through me. Though what I was afraid of, exactly, I'm not sure.

Mum bustles in. Now she's the one who seems agitated. 'Angels,' she says. 'What on earth were you doing in here?'

Reluctantly, I let them go.

'We were looking for Daddy,' they say.

'Your daddy?' Mum crouches down, pressing a hand to their foreheads in turn, as if she suspects a fever. 'Why would he be in here? This is your aunt's room.'

Cassia shrugs. 'We couldn't find him.'

'No,' Sylvie says. 'We couldn't find him anywhere.'

'We looked upstairs.'

'And downstairs.'

'In the cupboards.'

'And under the beds.'

'But he wasn't there.'

'He wasn't anywhere.'

'Well, don't you worry,' Mum says, soothingly. 'He's here. Right here.'

She points at Alfie, who steps forward into my bedroom. The girls draw back slightly. There's a look in their eyes I can't quite place – confusion, perhaps, or trepidation.

'That's not him,' Sylvie says.

'What?'

Cassia nods, wide-eyed, in solemn agreement. 'That isn't Daddy.'

Mum laughs uneasily. 'What do you mean? Who is it then?'

But the girls say nothing, as if they're afraid to answer – or not quite sure.

Mum lights a match and waves it wildly near Alfie's face.

'Look. It's him. It's him.'

I sigh, miserably, as I realise what's going on. In the gloom, I picture Alfie clenching his fists, trying to control his temper.

'The girls,' I say quickly, 'have an imaginary friend. Black Mamba.'

Mum doesn't even pretend to be surprised. 'I know,' she says, shaking the match till it goes out, leaving a bright ember and a line of smoke. 'They've told me all about him.'

'Well, today,' I explain, holding her shoulders lightly, 'they've started to call him *Daddy*. And Alfie ... they're calling by his Christian name.'

Mum looks aghast. 'I thought you were helping the girls.'

'I am.'

'Not much good, is it, then? This psychotherapy lark.' Even in the low light, I see her eyes glitter.

'Everything's fine,' I mumble. 'I have a handle on things.'

'Evidently.' She turns to the twins, ushering them towards her. 'What are you doing? We've talked about this: you mustn't be afraid of this creature. Remember, I've been praying to the Lord, our shepherd. You're under His protection. No demon can harm you – not while my heart still beats.'

'Mum,' I protest. But she silences me with an imperious flick of her finger.

She takes the girls by the hand. 'Let's find Black Mamba. Let's find him together.'

'But he turned out the lights,' says Sylvie, eyeing her grandmother dubiously.

Mum shakes her head, pressing on. 'He can't hide from us. We're in control, remember? And ...'

She leans in, attempting to exclude me with a whisper. (I still hear every word.)

'*Remember what I told you*. Demons can do incredible things. Change form ... speak to spirits ... return our loved ones to us. There's no need to give them something in exchange – a title, a kiss, a drop of blood ... Demons are our servants, and we are their masters. We can control them. Command them. *As long as we have faith.*'

'Stop this,' I say. 'Please. It's so late. They need to sleep.'

But I'm silenced again – this time, to my utter surprise, by Alfie, who lays a hand on my shoulder. 'No,' he says. 'It's okay. Let her try.'

That's all the permission Mum needs. Excitedly, she rolls up her sleeves, ushering the girls out onto the landing. 'Where did you see him last? Do you remember?'

A melee of shadows as they shake their heads.

'Well, then. Where did you see him first? Where has he appeared to you? Come on. Let's retrace your steps.'

'Alfie,' I whisper urgently. 'This isn't healthy.'

He touches my waist in the dark. 'It's okay. If Marian thinks she can command him—' He breaks off. A muffled sound: as if he's trying not to laugh. 'If she thinks she can smoke him out, let her try.'

I feel uneasy still, but I guess he's right. It might not be a bad thing for the girls to watch their grandma try, and fail. 'All right,' I say. 'Let's see what happens.'

The girls lead Mum into their bedroom, where they saw Black Mamba for the first time months and months ago, standing silently at the foot of their bed. Where he appeared to them as a bird, and bore them off into the night. Where he climbed into their bed, filling the cleft between them, in the form of a large, grizzled bear. Mum soaks in their every word, her eyes shining in the candle-light as they recount the stories. The girls' words are like brushes, painting the shadowy canvas of the house at night with their strange visions.

They lead her into the bathroom, where they saw him as a fish, and to the room where Pippa used to hang her laundry, where they drew him as a snake. Alfie disappears, then re-emerges shortly bearing two tiny torches, which he places in his daughters' hands. They take them reluctantly, clearly still wary of him.

Alfie stays disarmingly composed. 'Careful,' he murmurs, as the girls pull Mum keenly down the stairs. 'Grandma's not too steady on her feet, remember. We don't want her to trip.'

Next, the living room, where they saw Black Mamba as a monkey – where he destroyed the scarlet vase that Pippa had given Alfie on Valentine's Day. Then, the kitchen, where his portrait still hangs. I skirt around the table, running my fingers lightly over the varnished wood, until I'm standing face to face with Sylvie's sketch. The beams of the girls' torches light up the diamond pattern on Black Mamba's leathery skin. I close my eyes, my forehead inches from the paper. I press a hand to my churning stomach.

Mum raps the kitchen table. Her voice is breathy with anticipation. 'We're getting closer. I can feel it. Where next? Come on. Where next?'

This is what Pippa did with Dad, I think, *when we first moved in*. I can still remember how they moved from room to room – shaking the rattle at night; photographing the walls by day. Click. Click. Click. Searching for something in the air around them – something hidden from sight. Then, sequestering themselves for hours on end in the darkroom. Developing images, scouring them for peculiar outlines, hidden meanings. Always together.

The problem is never that a parent has a favourite; it's that their children know it.

'The cellar,' Cassia says.

'What?'

'That's where we saw him last.'

'The cellar?'

'Yes. It's where he showed us the door.'

They're leaving the kitchen now, leaving me behind. I follow them hastily.

'You can't.'

Mum raises her hands, her fingers stiffening like rigor mortis. 'Julia, please!'

'There is no door,' I say. Then, turning: 'Cass, tell her.'

Cassia stares at me impassively. Her lips are pressed together, as if sewn shut.

'Come on,' I say. 'Tell her. There's nothing hidden in this house. No demon. And no spirits.'

'Ah, but that's not true, is it?' Mum interjects. At the corners of her lips, a glimmering smile. 'If anyone should know that, it's you.'

Her words – sharp – slip out casually, and no one understands them but me.

'The dead,' I murmur, 'can't be reached.'

'Tell that to Sue,' Mum retorts. 'She talks to Michael all the time.'

Exasperation swells in me, but I try to contain it. 'Sue's not well. You know this.'

She glowers at me undeterred, standing by the door to the cellar, clenching her fist around the handle.

I turn to Alfie, who merely shrugs. 'It's the only place left to look,' he says, reasonably enough.

Smiling smugly, Mum opens the door.

Michael. Whenever I hear his name, I can't help but picture the pencil sketch that hangs in Crescent Place, above the grate in the sitting room. I see his round, smiling face, his smudged-graphite curls. He exists, in my mind, only in the form of that picture – bodiless, weightless. His face is blank paper and chiaroscuro.

I never think of the photo I saw. Why would I? I saw it just the once, when I was a little girl – and even then, I saw it for a matter of seconds.

It was a Sunday, and the church had gathered in Hart

House. Crescent Place was nowhere special, just another building. A real church is a congregation, a body of believers. The curtains were drawn; the candles were lit. The smell of incense was filtering through the house, hanging heavily in the hallway. Pippa and I were seated in the living room, side by side. We could feel the presence of our family around us: Mum, Dad, Auntie Sue, her daughters. All watching us.

Dad stepped forward and slipped blindfolds over our heads. The last thing I saw with any clarity, before a swathe of dark fabric covered my eyes, was *The Book of the Princes*, lying on the floor before us, open at a double-page spread: a drawing of seven demons, communing with each other. I still remember their hairy male bodies and their animal heads. One had the head of a wolf; another, the head of a bear. And each held an instrument: a rattle, a tambourine, or a trumpet pressed against his furry lips.

We held our hands up, at Dad's command, and he placed a photo in them. I gripped the bottom left-hand corner; Pippa, the right.

'What can you see?'

He was speaking to her, of course.

Oh, Pippa, with your drawings and dreams; your sensitivity; your *femininity*. She was the sun, and I was the moon – only ever reflecting her light.

She started speaking, softly. Describing the shapes that she could see in the dark. If only she could paint them for us! She sighed in the perfumed air, and the sofa seemed to sway with her fluttering breath; the tremulous beating of her heart. She was acting – possibly. But she wasn't consciously acting. So it made no difference.

I opened my eyes. I shouldn't have, but I did. The blindfold was thick but not opaque, and if I tilted my head right down I could see under a gap, and examine the photo we were holding. I recognised the boy at once; the likeness of the pencil sketch, above the mantelpiece in Crescent Place, was very good.

'Michael?' Alfie whispers. 'Who's he?'

'No one,' I mutter, my face going red. Not for the first time, I'm glad of the dark. *Surely Pippa would have told him?*

We travel down the steps in convoy, Alfie and I bringing up the rear with the light from our phones, the girls striding ahead with their tiny torches, and my mother, leading the way, holding a lit taper – her hand cupping the naked flame like Rubens' old lady with a candle. When we reach the bottom, she turns to Alfie and takes his hand.

'Michael,' she says, 'was Julia's cousin. He died before she was born.'

'Died?'

'Yes, it was an accident. A horrible, horrible accident.'

My fingernails dig into my palms, leaving impressions in the skin, and my eyelids crease until I see nothing but bars of blurry light.

Poor Michael. What must it have been like – to be standing, one moment, on a bed of solid ice; the next, to be falling through water? Plunging down, and down, with no means of escape, then swept away. Coursing down the gelid river. All the rivers run into the sea; yet the sea isn't full ...

'Poor Michael,' Alfie says, divesting his hand from Mum's and then patting her gently on the shoulder.

Mum turns to me and smiles eagerly. 'Tell him what happened, Julia. On the day your father died. Tell him what you saw.'

I don't answer, stubbornly refusing to engage.

'Julia saw him,' Mum says impatiently, turning back to Alfie. 'On the day her father died, she had a vision, here in this house. She had a blindfold on, but still, she saw his face.' Mum throws up her hands. Still marvelling, after all these years. 'Eric thought that Philippa had the sight. But it was Julia who saw him ... who felt his spirit. So how' – she turns back to me, inflamed again – 'can you say that the dead can't be reached? That there's nothing in this house? You know it isn't true. It isn't true.'

I say nothing. There's nothing left to say; nothing that will make a difference.

'On the day her father died ...' Alfie repeats the phrase slowly, as if he's fingering a cut of velvet.

Mum shifts uncomfortably. 'Another accident. He was excited, after Julia's vision. He pushed too far. He thought, if only he could simulate Michael's death – deprive himself of air – then he could reach him. Oh, it was stupid. Reckless. But he was on to something. He was. And everything the girls have seen ... Black Mamba ... that all proves it.' She turns back to the girls and starts to comb their hair, fussily, with her fingers, homing in on the knots with preternatural precision. They wriggle away. 'Come on,' she says. 'Where is he? Where's Black Mamba? Can you see him? Hear him?'

The girls circle the cellar, their torches flashing, illuminating Pippa's veiled canvases, a cardboard box. Then they settle on the stone floor in the centre of the cellar, beneath the bare bulb. They crouch down and press their ears to the ground, as though listening intently. They lie on the spot where their mother lay, the allergen coursing through her as she died.

I knew I'd set disaster in motion from the moment I opened my mouth and claimed to see my cousin in the gloom; mimicking Pippa's catching voice, falling off the sofa in a faux-swoon, calling for my father.

Daddy! He held me in his glorious arms, kissed my forehead, his eyes shimmering. *All the rivers run into the sea,* he crowed. *Yet the sea isn't full. Whatever you lose will come back to you.*

That was the last time I saw him, except in dreams, which only felt real in the dreaming of them. Mum couldn't be left on her own for years. Her grief was all-encompassing. So Pippa left, and I stayed. She met Alfie, had the twins, and I was happy for her – or happy enough. It was what she deserved, I told myself; it was what we both deserved.

Ever since the accident, I've tried to hold him and the girls at arm's length. But he's kept on inviting me in. I didn't come back because I wanted to; I came because he asked. It would be so easy, now, to just say yes – but I can't take her family from her, even in death. After what I did to Dad, how could I take anything from her, ever again?

There's silence for an age. Then the girls rise off the stone floor and brush down their legs. They look at each other. Then at Alfie.

A curious expression drifts across their faces suddenly, like a shadow passing over the surface of the moon. *A look of realisation.*

'Well?' Mum says impatiently. 'Could you hear him?'

'No,' they answer slowly – still staring at Alfie. 'We couldn't. He isn't here. Daddy's gone.'

'Black Mamba,' I remind them, wearily.

But Alfie comes up behind me and once again touches my shoulder. He stills me with the weight of his presence. His irrevocable hand. 'It's fine,' he whispers. 'Honestly, it's fine.'

'Are you sure?' Mum says, crowding them – cracking her knuckles anxiously.

They're sure.

The girls slip past her, and press themselves against my sides. A hot tingle runs through my body and I bite my bottom lip, so as not to cry. *They're not mine. I can't think of them as mine. If I do, I'll turn them into woozles of my own – proxies, dolls.* Yet their warm hands fold into my own, and they fit perfectly.

'Are you sure?'

'Mum,' I say, my voice rising, 'leave them now.'

And at last, she submits.

The girls yawn. Guiltily, I check the time.

'Jesus, Alfie. It's really late.'

'The devil's hour,' he says, distantly. I look up – but his whole face is veiled by the dark.

The girls yawn again, great heaving yawns, like the groans of ships bearing off into the mist, and Mum, too, seems suddenly spent. The light of her candle sags, as she leans wearily against the wall.

Alfie approaches me gently. 'Why don't you take the girls to bed? And I'll take your mother home.'

Mum grumbles, but when Alfie holds out his arm, she takes it.

'Thank you for coming when the girls called,' he says, leading her up the cellar steps.

She grunts derisively, but Alfie continues, undeterred.

'I mean it, Marian – thank you. For everything.'

Eighteen

Julia

It's a cold, crisp midwinter morning. The sun is shining on dark, wet pavements and the day is clear and windless, the perfect walking temperature. So, even though a van came first thing for my belongings, I'm making my way to my new home, which is also my old home, on foot. Alfie tried to stop me, but this was my final act of defiance before the inevitable dependency that the next few months will bring. I wouldn't be dissuaded.

My route takes me past Crescent Place where, nostalgically, I pause to sit on the low brick wall outside No. 2. A 'FOR SALE' sign is out the front and I notice, for the first time, that the brass plaque which read A CHURCH OF CHRIST has been removed. The brickwork where it once hung is pale, like an afterimage. I gaze wistfully at the heavy ivory netting, knowing that even if I were to ring the doorbell, it wouldn't twitch. No one lives here anymore; Mum died the night Black Mamba disappeared, six months ago, and Sue went into care soon after.

Exactly what happened, we're still not sure. Sue is a paradigm of the unreliable witness. We know that Alfie brought Mum home and took her to bed; he stayed with her until she fell asleep. But she must have risen in the night, because when Sue came downstairs the following morning – early, while it was still dark – Mum had collapsed in the kitchen. She'd suffered a second stroke. Sue phoned an ambulance, but it was too late. Mum couldn't be revived.

It was a shock, of course. Though within a day or two, I realised that the strange sensation I was living with – the light-headedness, the feeling of walking on air – wasn't the numbness of surprise, but relief. *Not the worst way to go*, I thought. *At least she's no longer in pain.* We laid her in earth at the hinge of summer, under an auburn sun, under the changing trees. *God will grant her a new body*, the priest said. But it was I who felt born again.

The harshest impact was on Sue, who couldn't live alone for much longer. I've visited her once or twice – her new home is a few miles west of here. But she no longer knows who I am. Half a year on, she recognises almost nobody, not even her own daughters; not even Michael, when they show her pictures – which, as she's the last person alive who could remember him, feels like an ending of a kind.

I ease myself off the wall and move on, wandering slowly through the familiar streets, through the abandoned graveyard, where the stone angels are dark as charcoal after the rain, and into Peter's Park. The leaves on the evergreens gleam and Hart House rises in front of me, like a tall wave of peeling paint. I've abandoned the thought that I might one day be free of it, and that acceptance is, in itself, oddly freeing.

Before I can ring the bell, Alfie opens the door with a smile. He kisses me brightly on my cheek, which, I realise suddenly, at the heat of his breath, is cold and stiff. He helps me out of my coat. Still a gentleman, I think, even after all that's happened. *No – more so.* He kisses me again, so gently, then touches my belly. The drinking has stopped, and with it, the chaos. His frame looks lean again, athletic; his movements are calm and controlled. He shaved his stubble long ago, and now keeps his face smooth. He looks young again – almost as young as the day I met him, in a restaurant in Soho, with Cubist prints on the walls and the tablecloth perfectly pressed. The cause of his physical renaissance is a mystery, for he insists that he sleeps soundly only when he's next to me, and there's no enchanted portrait in the house, as far as I've seen – only Pippa's old canvases, the ones he hasn't yet sold.

He says it's not about the money, which will go into a trust fund for the twins, but 'They ought to be on walls, in galleries. They ought to be seen.'

He closes the door behind me.

'All your things,' he says, 'are up in my room.' He pauses, corrects himself. 'Our room.'

I wince – an old reflex, hard to let go of.

'How are the girls?' I ask quickly.

He shakes his head at me, almost mockingly, and grins. 'Excited,' he insists. 'Go on. See for yourself.'

I make my way up the spiral stairs, pausing now and then for breath. On the first floor, I reach Sylvie's room, the walls of which are painted with enormous petals – yellow, red and coral pink. And Cassia's, directly opposite – my old room – is painted in an ornate kaleidoscope of blue and white.

Six months on, the girls are much improved. In some ways, the process has been gradual. Months of talking therapy with one of my colleagues, of patient listening from us; a roadblock here, a breakthrough there. But in large part they were cured the night Black Mamba disappeared, the night their grandma died. I've never been able to put my finger on it. The conversations I had with Sylvie in the park, and with Cassia in the girls' bedroom, seemed like milestones, even at the time. But still, I was unprepared for how suddenly, how completely, Black Mamba left us that night. It was like a fever broke. Just like that, their *folie à deux* was at an end.

In the days that followed, the girls made no mention of Black Mamba – nor did they mention him, in the months that followed, during any of their sessions at the clinic. We spoke of Pippa many times. Of how an ideal mother would never have died, and an ideal father would have coped, but how none of us can live up to ideals. They never once mentioned their imaginary friend. I wrote up their case, anonymised, as a study for the clinic; it's soon to be published. Yet documenting it all – how Cassia ('child A'), who brought Black Mamba into being, was the inducer in their *folie imposée* and Sylvie ('child B') was the acceptor – somehow made it feel even less real, like it had happened to another family. Like it had all been a game of make-believe.

Still. The girls' behaviours persisted now and then: the self-harm, the aggression. Even if their woozle had gone, the conditions that had created him remained, at least for a while – as if to remind me, to remind us all, that the events of the past year had not been a dream; they were real. Things are better now, though – much better. Sylvie's guilt and anger have shrunk steadily, and Cassia's self-esteem has grown and grown.

They're maturing. The separate bedrooms that I pass on my way up the spiral stairs are evidence of that. But it runs more deeply: at last, their childlike regression has reversed. The fantasies, the clinginess, the volubility, even the babyish voices that they used sometimes when speaking to Alfie, and which I loathed so much – reminding me, as they did, of the falsetto certain women adopt when speaking to their partner – have all receded. The girls are eight years old now. Soon, they'll be nine. They're becoming wiser, more worldly. Before long they'll hit puberty, and they'll ask how it happens, how I came to be in my condition. I'm surprised they haven't asked already.

I'm six months gone. My belly is a large, smooth dome, and I'm breathless after every flight of stairs. Though Alfie hasn't followed, I can sense him below in the hallway, observing my movement. We haven't spoken of that night, when he was conceived. We've barely even spoken of what's to come: the arrival of our son, the girls' brother. Yet there exists between us – in Alfie's ever-watchful gaze, and my decision to return to Hart House – a tacit acknowledgment that we should raise him together; that we should be together.

To celebrate would feel indecent, but we are happy. Wonderfully, improbably happy. I still have pangs of guilt most days; catch a glimpse of my twin in the bathroom mirror; feel like an imposter. But after the baby comes it'll be easier. I'm sure, one day, those feelings will end altogether.

At last, I reach the top of the stairs. The girls are in the bedroom – mine and Alfie's – sifting through my things, lining up my little pot plants and looking in bewilderment at my collection of film posters: *La Pointe Courte*, *La Belle et la Bête*, *Le Mépris*.

'We'll watch them together,' I say, 'when you're older.'

They look up. They hadn't heard me puffing up the stairs, evidently. They fling their arms around me before ducking down, pressing their heads against my belly.

'When's he coming?' Sylvie asks, tugging my wrist.

I pat her on the head and smile. 'Soon.'

'It'll be nice for Dad,' Cassia comments, with a fine air of maturity, 'to have another boy in the house.'

'Again,' adds Sylvie.

'Again?' I ask lightly – and then freeze.

Can they really mean Black Mamba? After all this time.

I lower myself carefully onto the bed and the child shifts inside me. Normally, I smile whenever I feel a kick. But all I feel at present is discomfort. The girls are at eye level. I scan their faces cautiously. But they both seem fine.

I take their hands and clear my throat, a little imperiously. *This is important.* The girls straighten up.

'Have you seen him,' I ask quietly, 'since that night?' For some reason, I can't quite bring myself to say his name. But it's all right: a look passes between us; they know who I mean.

'No,' they answer. 'Never.'

'We hear him, though,' Sylvie adds, after a moment. 'Sometimes.'

'Yes,' says Cassia, nodding astutely. 'We hear him moving, underneath the cellar.'

I frown; release their hands uncertainly. 'Black Mamba's ... underneath the cellar?'

The girls' eyes widen slightly.

'No,' Sylvie says. 'Not Black Mamba.'

A look passes between them, a look that excludes me – odd and impregnable. Then Cassia cups her hand to whisper in my ear. Her hot breath tickles the lobe, prompting a pleasurable shiver. '*Alfie.*'

She takes a step back. I stare at the girls in silence, too startled to speak. The boy shifts again, beneath my skin.

Then, all of a sudden, the twins erupt into peals of laughter and leap onto the bed behind me. They bounce giddily, pointing and howling; they seize the pillows. A low creak issues from the corner of the room, as the door opens abruptly. Alfie walks in, his face the very picture of bemusement.

'What on earth... ?' he asks. But they don't answer. They carry on bouncing back and forth, giggling, pounding each other mercilessly with the pillows until one bursts, erupting in a sudden drift of plumage – snow-white, downy, dazzling.

'Oh Auntie,' the girls shriek, their bodies shaking merrily beneath the whirl of feathers. 'We got you, we got you!'

Acknowledgements

My sincerest thanks to everyone who was involved in the writing and publication of *Black Mamba*. Everyone at Atlantic Books. Everyone at The Blair Partnership. I'm indebted to my editor, James Roxburgh, and my agent, Jordan Lees, for their wise comments on the manuscript and their abundant encouragement. Thank you both for your hard work on the novel, and for your faith in me. I'm also grateful to my copy editor, Amber Burlinson, for her astute comments and corrections.

Thank you to my sister, Anna, and her fiancé, Karl, for being among the novel's first readers. My parents, Jan and Mark, for a lifetime of love and support. My grandmother, Pauline, for always being there for me. My partner, Sam, for reading through every draft of every chapter with such care and patience, and always helping me find the time to write. Last but not least, thank you to my grandfather, Brian, who was so thrilled to know that *Black Mamba* would be published. The stories you told me and Anna as a child will always be in my heart, as will you.

Note on the Author

William Friend studied English, French and Italian at university. He lives in Hertfordshire with his partner. *Black Mamba* is his first novel.